AWAKENED

D1602900

Also by Morgan L. Busse

Daughter of Light

THE SOUL CHRONICLES:
Tainted | BOOK ONE

AWAKENED

THE SOUL CHRONICLES

———

BOOK TWO

MORGAN L. BUSSE

an imprint of
GILEAD PUBLISHING

Awakened by Morgan L. Busse
Published by Enclave Publishing, an imprint of Gilead Publishing,
Grand Rapids, Michigan
www.enclavepublishing.com

ISBN: 978-1-68370-076-0 (print)
ISBN: 978-1-68370-077-7 (eBook)

Cover design by Kirk DouPonce
Interior design/typesetting by Beth Shagene
Edited by Reagan Reed

Printed in the United States of America

For My Dad

CHAPTER
1

KAT LAY ON THE BED WHERE STEPHEN HAD PLACED HER INSIDE Captain Grim's cabin aboard the airship *Lancelot*, her skin pale against the deep red coverlet. He shifted his hold on her cold hand and looked up.

Would Kat ever forgive him for taking her to the Tower? For the pain he had put her through at the hands of her father? Stephen sighed and dropped his head into his free hand. He wasn't sure if he could forgive himself.

God . . .

A dull ache filled his chest. He glanced back at Kat. Her eyes were tightly shut and her dark hair splayed across the pillow. She reminded him of those fairy-tale stories where the sleeping princess waited for true love's kiss.

He shook his head and placed her hand down at her side, his middle twisting inside him. The bedspread moved, revealing part of her body. Blood stained the sides of her white gown and seeped into the sheets. He swallowed and pulled the cover back. More reminders that he had left her at the Tower and what they had done to her. What *he* had done to her.

No, this was no fairy-tale. No kiss would awaken Kat, and he was certainly not her prince. More like the villain.

The door burst open behind him.

Stephen glanced over his shoulder. Finally, someone with dressings for Kat's wounds.

A sailor stood in the doorway with a stern look on his face and no bandages in his hands.

Stephen frowned. "Where's your cook? And the bandages? Your captain said he would send someone to attend the lady."

Ignoring his questions, the sailor—Reid, he remembered—shot him an enigmatic look. "The captain requests your presence on deck."

Before Stephen could ask why, Reid disappeared, leaving the door ajar behind him. The deck above rumbled with shouts and gears grinded deep within the airship.

Something was wrong. Robert had said he would need a couple hours to restock his ship, so why were they leaving now?

Stephen leaned over Kat and pulled the coverlet up to her neck. He paused above her face. She was so pale that her lips were only a shade darker than her skin. The only sign she was still alive, not a corpse, was the slight rise and fall of her chest and the shallow breath that escaped her lips every few seconds.

Stephen let out his own breath. He was not her prince. He was not the one who could awaken her from this deathly sleep. But he could keep her safe. "And I will," he whispered.

He straightened and crossed the cabin, bypassing the large table nailed to the floor in front of the wall of tiny windows that overlooked World City, past the bench and desk built into the side of the ship. His revolvers sat snug on either side of his hips. Whatever the trouble was, he would be ready.

Stephen pulled the rim of his hat down low across his forehead and left the cabin and Kat behind.

The main deck bustled with activity as the crew of the *Lancelot* prepared for flight.

Reid, the sailor who had come for him, spotted him and pointed at Robert Grim. The captain stood near the port-side rail, his attention focused on the ground hundreds of feet below. Stephen crossed the deck and came to stand beside Robert.

Without saying a word, Robert handed him a spyglass made from gold and pointed where he had been looking moments before.

Stephen took the spyglass, leaned across the railing, and pressed the eyepiece to his right eye. Far below, at the bottom of the sky tower, were three figures.

"Blazes," he muttered, his fingers tightening around the metal rod. He couldn't see Jake Ryder's telltale tattoos from this high up, but he would recognize the bounty hunter's bearing anywhere. Piers Mahon was dressed in his usual impeccable white suit, hat, and pseudo-cane that hid his sniper rifle. And "the Judge" was with them, his cannon arm glinting in the sunlight.

Stephen pulled the spyglass away and clutched it in his hand. "How did they find us?"

Grim tapped a finger against his chin as he looked thoughtfully down below. "You know those men?"

"Yes," he said through gritted teeth. "They're World City bounty hunters. Jake Ryder, Piers Mahon, and 'the Judge.'"

Robert frowned and glanced at him. "Wait, Rodger Glennan is with them?"

Stephen handed the spyglass back. "You know the Judge?"

"I met him a couple of times. Never forgot that interesting prosthetic he had made for his arm." Grim tucked the spyglass into his side pocket. "Always wondered if I could find something similar for my eye."

Stephen blinked. How could Grim being thinking of that at a time like this? "If you know about Rodger's prosthetic, then you know you what it can do. We need to get out of here before he takes a shot at us. That cannon of his could put a serious dent in your ship. Or worse."

"You're right." Robert turned around and faced the deck. "You heard him, men. Move it! Let's put some distance between the platform and us. Now!"

The sailors scurried across the deck and more shouts erupted.

Ropes slithered onto the wooden planks while a group of men rushed to engage the pumps that would deflate the huge balloon that held the airship afloat while docked. The four small rotors, two on either side of the ship, began to spin with a thunderous whirring sound.

Stephen looked over the railing again. Jake, Piers, and Rodger entered the sky tower far below. "Here they come."

Robert finished giving instructions to two of his men and turned around. "Where are they now?"

"They just entered the sky tower. We have a couple minutes before they reach the platform." He glanced at Grim. "How far do you think we'll be from the tower?"

"It'll be close, but we're ready." Grim's face held no trace of fear. Instead, his one eye glinted with anticipation for the possible fight.

There was a sudden lurch across the *Lancelot* as the balloon deflated. Too heavy for the four small rotors to support alone, the ship began to sink. Stephen braced his legs, his heart flying up into his throat.

"Don't worry, it's always like this on takeoff," Robert said with grin. "There's a moment between the stowing of the docking balloon and the main rotors taking over. It's a bit of a thrill, really."

Stephen wasn't so sure, as his heart continued to beat against his ribcage. At this rate, would they be far enough from the sky tower before the bounty hunters arrived?

He drew out one of his revolvers, checked the chamber, and stood near the railing where a ladder had been moments before. He would be ready just in case.

From this vantage point, he could see the opening from the sky tower to the platform. The ship dipped farther below the wooden scaffold as the twin main rotors worked themselves toward flight speed at an agonizing pace. Stephen swallowed. Blazes! When were they going to take off?

He trained his revolver on the opening. When Jake and the other bounty hunters arrived on the platform, he would have little warning. They had the advantage of cover and surprise. Piers could stay in the shadows inside the tower and use that sniper rifle of his. And

Rodger . . . well, that cannon of his could take the *Lancelot* out of the sky.

Stephen went down on one knee behind the railing, keeping his body flush with one of the posts and his eyes level with the hand bar. The ship gave a hard lurch, cracking his forehead against the rail. Stephen grabbed the post and straightened himself as the air spun above his head, whipping his hair around. Slowly, the ship began to rise. Robert shouted more commands behind him, but they were gibberish in the hail of wind above him.

The ship was eye level with the platform when Jake appeared in the doorway. The moment he spotted Stephen, he went for his revolver.

Stephen shot first, aiming right past Jake's head and hitting the wooden doorframe behind the man.

Jake flinched and dove for the side.

Stephen peered between the railings, keeping his gun close and ready as the ship continued to rise and maneuver away from the sky tower. Piers and Rodger could show up any minute. He sent another bullet toward Jake when the man began to stand.

Another shot answered from the shadows of the doorway, whizzing past Stephen's head and pinging off the rotors above. Stephen twisted around and planted his back against the post, breathing hard. That shot could have only come from Piers.

The ship began to pick up speed. Stephen glanced between the railings. He glimpsed the barest hint of a man in a white suit standing inside the sky tower before something large and dark barreled past Piers.

Rodger stopped outside the doorway, glanced at the airship, and raised his prosthetic cannon.

Stephen couldn't hear the whine of Rodger's cannon over the ship's propellers, but he could see electricity arc around the prosthetic and knew what was coming next. So did Jake and Piers—they rushed toward their comrade to stop the blast.

"Brace for impact!" Stephen shouted and took aim at the cannon-arm. Maybe he could nick the weapon and throw it off target.

Stephen let his breath out, focused on the corner of the cannon, and shot.

The cannon went off and Rodger jerked back, sending Jake and Piers sprawling to the floor behind him.

A white beam shot toward the ship and struck just below the aft rotor. The ship rocked. Smoke rose into the air from the hole and the men shouted across the deck.

Far below now, Rodger stared up at Stephen, shouting. He could guess what the bounty hunter was saying, and it wasn't fit for a lady's ears.

Stephen snorted. Rodger should be thankful he only hit his cannon. Another man might have aimed for his heart.

There were two more pings along the deck, probably from Jake and Piers, but they were too far away to do any damage with a gun.

Stephen bowed his head and let his breath out. They had escaped.

He stayed on one knee beside the railing while Robert's crew finished stowing the balloon. The ship drifted steadily upward beneath him, a different feeling compared to undulations of a ship on water.

After a moment, the ship stopped ascending and began gliding along the air current. Stephen stood. The sky tower below was the size of a finger, blending in with the rest of World City, a landscape of thousands of rooftops and smokestacks. The sky above was robin's egg blue with only wisps of clouds hanging along the horizon.

The air was cooler up here, but not uncomfortably so, and the blades rotating around the ship had ceased their straining and settled into a loud hum now that they were coasting along.

A small plume of smoke still curled from the hole Rodger had left in one of the smaller masts near a rotor blade. Grim came up beside Stephen and tapped his chin, staring at the hole. "Yes, I would like a prosthetic like that very much. Next time I'm in World City, I need to find whoever created Rodger's cannon."

Stephen shook his head and put his revolver away, trying to picture Grim with a prosthetic eye that shot back.

For some time he remained there at the rail, watching the city pass by below. He should go check on Kat, but he couldn't make his body move in that direction. Invisible manacles held him place. Every time he closed his eyes, he saw that wounded look on her face and felt the gut punch all over again.

Like now.

He groaned and bowed his head. *What a fool I was! If only I could go back* . . .

He shook his head. No. There was no going back. What was done was done. He could only hope now to repair the damage between them. He looked up and clenched his hand. He would do whatever it took to mend the breach.

But would Kat forgive him?

They passed over the Meandre River. The airship turned and headed for the coast, where hundreds of ships rocked gently in the blue-green waters below. At this height, the ships looked like a child's toys left along the edge of a pond. Soon the airship would be past World City and start across the Narrow Strait.

Part of him wanted to stop the airship and head back to the city. He had saved Kat. What more could he do?

But that was the coward's way out. No, he owed her more. And . . .

Stephen pulled the brim of his hat down across his forehead. He couldn't deny what he knew deep inside. He loved Kat. Which made what he had done in the heat of hurt and betrayal even more heinous.

He straightened and turned around. The door that led to Robert's quarters was on the other side of the deck. The rotors swirled above him, powered by the solar panels Robert had brought out.

He stood rigid and stared at the door. *Go. Just do it. Tell Kat—What? That I'm sorry? I am. That I love her?*

Stephen pressed his lips into a thin line. He couldn't tell her that. Not right now. Not after what he had done. But he could be with her. And he would, at least until she woke up, then after that . . .

Then maybe we can talk.

But the thought of talking about what he did made his stomach clench hard and bile fill his throat. Nevertheless, he made his feet move. He would be there when she woke up, no matter what.

CHAPTER

2

IMAGES RUSHED THROUGH STEPHEN'S MIND, A BLUR OF COLOR AND figures. He was at the World City gala, dancing with a woman in blue. For one heartbeat, she looked like Vanessa; then her face morphed into Kat's. Kat looked at him up and smiled.

Before he could react, his mind rushed on to the next scene. Now he was in a dance hall. Kat sat next to him, dressed like his old school teacher. She leaned over, her eyes dark and wide, and whispered, "I started the fire."

His stomach dropped and he was in a dark room with a single green light that shone from a simple miner's lamp. A figure in white stood, her back to him, her dark hair falling in chocolate cascades over her shoulders. Slowly she turned.

His heart started thumping faster. Something wasn't right.

She looked at him with milky white eyes. Kat. The other Kat. "Everything will be fine, Stephen," she whispered.

Stephen took a step back and hit a wall.

She held up her hand and a flame appeared across her palm. "Which shall it be? Fire? Or—" She held up her other hand and clenched it into fist.

Stephen grabbed his throat. He couldn't breathe.

Kat laughed, that eerie, ethereal laugh when the other Kat appeared. "Or maybe both—"

The door clicked behind him.

Stephen's eyes shot open. He bolted up from the chair, grabbing his guns as he turned. He pointed both revolvers at the door that led into Grim's cabin.

A rotund man entered, a stained apron stretched across the broad expanse of his waist. He held up small wooden box and a wad of bandages. Sweat glistened across his bald head. "Captain Grim sent me to check on the lady. However, if this is a bad time . . ." His gaze focused on the barrels pointed at him.

Stephen blinked and glanced at his guns. "I'm sorry," he said, lowering the revolvers. "I must have fallen asleep, and you startled me."

"The captain told me you're a bounty hunter. Explains the reflexes." The man crossed the room and set his supplies down on the nearby table. "Fitzgerald, by the way. Cook and medic for the *Lancelot*. Everyone around here calls me Fitz."

Stephen put his revolvers away and took a deep breath, his heart returning to its normal beat. "Stephen Grey. And I apologize again for my reaction." He ran a hand through his hair. "It's been a long couple of days."

Fitz grinned. "I'm sure it's quite a story. It's not every day we pick someone up from the roof of the Tower." He laughed, and his belly jiggled in time with his chortle.

A smile tugged at Stephen's lips. "True enough."

Fitz caught his breath and wiped his face. "Now, tell me about the lady."

Stephen's smile disappeared. He slowly turned to look down at Kat, and the bile returned to his throat. "I don't know what's wrong with her."

Fitz came to stand beside him. He smelled like flour and yeast. "Hmmm."

"There were metal rods in her sides, but not deep. And tubing attached to her wrists."

Fitz frowned. "For what purpose?"

Stephen swallowed. "I don't know."

Fitz picked up Kat's hand and angled it so he could study her wrist in the light of the chandelier behind him. "Well, these wounds don't look deep, and they're pretty clean, all things considered. Let's check the others."

He placed her hand down and drew back the bedspread.

The white gown Kat wore barely reached her knees and was so thin Stephen could make out the contours of her body underneath. He shifted his gaze away and clenched his hands. Her father hadn't even had the decency to cover up his own daughter!

"She's lost a bit of blood. I need to cut away some of the fabric to see how bad the wound is. Could you hand me the shears from my box over there?"

"Sure." Stephen turned and headed for the table, anxious to do anything but stand there and stare at Kat. He opened the wooden box and found an array of vials, small pouches, a stone mortar and pestle, and a pair of shears. He pulled out the shears and brought them back.

Fitz took them without a word and cut away the gown while Stephen stared out the windows to his right.

"Metal rods, you say?" Fitz said a minute later.

"Yes, along both of her sides. I had to pull them out before I could move her."

Fitz made a clicking noise with his tongue. "What in all of God's green world were those scientists doing? To a young woman no less!"

Stephen licked his lips and shook his head.

"I'll put some antiseptic on the exit wounds and give each one a stitch or two, then bandage them up."

"Do you know why she's not waking up?"

Fitz glanced over at Stephen. "I have no idea. Trauma, perhaps, or something more. I'm afraid I know very little. Just enough to get by. I'll need you to stand by her head and be ready to hold her just in case she wakes up from the needle. All right?"

Stephen nodded and walked around Fitz to the other side. He pushed the chair away, went down on his knees, and placed his hands on the bed by Kat's head. She took a shallow breath every few seconds.

"Ready?"

"Ready."

Stephen watched Kat breathe while Fitz retrieved the necessary stuff from his box and started stitching up the wounds on her side.

Five minutes passed when Fitz stood up and stretched his back. "All right. You said they placed rods on both sides of her ribcage?"

"Yes."

"Then we'll need to gently turn her over."

Stephen's stomach tightened, but he nodded. He held onto her shoulders while Fitz reached for her side.

"One, two, three."

They carefully rolled Kat over and Fitz brought the bedspread up to her hips before cutting away the bloody fabric.

Stephen turned away. He couldn't watch anymore, and that sheer gown of hers left little to the imagination, which only fueled his anger, both at himself for looking, and at Dr. Bloodmayne for treating his daughter this way. Minutes ticked by and Fitz whistled softly under his breath. "There," he said just as Stephen debated heading out onto the deck. "Stitched up and bandaged. Now, let's make her comfortable."

Stephen looked back, keeping his eyes on Kat's head. Her hair spread across her back in dark, thick curls. He moved forward and helped Fitz turn her back around.

Fitz fixed the bedspread across her body, tucking it in close and leaving her arms out along her sides. He took a step back and let out his breath. "Now we wait."

"I'll stay with her."

Fitz nodded. "That's a good idea. It will help her to wake up and see someone she knows."

Stephen's stomach knotted up. He wasn't so sure about that. He doubted his face was the first one she would want to see. But he would stay here, at least until then.

Fitz placed his supplies back in his box. "I'll bring you something to eat, and every few hours I will check on her." The door shut behind him with a quiet click.

Stephen pulled his chair back to Kat's side. He reached over and brushed a dark strand of hair away, then settled into his chair. His stomach rumbled, but he couldn't bear the thought of food. All he wanted now was for Kat to wake up.

CHAPTER

3

KAT PLUNGED INTO THE COLD, DARK WATER. GASPING, SHE FLAILED her hands and kicked out, but the water sucked her in like a whirlpool in the middle of the ocean. The swirling wall of water roared around her. Beyond the coursing waves, the sky above was as dark as night.

She screamed and sucked in cold salt water. Her sides ached along her ribcage, as if fiery pokers pressed against her skin. Adrenaline coursed through her body and she gasped again.

Water sprayed up around her and she sank deeper into the whirlpool. She fought against the tide, but her limbs shook with fatigue and her fingers were stiff with cold.

She swallowed another mouthful of water and choked. Her legs seized up. She looked up to the patch of darkness above. So far away.

Just let go.

That voice. She knew that voice. It was her voice. The one she heard in her head when the monster inside her awoke.

Why fight? Just let go and sink into the water.

For one heady moment, she wanted to. She was cold and numb. Especially her heart. She could barely feel it. It would be so easy to just sink beneath the water and be finished.

"No!" Kat kicked out with legs and arms and lifted her head above the water's surface. Her lungs burned with icy cold air. *I don't want to die!*

But Kat, you're already dying. Why not end it now and be done with it?

Kat blinked. What was this place? Was this the passage between life and death? Had her father . . . killed her?

She looked at the small opening high above, between the rushing waters. Something burst inside her, that last lunge of life. She held up an open hand toward the sky and sobbed. "God, please save me!"

The water collapsed above her and swept her under.

Kat sat up with a gasp. Her body convulsed with chills and her teeth chattered so hard her jaw hurt. *Cold. So cold. Wait . . . I can breathe!*

She sucked in sweet air until her lungs filled to bursting. Then she let out her breath and took in another. Her body tingled as it thawed beneath something thick and warm. She was on a bed. A red feather-down coverlet lay across her legs and midsection. She drew the coverlet up to her neck, and gradually her body stopped shaking.

"Kat . . ." a tense voice said beside her.

Her throat went dry. Slowly she looked over, and her heart stopped.

Stephen.

He sat in a chair a couple feet away, his eyebrows drawn up, his fingers gripping the arms of his chair. Dark circles traced the bottom of his eyes and blond stubble covered his jaw. He looked like he hadn't slept in days.

Of all the people . . . How in the world was Stephen here?

He stood abruptly and rubbed the back of his neck. "I'll go let Fitz know you're awake."

Before she could say anything, he turned and headed for the door across the room.

Kat watched him until he disappeared, her heart vacillating between strange thudding beats and deep hurt.

Why was Stephen here? Last she remembered—bile filled her

throat—he had left her at the Tower. So why was he here now? She glanced around. And where *was* here?

The room appeared to be a bedchamber, but more. A simple chandelier hung above a polished metal table with matching chairs on either side. On the other side of the room was a large desk and a bench that looked built into the wall. Swords and tapestries depicting high adventure decorated the wooden panels.

To her left, past the table, was a wall made of small square pieces of glass. But there were no buildings outside. Not even a street lamp. Just darkness.

She closed her eyes and gripped the blanket, breathing in the strange, sweet scent the fabric held. Wherever she was, she wasn't drowning. She was still alive.

Kat pressed the coverlet to her eyes and wiped away the tears that had emerged along her lower eyelids. It had been just a dream. A terrifying, horrible nightmare. It wasn't real . . . but that voice . . .

She pulled the blanket away. That same voice—the one that always urged her to set the world on fire—it said she was dying. But she couldn't be. Could she?

She held up her hand and moved her fingers, then mentally checked her body. Her wrists and her ribcage were sore, but everything seemed well enough. Everything except . . .

Kat frowned and placed her hand just above her heart. Her skin felt smooth beneath her fingers, but when she pressed a finger into her sternum, she couldn't feel the pressure. In fact, the whole area above her heart felt numb, and her skin was chilly to the touch.

Casting a glance around the room to make sure she was alone, Kat pulled the coverlet away and lifted the neckline of the simple white gown she wore. Her skin looked fine. No bruises, no cuts or wounds along her chest, though her ribcage was wrapped with bandages. She ran a finger along her side above the bandages. A sharp twinge of pain erupted beneath her touch, and she gasped and pulled back. Somehow she had been injured along her sides.

She frowned and glanced at her chest. That didn't explain the numbness around her heart.

She raised her hand and forced her thumbnail into her skin, right above her heart, until it left an impression. She should have felt that. Instead, she felt nothing.

Her mouth went dry as she drew her hand back. What was happening to her? Was the voice right? Was she slowly dying?

The door opened and she jerked the coverlet up over her chest. Stephen?

She glanced back. No, definitely not Stephen. A short, stocky man walked in, the low light of the lamp on the table gleaming off his bald head, which was almost perfectly round. He wore a stained apron over his white shirt and dark trousers. In one hand he balanced a tray, while he closed the door with the other.

Kat shrank against the bed frame and held the blanket close to her body, her mind flashing back to other trays—to syringes and needles and cruel instruments.

The man glanced up and caught sight of her. He smiled, and something about the gap-toothed expression calmed Kat's fears. Wherever this was, it wasn't the Tower. This man's apron was stained with broth, not blood. As he drew near the bed, she spotted a simple teapot on the tray with wisps of steam emitting from the spout. Next to the pot was a matching teacup, plain and somehow homey.

"So you're finally awake."

Kat wasn't sure how to respond, so she gave him a small nod. She also kept a close eye on the door, ready to run if the man proved to be here for reasons other than tea.

His smile broadened, revealing more stained teeth—one of which was missing entirely—and he placed the tray on the table nearby.

Kat caught the earthy scent of black tea and—dizziness washed over her—scones. She hadn't eaten since, well, she wasn't sure. How long had she been out?

The man picked up the teapot and poured the hot, black liquid into the teacup with a gentleness that belied his bulk.

He looked over his shoulder. "Do you take cream with your tea? And sugar?"

Her mouth moistened. "Cream, please. And one lump."

He picked up the creamer and poured, then placed a sugar cube into the cup and stirred.

"Here you go."

Kat reached for the cup, breathing in the bittersweet scent and letting the warmth from the porcelain soak into her fingers. She wanted to take a sip, but was it safe?

"By the way, my name is Fitzgerald, but the crew calls me Fitz."

Kat looked up. "Crew?"

"Yes. You're aboard the *Lancelot*, captained by Robert Grim."

Her brow furrowed. "I've never heard of the *Lancelot*. How did I get here? And *why* am I here?"

"First, food. If you want to gain back your strength, you need to eat. I thought a proper lady like yourself would enjoy a simple meal." Fitz placed one of the delicate golden biscuits on a small plate and handed it to Kat.

Kat held the teacup in one hand and set the plate on her lap, careful to keep the coverlet in place. She stared at the scone, her mouth watering, her stomach tightening with the thought of food, but she didn't reach for it. How could she know if it was safe to eat? She could sniff it, maybe—

"It's not poisonous."

Kat looked up and blushed.

"It's my mother's recipe, and the captain's favorite."

She hesitated.

Fitz took one of the other scones, showed it to Kat, then bit in. Her stomach growled as she watched him chew. He swallowed and smiled. "There, you see? Go on." He waved his hand. "Eat."

Kat gave in. She picked up the scone and took a bite. The scone was still warm and flaky and she longed to stuff as much into her mouth as she could, but years of etiquette held her hungry thoughts back. She finished the first bite, took another small one, then sipped a little tea to wash the sweet biscuit down. She glanced back up at Fitz. "This scone is delicious."

Fitz took a seat in the chair Stephen had vacated and folded his arms. His smile spread across his entire face. "I'm glad you like it."

Kat took another bite, savoring the buttery sweetness. "So you made these?" she asked, holding up half of the scone.

"Yes, ma'am. I'm the cook for the *Lancelot*. And the medic. I'm the one who fixed you up when you arrived, and both Stephen and I have watched over you the last two days."

"Two days?" Kat sucked in her breath. She had been out that long?

"I've seen a lot of stuff in my day, but never the wounds you had along on your sides. They weren't too bad, but we still couldn't awaken you. How do you feel now?"

Kat set the plate down, now covered in crumbs, and felt along her sides where the bandages were. "Well, I'm awake now. And my sides don't hurt much." She wasn't about to tell him about the numb, cold area around her heart.

"Good. I . . . uh . . . was very careful when bandaging you." His face turned red, spreading up across his bald head. "I usually only treat men, mainly the crew."

Kat took hold of the situation and gave Fitz a small nod. "Thank you for being a gentleman." She paused. "You mentioned Stephen was here as well, watching over me."

"Yes. He only left your side for minutes at a time."

Kat lowered her head, her lungs constricting, making each breath difficult. It didn't make sense. Stephen had left her at the Tower. He *had left her.*

"Would you like another scone?"

Kat glanced up and swallowed. Her mind was a muddled mess at the present. Later she would figure it all out. "Yes, I would. Thank you."

When Fitz returned to his duties, Kat fell into a fitful sleep. Fire and waves swept across her mind. And that voice again . . .

Kat, you're already dying. Just give up . . . give up . . .

She opened her eyes and stared up at the ceiling. Pale light filtered through the wall of windows nearby. The lamp on the table had been snuffed out.

The door opened behind her. She twisted around and looked over her shoulder. Fitz walked in, holding an armful of clothing. Tucking the comforter under her arms, Kat sat up. She might have slept, but she still felt as tired as ever.

"Good morning, miss. I brought you some clothing." He placed the garments on the table. "It's not what you're accustomed to, but it's better than what you're wearing now. That is, if you want to leave your room."

"It's morning?"

"Bright and early." Fitz placed a pair of boots beside the clothing, then used his sleeve to polish the toe of one.

"Fitz?"

"Yes?" he said and turned around.

"How did I end up here?" Her face wrinkled. "I do not know a Robert Wim, Limb . . ."

"Grim."

"Yes, that."

He gave a chuckle. "That is quite a story. In a nutshell, Stephen Grey rescued you from the Tower, and we picked you both up by way of the roof. The crew is still talking about that rescue."

"Stephen rescued me?"

"He sure did."

So it wasn't a dream. She sat back against the headboard. She remembered seeing Stephen's face before passing out, and the deep hurt it invoked. Even now, dredging up his face made her feel sick. Stephen had turned her in to the Tower, and he had never even told her why. He had left her with her father, who then . . .

Kat clenched the coverlet tight between her fingers and swallowed. *No, not now. I don't want to remember.* She forced the memories of that dark room from her memory. Instead, she focused on the windows. Faint, downy white fluttered by outside.

She sat up and stared. "Fitz, is it foggy outside?"

Fitz turned and looked out the windows. "No, just clouds passing by."

She blinked. "Clouds? But how?"

"*Lancelot* is an airship. We're making our way across the Narrow Strait right now."

"We're up in the air?" Kat sucked in her breath. Ms. Stuart had never let her travel by airship. Too dangerous, she used to say. That and, Kat believed, Ms. Stuart had a fear of heights.

Ms. Stuart.

Her shoulders sagged and the elation from moments ago vanished. There was no longer that sharp pain whenever she thought of Ms. Stuart. Her housekeeper and friend was at rest now, along with her mother. Gone to that dark place where science could not reach.

So her father used to say.

Kat, let go—

She squeezed her eyes shut against the voice. *Quiet. Now!*

"Everything all right, miss?"

"Yes." She opened her eyes and concentrated on the windows.

"First time up in the air?"

Watching the clouds soothed something inside her. "Yes."

"Would you like to see more?"

A small smile crept across her face. It felt odd and foreign after the tumult of emotions raging through her. She looked at Fitz and nodded. "Yes, I would like that very much."

Fitz stood and straightened his apron. "Go ahead and dress and I'll meet you out in the hall."

The moment the door shut, Kat moved from the bed. Her head spun for a second and she clung to the bedpost. Once the room came to a standstill, she moved toward the windows. Wisps of clouds slid by the glass, set against a backdrop of pale blue. She stopped a foot away and peered down. Like a broad, rumpled blanket, darker blue spread beneath the delicate fog. The Narrow Strait.

There was something small below. At second glance, it looked like a ship. Her smiled widened. It looked like a toy from this high up. And the clouds . . .

She reached out and touched the window. A thin film of condensation coated the glass and melted away at the heat of her hand, leaving rivulets along the pane. Amazing. If only she could reach out and actually touch the cloud.

Maybe she could, if she dressed quickly.

Kat turned and eyed the clothing Fitz had left on the table, a brown skirt with a matching brown corset and boots. Dark stockings and a white blouse with ruffles down the front lay folded beside the brown clothing. There was even a tortoiseshell comb for her hair.

Kat crossed the room, checked the door and slid the chain across, then went back to the table. There was no way to cover the windows, although how a person would be able to view in, she didn't know.

She carried the clothes to the bed and laid them out. Standing between the bed and windows, she pulled the blouse on and buttoned it up. The ruffles felt extravagant after the plain blouses she was used to wearing. And the neckline, although not low enough to be considered improper, was certainly lower than any World City lady would wear. It was more the current style in Austrium, or so Marianne had said one morning at the academy while browsing one of those new fashion catalogs.

Wary, Kat picked up the skirt next and held it against her hips. It fell to mid-calf. She let out a sigh. At least the skirt was long enough. Most Austrium women were wearing their skirts at knee length. An image of the ladies from the dancing hall Stephen had dragged her into darted across her mind, with their legs flashing beneath their short skirts.

She blushed. It could be worse.

Kat pulled on the stockings, buttoned her boots, and pulled on the skirt. Lastly, she placed the corset over her blouse and skirt, working the clasps in front then tugging on the laces in back. Most young women grew up with a maid to help them dress, but her father never saw a reason to hire more house help apart from Ms. Stuart. Ms. Stuart taught her how to dress herself, and given that she was on the run now, she was thankful for her independence.

She pulled on the laces, tightening both the top and the bottom of the corset at the same time until the two sets of laces were taut in the middle, right at her waist. She adjusted the corset one more time, checked the laces, and tied the laces into a bow.

There.

She fingered the belt loops and thin brass chains that hung from the corset, and the pouch that sat snug against her right hip. What were they for? Perhaps she would ask Fitz.

Kat smoothed her skirt one more time, then ran her fingers through her hair. Satisfied, she pulled the strands back into a simple chignon and pinned it in place with the comb.

She breathed in deeply and let it out with one long sigh as she glanced at the door behind her. There was one person on this ship she didn't want to see, but chances were she would run into him.

Stephen Grey.

CHAPTER
4

THE MOMENT KAT STEPPED ONTO THE DECK, ALL THOUGHTS OF Stephen vanished from her mind. Wispy clouds floated by, just beyond the edge of the ship. Mesmerized, she walked across the deck and grabbed the railing. She held out one hand. The cloud was more like mist—cold, wet, and semi-opaque. A moment later the air grew clear.

"I would hate to see such a lovely lady fall."

Kat gasped and turned around, holding her hand to her chest as if she had burned it. A man stood a couple feet away, a black patch over his right eye. He wore a long, black duster that rustled in the wind. His dark, shaggy hair hung around his face and his one good eye—brilliant blue—studied her.

He bowed. "Captain Robert Grim." He looked up. "And you are Miss Bloodmayne."

Kat pulled her shoulders back, years of etiquette grilled into her by Ms. Stuart taking over. "Yes. A pleasure to meet you, Captain Grim. I take it I owe you my thanks."

Captain Grim straightened. "Nonsense. You are a guest here on the *Lancelot*. Have you ever flown before?"

A smile touched her lips. "No, I haven't. This is incredible!"

Her words appeared to have a positive effect on the captain. He grinned and held out an arm. "I'm afraid Fitz had an emergency to take care of, so now I have the pleasure of taking you on a tour of my ship."

Kat took his arm and before she could say another word, Grim whirled her around and headed for the top deck. Her skirt spun around her boots, and a light wet mist pressed against her face.

"I'm glad to see my sister's clothes fit you."

Kat glanced down at the ruffled blouse and corset. She touched one of the thin brass chains that hung near the pouch.

"Sarah used to fly with me until she married a gent last year. I had that corset especially made for her. She was never content to just fly; she had to be doing something on the ship. Always had a tool in her hand. Those chains, belt loops, and pouch are where she kept her gear."

Kat's face softened. "I see." She had a feeling she would have liked this Sarah.

"She left a chest of clothes behind, so let Fitz know if you need anything else."

"Thank you."

Grim led her up a set of stairs toward the top deck, which stretched out across the front of the ship, about twenty feet wide, coming to a rounded point at the end. The ship's wheel was set in the middle. A man, tall, with long brown hair tied back, stood behind the wheel with his hands on either side of the helm. He wore a loose white shirt that rippled with the wind. A tattoo flowed along his neck and disappeared into his shirt.

He spotted Grim and Kat and nodded. "Captain. Miss."

"Anders," Grim said, then glanced at Kat. "Anders is my first mate. Been with me almost as long as I've been a pirate."

Kat felt as though she had been punched. "A p-pirate?"

"Oh, yes." Grim's one good eye crinkled. "Did I forget to mention that?"

Yes, and so had Fitz. Convenient. Did Stephen know Captain Grim? Or had this ship just been a convenient way to flee World City?

Grim chuckled and Anders gave her a wink. "Don't worry, we are honorable pirates."

"Is there such a thing?" She said the words before she could stop her tongue.

Grim laughed again and Anders joined him. "There can be, and there is."

"Is Stephen paying you for this voyage?" The thought of Stephen paying her passage made her feel ill.

Grim sobered. "No. Stephen and I are old friends. He telegraphed me stating you were both in great danger and needed a fast getaway. I happened to be in World City, preparing for a blockade run, when Stephen contacted me. And now here you are on my ship, safe and sound."

"I see." Fitz had said something about a rescue, and from the top of the Tower.

"So what exactly happened?"

Kat glanced back at Captain Grim. "Pardon?"

He folded his arms. "Stephen hasn't said a word about what happened back at the Tower, or why you were there. All I know is you came aboard my ship unconscious and near death." He watched her with that one eye of his.

The blood drained from her face. She wasn't ready to share with anyone what had happened to her at the Tower, certainly not with a man she hardly knew.

Grim dropped his hand. "Well, whatever happened back in the city, it unnerved Stephen. I've never seen him run from a fight before, but he did run. To save you."

She brushed the base of her neck. "I-I didn't know." She glanced over the railing at the blue sky. Why? Why had Stephen come back? Why did he save her after he had left her there? She couldn't remember anything after her father had come and talked to her in the lab.

She still couldn't believe what she had witnessed of her father. Yes, he had been absent most of her life, so she barely knew him. But the man who had stood over her—his cold, calculating stare, his words twisting inside her mind—that had not been her father. Not the one she had always dreamed about.

"You are the culmination of my life's work."

Her hand tightened around her throat. An experiment. That's all she had been to him. Then he had started the tests.

"Anyway . . ."

Kat turned back.

Grim brushed his coat and readjusted his cuffs. "You are a guest here on my ship. You're safe, just as I promised Stephen you would be."

Anders had quietly slipped away from their conversation, his hand holding the wheel steady, his gaze set across the ship toward the bow.

"Thank you." She wanted to feel safe, but what her father had done back at the Tower had left her feeling tainted inside. She was a monster, and it was only a matter of time before it came back to the surface.

He smiled and held out his arm. "Come, let's finish our tour."

Kat took a deep breath and nodded. A tour would be a welcome distraction.

Kat had never been on a ship before, neither in the water nor in the air. The *Lancelot* was large, with a full deck, another top deck, and two levels below those. The bottom level held the cargo, the middle level the living quarters for the crew, the galley, and the motor house for the ship. On either side of the main deck were the captain's quarters and the navigation room. The top deck and helm were located above the captain's cabin.

Two main towers rose from the deck with a rotor on top of each. Four smaller towers were attached to the sides of the ship, two on each side, all four with smaller rotors.

The rotors filled the air with a steady hum as they propelled the *Lancelot* through the sky. Wherever the ship was in relation to the sun, panels were propped open to catch the light and transform it into energy. Kat watched two of the sailors prop open a set of panels along the side of the deck. Back home in World City, almost everything ran on steam, gas, or the new source of power, electricity.

"How do you use panels to catch the sun's rays?" she asked Grim.

Grim leaned back against the railing on his elbows. "I had a drink with a young man down south a couple years ago. He was fiddling with the concept, and I offered to back his project on the condition that if he was able to turn the sunlight into energy, I wanted to add it to my ship. What could be better for an airship than a way to harness free power here in the sky? A little over a year later, he tested his panels on *Lancelot*, and we've been flying with them ever since."

Kat studied the panels, tapping her chin as she did so. It was a brilliant idea. If only she could get a closer look at one of those pa—

A figure stopped near the stairs, just a shadow in the corner of her eye. Before she could think, Kat swerved her head—and froze.

Stephen stood at the bottom of the steps that led to the top deck. He stared back, his expression unreadable. His blond hair whipped around his face. His leather duster swirled above his boots, blowing back every few strokes to reveal a white shirt, trousers, and his gun holsters.

He turned abruptly and headed up the stairs.

Kat stood there, her feet nailed to the spot. A sharp ache clawed its way up her middle. Stephen may as well have walked over to her and slapped her face.

He disappeared beyond the top deck.

Why had he saved her? Out of duty? Regret? Kat turned, gripped the railing, and closed her eyes. Maybe he should have left her at the Tower.

No. Not there. Never again. Even if it meant Stephen's cold presence.

"Interesting," Grim said quietly.

Kat took a deep breath. "Where are we going?" She grit her teeth against the tears threatening to spill from her eyes.

"Austrium, my dear."

"Austrium?" She turned and looked at Grim.

"I'm technically a blockade runner for World City. A privateer. However, I prefer the title pirate. Sounds more adventurous,
wouldn't you agree?"

Kat frowned. The ache that had been building inside her vanished near her heart, washing away all feeling. She glanced again at
the deck where Stephen had disappeared, but felt only a hint of the
ache that had pierced her moments before.

Strange.

"Are you all right?"

Kat glanced at Grim again.

He stared back with a concerned frown. "Perhaps we should get
you back to your room."

"But isn't it your room?"

He cocked the eyebrow over his one good eye. "Would you rather
sleep with the crew?"

Kat blinked, an image of the hold below lined with hammocks,
each one with a man sleeping inside flitting across her mind.

Grim smiled. "I didn't think so. Come, I'll take you back and
have Fitz bring you something to eat."

He held out his arm and Kat took it, grateful for something to
hold on to. "You're right, I am feeling a little fatigued."

Grim gave her a polite nod and led her across the main deck
toward the door that led to his private quarters.

Kat stood before the mirror late that evening in just her borrowed
undergarments and a long bandage wrapped around her middle. A
nightgown and robe draped across the nearby bench. She touched
the area above her heart with her fingertip. She still couldn't feel
anything.

"What's happening to me?" she whispered to her image. Not only
did she feel nothing physically near her heart, she didn't feel anything inside either. She remembered Stephen's look, and a ghost of
the ache filled her belly. But it wasn't as strong, not as intense now.

As if there were a hole where her heart used to be, sucking in all feeling.

But how? Why? She rubbed her face and turned away from the mirror. Her mind raced through everything she could remember from school, but none of the scientific journals or lectures came close to explaining what was happening to her.

The voice from her dreams said she was dying. Was it possible? Was she dying from the inside out?

Kat spun around and grabbed the nightgown. After she pulled on the light garment and robe, she headed back to the table. Fitz had been kind enough to procure a pen and a couple pieces of paper for her. She sat down and stared out at the inky blackness beyond the glass bulkhead, pen in hand.

What did she know?

She turned back to the paper and started writing. She knew her father had been experimenting, trying to unlock the power around death. Kat paused. What did that even mean? She shook her head and continued.

He experimented on corpses, eventually moving on to those close to death. She clenched her jaw, the pen moving furiously across the paper. He never explained what he did during his experiments, but he did hint that he had moved away from scientific methods to the mystical, and in doing so, had somehow opened up a door into the unknown.

Kat held the pen above a paper filled with notes. "Father, what did you do?" she whispered. "What did you do to me?"

Was it even possible to find an answer? After all, her father had strayed from science, and because of that, perhaps the answer could not be found in science.

Her fingers tightened around the pen. If her father had used mystical methods to change her, she wanted nothing to do with that sort of research. She would stick to measurable science. There had to be an answer somewhere. All she had to do was find it. And she would continue to search for Dr. Latimer, alone, once she left this ship. He was a man of science as well, even with all that talk of souls in his articles.

She tapped the end of the pen against the table. Then again, maybe this . . . thing, this numbness, would eventually heal, and she would be back to normal again. Or sort of normal.

Kat dropped the pen and held her head in her hands, her hair covering her face. *What am I thinking? I've never been normal.*

Her heart sank. *And maybe I never will be.*

CHAPTER

5

Kat always seemed to miss Stephen when she left the captain's cabin. When she stepped out on the deck, he disappeared through the door down to the lower levels of the ship. When she entered the galley, he left through the back. In some ways, it was a relief. As much as she wanted answers, she wasn't ready to see him, not yet. The very sight of him brought on a hurricane of emotions. Emotions that could trigger the monster inside her. A monster she did not want awakened.

She spent most of her time evaluating everything she knew and could remember from her brief time at the Tower, writing down her thoughts on the handful of paper in her possession. If only she had access to the Tower's library. With what she knew now about what her father had done to her, perhaps the texts and books she'd read previously would provide new insight and possible answers to her condition.

But what if there was no answer to be found in the physical world?

The thought niggled the back of her mind, growing like a weed in the shadows. Her father had tapped into something powerful, something that went beyond her limited understanding.

Did souls really exist inside people? And could they be damaged? Or worse? Was her soul dying?

No! Kat slammed her hand on the table, rustling the papers beneath her palm. *I won't go there, not yet. Not until I have exhausted every other possibility.* Her head throbbed above her right eye. *I just need a break to clear my mind. Then I'll keep working.* She stood and stretched her back before heading for the main deck.

Once outside, a smile spread across her face and the tightness along her back loosened. Cool wind rushed across her face. Distant clouds billowed over the open sea. The rising sun spread its glorious rays across the ship, making her wish her life were different. What she wouldn't give just to stay on the *Lancelot* here in the clouds, away from the city and the people and the problems back home. Not once had the monster stirred since she had come aboard the airship. Perhaps it, too, was calmed by the rhythmic rotors and the freedom of the skies.

Kat held onto the railing and closed her eyes. The rotors pulled curls out from her hasty chignon and twisted her skirt around her boots. She breathed in the cold, sweet air, and smiled. Ms. Stuart once said that God lived in heaven. When she had asked where heaven was, Ms. Stuart had stammered, then said somewhere in the sky.

Yes, she could believe that. If she were God, she would want to live up here, too.

Something moved behind her. Kat opened her eyes and turned. Stephen stood a couple feet away.

Her smile fell as heat rushed through her body.

Stephen stared at her, a pained expression on his face.

Her hands began to tremble. Kat clenched them together and turned back toward the railing. The calm from moments ago vanished, its vacuum filled with an aching hurt.

Her palms felt like they were on fire. She glanced down and found a wisp of smoke curling between her fingers. "No, no . . ."

She backed away from the railing and held her hands out, each breath fast and raspy. "Can't lose control, can't lose control!" *Just breathe and get to the cabin. Now!*

Kat turned and headed for the door.

"Kat! Wait!" Stephen called. "Can we—"

She shook her head as she dashed by. Stephen didn't understand. She had to get herself under control before the monster emerged.

She reached the door below the top deck and went for the handle. Wait, did Stephen want to talk? Now? After all the distant glimpses they'd exchanged on the ship?

I can't! I don't want him to see me like this!

Kat held the doorknob, torn between turning back and fleeing inside. She opened the door, then glanced back.

Stephen stood beside the mast that held one of the main rotors, his back to her, his hands in the pockets of his duster.

Her heart stirred. Those feelings from the coach came back to her—feelings from that night before she'd realized where Stephen was taking her.

He straightened and looked at her.

Kat froze, all blood draining from her face. She wasn't ready. Not yet.

His face fell before he turned and walked away.

Kat wrenched the door open and flew down the hall to the captain's cabin. At least her fingers had stopped tingling.

She hurried into the cabin and slammed the door shut behind her. Her body began to shake. She pressed her back against the door and slid to the floor. How could she bridge the gap between her and Stephen? *Did* she want to bridge that gap?

"It would easier if he . . . if he had never . . ." Kat pressed her palms against her cheeks and cried. Stephen was the first man she had felt anything toward, and she had trusted him.

If only I knew why. Why did he do it? Why . . .

She drew her hands away and stared at her palms. Her face was wet, salty, and hot.

Why did he come back for me?

She blinked. Something had to have happened. Yes, Stephen took her to the Tower. Her throat tightened. She remembered the moment she realized where they were heading. But he hadn't left her there.

He had come back.

What made him change his mind?

She let out a long breath and looked across the room toward the wall of glass. Gray clouds filled the horizon beyond the windows.

Stephen had come back for her. He took her away from the Tower and brought her here. Why?

Kat wiped her eyes and stood. She made her way to the bed. The scarlet bedspread was rumpled from last night's sleep. She lay down and curled up on her side. She still could not feel her chest. Even now the ache brought on by Stephen's appearance was rapidly dissipating.

She sniffed and closed her eyes. Yes, they needed to talk. She wasn't sure they could ever go back to where they had been before. That bridge had burned. But maybe, just maybe, they could rebuild it.

CHAPTER
6

ROBERT STOOD BESIDE THE SHIP'S WHEEL, HIS BLACK HAIR FLUT-
tering across his eye patch. "So you're ready to talk?"

Stephen leaned against the nearby railing of the top deck and
looked out over the sky. Cool air brushed his face and he readjusted
his duster across his shoulders. Dark clouds gathered along the horizon. "It's a long story."

"I have plenty of time."

Stephen let out his breath and dipped his head. "I'm the one who
turned Kat in to the Tower."

"The same Tower you rescued her from?"

"Yes."

Robert was silent as he gently turned the wheel. Stephen could
almost imagine the thoughts flashing through his friend's mind.
Why? How? But Robert simply said, "Go on."

"Kat had a bounty on her. I discovered this down in Covenshire
shortly after I met with you. A hefty bounty, for murder." Robert
didn't react, so Stephen went on. "I also witnessed something—
something I still can't explain." He ran a hand through his hair.
Would Robert even believe him? "I think Kat was experimented on
by her father. And it changed her. She can do things I've never seen
a person do."

Robert tugged the wheel to the right. "Such as?"

"Those three bounty hunters who shot at the *Lancelot* a couple days ago? They found us in Covenshire, at Marty's inn. They were after Kat's bounty. A gunfight started and I was pinned down behind a table. Then Kat came downstairs and . . ."

Stephen looked up, the scene replaying in his mind.

He let out his breath. "She has the ability to move things. With . . . her mind. She froze everything inside the dining hall. She picked up every man in that place and flung him against a wall, knocking each man out. She also stopped a bullet meant for me. All without touching a thing."

Robert frowned and looked in Stephen's direction. "Are you sure that's what you saw?"

Stephen nodded. "Yes. I was paralyzed in place and watched the whole thing." He didn't bother to tell Robert about Kat's transformation, about the eerie laughter or the crazed look in her eyes. "Then she cried out to God and collapsed on the floor. Apparently, this power saps her energy because she passed out shortly after. I picked her up and brought her back to World City. Half way, I received Jerod's telegram about the bounty out on Kat, placed there by her own father and the city council. A bounty for murder. Considering what I had just seen, I could believe it. So I decided to turn her in."

Robert shook his head and whistled. "That is quite a story, and if it were any other man telling it, I would call him a liar. But you were never one for telling tales, even when we were kids." He turned the wheel slightly to the right and the ship followed his course. There was a moment of silence before he spoke again. "So what made you decide to rescue her? It sounds like the Tower was a better place for her, as much as I despise the place."

Stephen sighed. "Because I was wrong." He rubbed his face. "Kat warned me about her father's dark side, about the experiments he had performed on humans, but I didn't listen. When I discovered the bounty on Kat, all I could see was Vanessa, and how she had lied to me. I equated Kat to Vanessa, and in my bitterness, I turned her in. I tried to convince myself it was better for Kat and society, but when I arrived at the Tower and saw exactly what Dr. Bloodmayne was doing to his own daughter—"

His throat tightened and he looked away. Far below, the Narrow Strait's blue water sparkled in the sunlight. More dark clouds gathered in the distance.

"I see," Robert said slowly. "So you think the Tower did this to her?"

"I do."

"Are they creating more humans like her? With power like that?"

"I think they are trying, but Kat is the only successful one." He clenched his hand. "Remember those missing people I was looking for a couple years ago? I think the Tower used them."

Robert scowled. "I don't want to think about what the city council would do with an army of humans like that."

I don't either. At least Kat tried to control the power inside her. What would happen if someone just chose to let it loose?

The rotors hummed around them, whooshing with each blade rotation.

"Is Miss Bloodmayne still a danger?"

Seconds passed. "Right now she can control it." *Barely.*

"But?"

Stephen swallowed and turned. "I made a mistake when I turned Kat over to the Tower. Who knows what they did to her before I came back. Kat needs help, but the Tower—and her father—were the wrong solution."

"So this is why you are searching for this Dr. Latimer?" Robert steadied the wheel between his hands. "You think he can help her?"

"Kat believes he can. And I'm willing to help her find the doctor."

Robert reached for a brass lever to the right of the helm and pulled it back. The airship began to ascend seconds later. Stephen braced himself against the railing, his feet feeling like they were pulling into the deck as the ship tilted upward. He glanced toward the bow. Storm clouds gathered ahead. Looked like Robert was planning on gliding over the storm.

"If you're still looking for Dr. Latimer, I have some good news for you."

Stephen turned back. "You know where he is?"

"Not exactly, but I know what happened to him." The *Lancelot* continued its slow, steady climb.

"All right, what do you know?"

"He disappeared from society for a couple years, then turned up a year and a half ago serving as a civilian doctor in the World City military over in Austrium."

"He's in Austrium?"

"Yes, but I don't know where."

"Austrium is a big country."

"It is. But how many civilian doctors are there serving our soldiers?"

"True. That narrows down the places Dr. Latimer could be." Even then, the task seemed daunting.

"Fortunately for you, I am transporting the medical supplies needed at the Ironguard Base. It's as good a place to start as any."

"You're running medical supplies?"

"That I am. I can send you and Miss Bloodmayne down with the shipment once we reach the rendezvous point."

Stephen's eyes widened. For the first time, he felt like they had a chance. That *Kat* had a chance. "How long before we get there?"

"We're still a couple days out. And Ironguard is two days inland."

A smile broke across Stephen's face.

Robert looked over and winked his one good eye. "Why don't you go tell the little lady?"

His smile ebbed away. He rubbed the back of his neck and looked down. "Things are . . . awkward . . . between us at the moment."

Robert lifted his eyebrow and huffed. "Of course they are. So go fix it."

Stephen looked up. "How?"

"How many times have we scuffled over the years?"

Stephen thought back. He'd known Robert almost all his life. They were good friends, but when they fought, they fought hard, then made up afterward, usually with him buying Robert a drink. "But how do I patch up things between me and Kat? It's not the same as you and me."

"Yes, it is. It's the way with all humans. Own up to what you did wrong and tell her you're sorry."

Stephen snorted. "And what if she doesn't forgive me?"

Robert's face grew serious as he worked the lever again beside the helm. There was a shift in the angle of the ship's ascension, a little steeper. "She might not. But you need to give her the chance."

Robert was right, and Stephen knew it. It was fear and shame that kept him away. Every time he thought about talking to Kat, his insides clenched up and a sour taste filled his mouth.

"Do you love Miss Bloodmanye?"

He wanted to deny the fact. It would make everything easier. But he couldn't. Stephen sighed. "Yes, I do."

"Then she's worth fighting for. Even if that fight is with yourself."

He straightened up, his hand still on the railing. "You're right." But fear still gripped his insides with an iron hold. He turned and headed down to the main deck. Sailors' shouts and laughter mingled with the constant whir of the rotors above. Wind blew across the deck, cool and pressing.

More shouts. More laughter. Constant motion.

Stephen stopped at the bottom of the stairs and clenched his hands. He closed his eyes and breathed in deeply through his nose. Silence. He needed silence. Just a place to think first and figure out what he would say, instead of barreling after her like his first woeful attempt. But where? The bunkroom was out of the question. Twenty-plus men squeezed into a tiny room filled with hammocks did not equal silence. And certainly not Robert's private room. Kat was there and he wasn't ready to see her, not yet.

Maybe the galley?

Yes.

Stephen walked across the main deck, opened the door, and entered the galley. For being inside the ship, the galley was actually warm and lighted, most of the light coming from the small square windows along one side of the narrow room. Gas lamps swung from a low ceiling over three long tables nailed to the floor. Benches lined either side of the tables.

Toward the back a counter divided the dining room from the cooking area. Above the counter, pots and pans swayed on their ceiling hooks. A man stood beyond the counter, his white shirt tucked into a pair of faded trousers with apron ties just above the belt line, his back to Stephen.

Stephen would recognize that round, bald head anywhere. Fitz.

Fitz turned and placed a wooden bowl on the counter. He didn't seem to notice Stephen as he began to mix something in the bowl.

Stephen retreated. Even Fitz was one person too many. Leaving the galley, Stephen headed lower, toward the bottom of the ship where Grim stored his cargo for his runs across the Austrium blockade.

The place was dark, save for a little bit of light filtering in from the door above. A musty, woodsy smell filled the hold. Crates and boxes lined either side of the large area, all tied to the walls and floors to keep them from shifting during flight.

Stephen sat on the bottom step and placed his head in his hands. Before he could even ask for Kat's forgiveness, there was an issue unresolved in his own life.

Vanessa.

Two years. He pressed his fingers into his eye sockets. It had been two years since Vanessa had shattered his heart. Two years since he had last spoken to God in anything other than anger or desperation. Two years since he had darkened the doorway of a church.

Only now, when he felt like he had hit rock bottom and betrayed the one person he loved—yes, he loved Kat; after all, he'd been honest with Robert, he might as well be honest with himself—only now was he finally looking up to God.

He moaned softly in his hands. "I don't know what to say." He had fallen far, far away. He knew God always welcomed back the prodigal—he recalled a story somewhere in the Bible about that—but the shame . . . How did one erase the shame of the past?

"*Mreow.*"

Stephen looked up. It took a moment to catch a glimpse of yellow eyes peering at him from across the path between the crates.

He glanced around the hold again, then back at the cat. He could barely make out the outline of the dark feline's body. Of course there would be a cat down here, to keep the rats out of the food stores.

The cat raised a paw and began to clean each toe with delicate precision.

Stephen bent his head again, his heart churning into a ball of lead inside his chest. Each word he tried to conjure lodged in his throat. What could he say? Even after all this time, he still hurt over Vanessa's infidelity.

Something rubbed against his legs and let out a soft purr.

Stephen opened one eye and stared down at the cat now doing figure eights between his legs. As if sensing his stare, the cat glanced up and meowed again. It arched its back, waiting to be petted.

Stephen sighed and reached down. The cat rumbled beneath his hand and turned around for another rub along his legs.

Just let go.

The words filled his mind.

Let go and turn back.

Stephen let out a dejected snort and scratched the cat behind the ears. Could it really be that easy? Could he turn around after two years of bitterness and find God behind him, waiting?

He paused and looked up. The cat continued to run its back beneath Stephen's stilled hand. He blinked and held his breath.

Maybe, just maybe it was.

His mind tore through his memories, trying to remember more clearly the story about that prodigal son. The old family Bible he had inherited on the death of his father was tucked inside a wooden chest back in his flat, buried deep beneath a quilt his mother had sewn just before her death. Not once had he taken it out since Vanessa's betrayal.

If only he had it now.

He recalled bits and pieces. Something about the young man leaving, then falling into hardship and remembering his father. The young man returning . . .

"Gah! I can't remember."

The cat stopped and looked up at him.

"You don't have to think about this kind of stuff, do you?" Stephen scratched the cat beneath the chin. Eyes closed, the creature tilted its head in ecstasy.

No, a cat didn't think about such things. Cats, dogs, all critters probably never turned from their creator. Only humans did that.

He let out a dark laugh. And he was definitely human. A human who had blundered badly.

Just let go.

Stephen shook his head.

Turn back.

Wasn't that what the son eventually did in the story? And he found his father waiting for him with open arms and more.

Stephen swallowed. He was on the edge of doing just that, he could feel it. But was it because he wanted acquittal for what he had done to Kat? Or did he really want to return to God?

Could a man really know his own heart?

I want to make up for what I did.

He sighed. No, he could never make up for what he'd done. He could never erase the wrongs Kat had suffered because of him. He could only ask for her forgiveness.

The cat butted against his stilled hand, and he felt an answering nudge on his spirit. How could he ask Kat to forgive him when he himself was unwilling to let go of his own bitterness?

He had to forgive Vanessa. And to do that, he had to return to the source of all grace.

He had to turn back.

CHAPTER
7

STEPHEN WASN'T SURE HOW LONG HE HAD KNELT ON THE FLOOR OF the cargo hold when a loud bell began to chime somewhere above him. At the sound, the cat lying next to his knee bounded for the crates nearby.

One, two, all the way to seven. He blinked against the darkness and staggered to his feet. The eighth bell was long and low. Muffled boots stampeded across the decks above.

Instinct twisted Stephen's gut. He turned and headed up the stairs two at a time. He started across the second hold and past the hammocks when the bell started again, repeating the same pattern. At the same time, the ship tilted back at a steady incline. He placed his hands along the wall and made his way to next set of stairs.

At the top, he emerged onto the main deck. The air felt cooler than it had earlier, almost with a bite to it. The dark clouds that had been a thin line on the horizon now loomed across the entire sky ahead. Sailors ran this way and that across the deck, pulling on ropes or shouting commands. Anders, Robert's first mate, ran past Stephen toward the top deck. Stephen followed.

Robert stood alone at the helm, the wind pulling his dark hair back away from his face, his gaze forward.

Anders came to a stop near the helm and brought his hand up to his forehead in a salute. "Captain?"

"We have company," Robert said without taking his eye off the skies ahead. He reached over to his left and cranked on the large gear attached to helm, next to the lever. The bell began to ring again. While it rang, he brought the ship level above the first tier of dark gray clouds.

Stephen glanced over the railing. The gray expanse looked more like the ocean on an overcast day than a storm.

"We've been spotted by the Austrium blockade." Robert returned his hand to the wheel. "They're sending a squadron of wasps our way from the port side. Tell the men to prepare."

"Aye, Captain," Anders said. "But, if I may ask, how did they find us?"

"I don't know. Austrium must have established a new base nearby. Right now we need to concentrate on those wasps. We'll figure out the logistics later, after we have escaped. And Anders?"

"Yes, Captain?"

"I'm going to try to keep us above this storm for as long as possible. But if we can't shake those wasps, I'm going in." His face tightened. "The men need to be prepared for that as well."

Anders' face paled. "You don't mean to actually fly into the storm, do you, Captain?"

Robert set his jaw. "Not unless we absolutely have to."

Anders saluted again. "Aye, Captain." The first mate disappeared below the deck.

Stephen turned around. "Where do you want me?"

Robert answered without looking his way. "Galley. It's one of the safer places and Fitz might need help if we have wounded."

"And Kat?"

"I'll send one of my men to escort her to a safe place. You just get yourself to the galley."

Stephen hesitated, then nodded, leaving Robert at the helm with a grim expression on his face. Already he could hear a buzz in the air over the rotor blades. Must be the wasps Robert had referred to.

He descended from the top deck and dashed toward the galley door. Sailors raced to either side of the ship and started pulling on a complex set of ropes and pulleys.

Halfway to the door, a large buzz sounded to his right. Stephen glanced over.

A yellow and black aircraft the size of one of those steam-powered phaetons whizzed by on wings similar to that of a wasp. A second later a volley of bullets erupted across the deck. Stephen dove for the door and covered his head.

"Get those panels up now!" Anders shouted.

Stephen lifted his gaze. Using the pulleys and ropes, the sailors heaved up three large panels, each the size of a bedroom wall, from the port side of the ship. Another crew of sailors did the same on the starboard side.

"Goggles on!"

Stephen straightened up and reached for the door just as the ship dipped beneath his feet. For a split second he felt like he was falling. Then the ship rose a micro-foot and caught up with his feet. His knees buckled on impact and he tumbled forward, hitting his head against the doorway.

Throbbing pain shot across his right temple. Stephen twisted around and gripped his head as stars popped across his vision. Blazes, but that hurt!

"Light the panels, now!"

A bright, searing light appeared across the panels on either side of the main deck, bright as the noonday sun. Throwing an arm up to cover his eyes, Stephen stumbled back until he hit the door behind him. Flashes of light joined the stars dancing across his vision.

"Good work, men! We've dazzled them!"

Stephen pressed his palms into his eye sockets. What just happened?

The ship lurched again, but this time he planted his feet and stayed put. The moment his sight cleared, Stephen went for the door.

"Get ready to light the panels again on the next go around," Anders yelled.

Stephen wrenched the door open and dashed inside, shutting the door behind him. Lamps swung above his head as he staggered between the tables, using his hands and the wall nearby for balance.

In the back, the dangling pots and pans tilted away from the dining room as the ship continued its ascent. Ignoring the imminent possibility of being brained by his own cookware, Fitz calmly lifted his black medical box and placed it on the counter. He looked up as Stephen entered.

"The captain sent you down here, eh?"

"Yes."

The box—and the pans above—began to tilt to the side as the airship changed directions. Fitz stopped the box from sliding with one hand and flipped open the lid with the other. "I assume we are under attack."

"Yes." Stephen made his way to the counter. "From something Robert called wasps."

Bright light flared outside the windows surrounding the galley, lighting up the area in almost blinding light.

Halos remained in Stephen's vision as the glare outside dissipated. "What is that?"

"An invention of the captain's. We have a limited arsenal, which we save as a last resort. So before we shoot the guns, we dazzle the enemy airships first."

"Dazzle?"

"Using reflective panels, similar to a looking glass, we intensify the sunlight and flash it across the panels. The effect is a wide display of bright light that temporary blinds the pilots."

"Does it work?"

"Most of the time. As a blockade-runner, the *Lancelot*'s strength is in stealth and speed. Usually the dazzle gives us enough time to outrun the enemy."

Another brilliant burst of light flashed across the galley windows.

"How are the men not blinded by the light?"

"Special goggles."

That's right, Anders told the men to place their goggles on before the light show began.

As his vision cleared, Stephen heard Fitz clicking softly with his tongue as he perused his medical box. "Yes, that should be good enough." He snapped the lid shut with a click and glanced at the windows with a furrowed brow. "We should have outrun them by now."

The airship leveled out beneath his feet. Stephen straightened up. "There's a storm outside."

A gleam entered Fitz's eyes. "Well, well, this could get interesting."

CHAPTER

8

KAT JERKED AWAKE. SHE STARED AT THE CEILING AS THE AIRSHIP shifted beneath her. Her stomach felt like it was pulling back into her spine and sliding toward her throat. One of the maps on the table nearby slid toward the edge and fluttered to the floor. The armillary sphere followed seconds later with a loud crash.

A spray of *thunks* beat a rapid staccato above her, followed by a flash of brilliant light that streamed in through the glass bulkhead, illuminating the captain's cabin with a painful glare. There was shouting and stomping of boots, then another flash of light.

Bracing against the wall to her left and the bed behind her, Kat sat up, an empty feeling expanding across her middle. What was going on? Were they under attack? What was that light outside?

She twisted and placed her feet on the ground. The ship dipped beneath her, and for one long moment, she felt suspended in air. The ship yanked up again and she landed on the bed.

The chairs and the table nearby shook but didn't budge from their hooks. The metal chandelier swung back and forth, and another map, along with her research, fluttered to the floor.

Kat stood, testing the wooden planks beneath her. There was a steady, low rumble across the floor, but thankfully the dipping had stopped for now. She stretched an arm toward the back of the closest chair and gripped it. Then she reached for the next chair, using them to make her way toward the glass bulkhead.

The door opened behind her. "Miss!"

Kat glanced back. One of the sailors stood in the doorway, a small, thin man with mousy brown hair pulled back at the nape of his neck.

"Miss, we need to get you to safety."

A large black and yellow metal cylinder the size of a phaeton whizzed by the glass bulkhead, disappearing before she could figure out what it was. Seconds later, the wall to her left reverberated with another dozen *thunks*.

Kat wanted to let go of the chair she clung to, but her fingers refused to cooperate. Another blaze of light flashed across the glass.

The airship tilted to the right and she stumbled toward the table, hitting the edge with her hip. Intense pain blossomed across her side and she gasped. The rest of the maps and navigation tools fell to the floor and slid toward the bench on the other side of the room.

The sailor staggered to her side and grabbed the table. "Are you all right?"

"I think so."

"We need to get you out of here."

She caught sight of her research papers. "Not yet! I can't leave without my work."

Another black and yellow flying machine came into view. The machine hovered in place, its wings on either side flapping so fast that they were a blur. A person sat in the cockpit behind the black-tipped cylinder, a set of goggles obscuring his face.

Kat gasped. "What in the world is tha—"

The sailor shoved her as the glass bulkhead shattered under the barrage of bullets. Kat fell to the floor, arms over her head. The sailor grunted behind her. A cold wind blew into the open space and whipped around the cabin. She began to slide toward the broken windows. Heart thudding against her chest, she reached out and snaked her arm around one of the hooked chairs. Her skirt billowed around her legs before she locked her left leg around another chair.

Adrenaline raced along her limbs like arcs of electricity. Kat looked back. The flying contraption was gone, but so was most of the bulkhead. The wind seized whatever it could and ripped it out of the ship. Papers and maps danced through the air and out the opening.

Then her research flew into the air.

"No!" Kat cried, frantically reaching for the whirling papers. One by one, they whipped through the air before racing out the opening. Her fingers brushed the last paper as it followed the rest. It hovered there, between the ship and open sky, as if mocking her. Then it flew into the raging storm below.

Kat stared at the opening, a painful lump in her throat. All of it—all her thoughts, all her hard work over the last few days—gone. As if the universe were saying no knowledge or science or pill could heal what was wrong inside her.

That she was on her own.

She stared at the open space, her hair fluttering around her face in a frenzy.

The ship dipped downward, yanking her attention back to her peril. Her leg came loose and she slipped farther toward the broken bulkhead. Shards of glass like teeth glittered around the edges. Far below, dark gray clouds churned.

The sailor slid by her. He scrambled for a hold, but his fingers, red with blood, slipped with every grab. He cried out as he disappeared through the opening, a look of wild terror on his face.

A scream from the depths of her soul tore through her lips. Kat continued to scream as she locked her arms around the metal chair next to her. It strained against the hooks that held it to the floor.

The airship continued its descent. Wind blasted across her body and her skirt flew up around her thighs. Her arms began to shake. Kat looked back toward the door that led to the main deck.

Only twenty feet away, and yet so far. Her arms were starting to go numb.

She was going to fall out of the ship, just like that sailor.

Kat squeezed her eyes shut and clung to the chair. *I should have gone with him when he first asked instead of going for my research. Now they're both gone.*

But maybe it wasn't too late for her. Kat raised her head. She could save herself. All she had to do was let her fear trigger the power inside her. Just open herself up and let the frigid darkness take over and do the rest.

One arm shifted on the metal leg.

A trickle of sweat slid down her face, and with it a crack formed deep inside her.

The power responded. Instantly she could feel every particle in the room: the air, the furniture, even her own body, the focal point. She could do it, just move the particles and—

Kat squeezed her eyes shut and clutched the chair. The wind continued to howl around her. Already an aching chill had begun to spread across her body in anticipation of the release.

No. I need to find another way.

She opened her eyes. They were now inside the storm. The ship juked and jinxed along the currents within the clouds. A moment later and the ship evened out.

This was her chance.

Kat scrambled to her feet and dashed for the door. Anywhere had to be safer than here.

She bypassed a patch of blood on the floor on her way to the door. The sailor must have been hit when he'd shoved her out of the way of the bullets. She tried to dredge up remorse, but only a hint of the feeling passed through her as she reached the door and wrenched it open. She flew down the dark corridor toward the next door and tugged at the handle, but the door was stuck fast. "What do I do?" She panted and held a hand to her temple. The ship began to tilt again. No time to think. She had to get out of here!

Kat raced down the rest of the corridor toward the deck ahead. The galley. That had to be a safe place, right? Right there in the middle of the ship. Fitz would be there, and maybe some of the sailors. Someone who could help her.

She breathed furiously as she fumbled with the outer door. The ship dipped again. She let go of the handle and slammed into the wall. Blood whooshed through her veins and the cold ache beat inside her. She brought her hands out in front of her and her fingers uncurled. The wind died around her, the air particles slowing at her command.

A smile spread across her face and a laugh gurgled up inside her throat.

No! Kat shut her eyes and closed her hands into fists. The air blasted across her again. She would not use her power.

She twisted around and went for the door. The knob turned and she flung the door open.

A gust of wet wind slapped her face. Rain pelted the deck in a harsh staccato while dark clouds swirled around the airship. Not a person in sight. Across the deck, she spotted the door that led to the galley. Then she glanced at the deck again. Rivulets of water raced across the wooden planks in waves.

She gripped the doorway. She couldn't do it. There was no way across—

The airship hit a bump and Kat slipped out onto the deck. The ship tilted sideways.

Her feet went out from under her. Down she went and began to slide toward the railing.

Faster, faster.

Kat screamed and twisted, scrambling to her knees. Rain showered her face and body. In the downpour, she spotted one of the main rotor masts a couple feet away. If she could reach it, she could cling to the thick rope tied around the post until the ship righted itself, then make a dash for the galley.

Kat reached out her hand, her fingers numb with cold. Her knees slipped and she fell onto her belly. Like butter, she slid farther across the deck and away from the mast. Heart in her throat, she glanced behind her.

The railing was a mere twenty feet away and approaching fast. All blood drained from her face.

I'm not . . . going . . . to make it.

It was just like her dream, only instead of being sucked into the ocean, she was going to slip off the airship and fall to her death. Just like that sailor. His face played over and over again in the back of her mind as the voice from her dream cooed inside her ear. *But Kat, you're already dying. What does it matter?*

Her nostrils flared. "No, I'm not!" she shouted at the sky. "I can't die! I—" She sobbed and curled her fingers like claws, gripping the deck with all her might. Rain slammed down on her and rushed across her face. She couldn't move forward, not without letting go of her grip, but at least she wasn't moving backward anymore.

She blinked away the water and took in a lungful of air. The storm raged around the ship, dark clouds rolling over each other, sparks of lightning flashing. The wind tore across her face, slamming the raindrops across her cheeks until her skin burned.

Even if she were to release her power, it could not save her from this storm. She could only control one element—either the rain, or the ship, or the wind—but not everything. And if she did, could she stop herself? It was only a matter of time before—

The ship bucked beneath her and her fingers slipped.

"Noooo!"

She gripped the deck again, shoving her fingers as far as she could into a wedge between the wooden planks. But she could not get a footing with her feet. Her arms began to shake from exertion and her fingers were numb. Maybe she should just let go. Who would miss her? The world would be rid of a monster.

"Kat!"

Kat blinked against the torrent. A figure emerged from the galley door. *Oh, God . . .* Her arms began to shake. Someone was coming to save her. *Thank You.*

The figure slowly made his way across the deck, a rope trailing behind him. There was flash of light, illuminating the man coming to get her.

Her stomach dropped.

Stephen.

CHAPTER

9

MORE AND MORE CREW MEMBERS PILED INTO THE GALLEY. Moisture from their clothing and the heat of their bodies created an oppressive humidity that made it difficult to breathe. Stephen stood in the back corner, careful to keep out of the way.

Outside the window, dark gray clouds rose up as the airship dipped into the storm. Moments later the galley grew dark. Condensation spread across the glass.

The ship bounced once and a couple men toppled over.

"Brace yourselves," Reid called out. "We're in for a bumpy ride."

Stephen moved forward and grabbed the table in front of him. Another sailor joined him.

Lightning flashed outside the window and the ship juked again.

"This is crazy," Stephen muttered under his breath.

"You're right about that one," the sailor said next to him. "But that's the captain for you. He would rather face a storm than let a bunch of Austrium wasps take him out."

"So that's why we're entering the storm?"

"Yeah, there were too many of them to dazzle them all, and they took out one of our rotors. Captain decided it was time to shake them off. They would be crazy to follow us into this storm."

That might be true, but were they just as a crazy?

Anders poked his head into the galley and let out slew of unsavory words. "We have an emergency! The woman civilian is out on the deck. Reid, get me a rope. And you—" he motioned toward the sailor closest to Stephen. "Find me a place to anchor it."

"Yes, sir!" Both men immediately moved to obey.

Stephen stared wide-eyed at Anders and the storm raging behind him through the doorway. Kat . . . was *outside?*

He blinked and sprang into action, making his way toward the door. Anders could not go out and get Kat. If Kat was out there, she had to be terrified out of her mind, and that could trigger—he took a deep breath and shuddered, remembering the inn at Covenshire a couple weeks ago.

She might go all-powerful.

"Let me get her." Stephen approached Anders, using the walls and table to brace himself. "Send me out to retrieve her."

Anders scowled. "You have no experience with this kind of rescue."

"I need to do it. Miss Bloodmayne is no ordinary woman." At Anders' sharp look, Stephen pressed on, "I can't explain now. All I can tell you is that she could put this ship in jeopardy."

Anders' nostrils flared. "We're already in jeopardy, and there's no way I'm letting you go out in that storm. The captain would strip me of rank if I allowed his friend to place himself in danger."

Stephen gripped the man's forearms. He leaned in so the other men couldn't hear. "The captain knows about Miss Bloodmayne's condition. If he were here, he would tell you to let me go to her. There is a reason we are on the run from the Tower. I am the only one who can help her." *I hope. Or maybe I'll just make things worse.*

Anders narrowed his eyes as Reid brought him the rope.

"I will take full blame for anything that happens to me."

Anders scowled some more, but he yanked out the end of the rope and began tying it around Stephen's waist, leaving a long tail. "Not sure how you'll take the blame if you end up dead. Make your way to the lady, tie her to you with the tail end of the rope, and bring her back, do you hear?"

"Yes." Stephen let out his breath.

"Reid, check the knots on Mr. Grey here. He'll be the one retrieving the lady."

Reid gave Anders an incredulous look, but he approached Stephen and began checking the knots, tugging them tight. "Watch yourself out there. The deck will be as slick as lard."

Stephen nodded and turned. A gust of wind came through the door with a blast of chill and water. The ship dipped and the men tumbled to the side, Stephen included.

Stephen reached out and grabbed the doorway, clinging to it with his fingertips. His stomach churned. Dark mist encompassed the ship as Grim took the *Lancelot* deeper into the storm.

He scanned the deck. There she was, on the starboard side near the railing. Another gush of wind and rain struck him as he exited the galley. The air roared with the storm and the rotors churning above.

With his hands out, Stephen slowly made his way across the deck, past the first mast, slipping once on the slick wooden planks. He caught himself and continued toward Kat.

She was on her stomach, her fingers wedged into a thin opening between two planks, her dark hair plastered to her face.

"Kat!" he yelled as lightning flashed across the deck, followed by a deafening boom.

She looked up, fear emblazoned across her face.

Twenty feet away. Ten feet away.

One of her hands slipped and a scream rent the air.

Throwing caution away, Stephen sprinted the rest of the way, dove onto his side, feet first, and slid right next to Kat as she began to slip toward the railing. He threw his arms and legs around her and pulled her flush against himself.

They continued to slide toward the railing.

"God, please help me!" Stephen cried. He tightened his grip around Kat as he glanced down and scrambled his legs into position to catch the railing rapidly approaching them. The rope had more slack than he had anticipated. *Don't let us die before I have a chance to speak to her.*

Right as they reached the railing, the ship shifted back. They slid to a stop, the rope still trailing behind him as Stephen's boots hit one of the railings.

Kat lifted her head, her eyes wide and terrified.

Stephen scrambled to his feet and pulled her up. She clung to his forearms as he glanced toward the galley where light spilled out from the open door. All they had to do was reach the galley and they would be safe—

A strong gale swept across the deck, followed by a resounding crack. One of the main masts began to fall, right between Stephen and Kat and the galley.

His breath left his lungs, and a chill unrelated to the wind and rain spread across his body.

The mast hit the deck with a boom, and the airship shuddered. The rotors continued to run, tearing through the wooden planks. Chunks and splinters of wood flew into the air.

Stephen grit his teeth. With every bit of strength he had left, he pulled Kat away from the chopping blades, terrified that the ship would shift and send the dying rotor their way. Even as the thought crossed his mind, he felt a jerk around his middle. A second later, he spotted the rope flying in the wind. One of the blades had cut through the cord. If the ship tilted again, they would slide right off and there would be nothing to save them.

Time to act. He made for the captain's cabin.

"No!" Kat pulled back and pointed to the cabin door. "We can't go there!" she shouted over the storm. "The bulkhead is gone!"

What? Blazes!

Stephen looked around. The ship dipped again. The other mast remained, about ten feet away. He would have to tie them to the mast and wait out the storm.

"This way!" he shouted, his arm around Kat's waist, and headed for the remaining mast.

"What are we doing?" she shouted back, but he didn't answer. His clothing was soaked through and his hair whipped across his face.

They reached the mast and Stephen pulled Kat closer to him. "Hold onto me!"

Kat hesitated, her eyes on him, her body shaking. Lightning flashed within the clouds and boomed across the deck. She closed the distance between them and gripped the front of his shirt. He worked the rope around the mast, then around the two of them, his fingers growing numb from the cold.

There. He let out a sigh of relief. The fallen rotor had stopped chopping into the deck. Robert or someone else must have turned off the machine inside.

He put his arms around her and held her tight. Now to pray Robert could take his crippled ship out of this storm.

CHAPTER

10

"HOLD ONTO ME!" STEPHEN YELLED.

Lightning flashed nearby, illuminating Stephen's face only inches from hers. His overcoat whipped around him, and his hair was slick with rain.

Kat froze, the hurt from the last few days surging inside her.

Why him? Why couldn't Captain Grim have been the one to save her? Or Fitz?

A boom followed the flash of light.

Heart racing and ears ringing, she closed the small gap between them and gripped the front of Stephen's shirt.

He wound the rope around and between them until they were tied to each other and to the mast. When he finished the knot, he wrapped his arms around her. Still the storm raged, the ship bucking and diving beneath them.

Kat closed her eyes, torn inside. She didn't want to be here with him. She didn't want to touch him. But self-preservation took over, and she continued to grip his shirt. A gust of wind swept across the deck and Stephen pulled her in as close as he could.

Why? Why had he turned her in? Now she wished she'd taken the chance to ask. But every time the words had pressed against her lips, they'd been accompanied by bile. And yet . . .

She couldn't hate him either. She wanted to—blazes, she wanted to! But it was as if the very hand of God were stopping her. Maybe that was a good thing. Ms. Stuart said hatred destroyed the heart, and her heart was damaged enough already.

Stephen cupped the back of her head and held her against his chest. Another gust of wind rushed across the deck. He didn't let go after it passed.

Kat stood there, next to Stephen, her head pressed against his heart to the point she could almost imagine she could hear each beat. A sob filled her chest, different than the bile. It rose until it burst from her. She dug her fingers into his drenched shirt and cried.

"Why?" She raised a fist and hit his chest. "Why? Why? *Why?*"

He didn't react.

She looked up and blinked back the water. "Why did you leave me?" she shouted. "Why did you leave me there, at the Tower?" Could he even hear her over the storm?

A pained expression filled his face, that same one from when she'd first spotted him on the ship. He placed his hand across her cheek and leaned in until his nose brushed hers. "I'm sorry."

She barely heard the words, but she could see him mouth them. Two simple words. Words never spoken to her before.

Did he really mean them?

The airship fell beneath them.

Kat screamed and gripped Stephen. Her heart thrashed inside her ears. Every beat moved her blood, and the coldness awakened deep inside of her.

The ship continued to fall.

The dark power surged through her, riding along the adrenaline buzzing across her body. Her fingers tingled.

Kat brought her right hand up. Flames licked the tops of her fingertips. Not even the torrent of rain could dampen the fire now spreading across her hand.

She let out a raspy breath. No, no! This couldn't be happening!

Stephen's eyes widened at the sight of her fingers.

Kat crushed her hand into a fist, but the fire blazed around her skin, steam rising where the water hit her knuckles. The cold ache throbbed inside her chest. One flame, then another fell from her hand onto the deck. Like a red flower opening its petals, the flame spread in a small circle.

She looked up at Stephen, an invisible hand clutching her throat, making it hard to breath. "Stephen, please help me! I-I'm losing control!"

He lifted his hands and placed them along her cheeks. Using his thumbs, his tilted her head upward. "Focus on me," he shouted. "You're stronger than this. I've seen you control yourself before. You can do this."

Lightning flashed again, followed by a boom that set her ears ringing. Water traced Stephen's face, dripping from his chin and nose. His eyes were set on her. There was no fear in his gaze. Just resolute confidence.

He believed in her.

Kat gripped onto that belief and took a deep breath. She clenched her hands tighter and focused on the cold ache inside her chest. She would not let her fear get the best of her.

Calm, focused breaths.

The wind howled and rain splattered across her like a dozen tiny bee stings.

Breathe.

The tingling retreated from her fingers.

Just breathe.

She glanced at Stephen again, and was struck by how similar he was to his aunt, Ms. Stuart. They hardly looked alike. His features were lean and angular, his facial hair giving him a distinct male look, whereas Ms. Stuart was round and . . . comfortable. Yes, comfort. But they both had a way of looking into her eyes and giving her strength.

She still wanted to know the reason Stephen had left her at the Tower, but there was no denying one fact. He had come back for her.

Maybe, just maybe, she could trust him again.

The ship tilted to the side and dropped again. Something in the pitch of the remaining rotors changed.

Stephen and Kat lurched to the side but caught themselves. With sound strangely muffled by the wind and rain, an explosion flashed through the engine powering two of the three remaining secondary rotors. The airship began to descend at a chaotic speed.

Kat swallowed the scream inside her throat. She grabbed the front of Stephen's shirt again and hid her face in the wet fabric. Terror blazed across the edges of her mind. No. She squeezed her eyes even tighter. She would not lose control again.

The ship juked the other way, sending them both staggering back against the mast. Stephen steadied them before they went crashing to the deck.

Faster, faster the ship went, diving deep into the clouds.

No, not diving. Falling.

Kat's limbs shook and black spots appeared across her vision. "We-we're falling," she said through chattering teeth.

Stephen licked his lips and nodded.

Kat wanted to collapse and curl into a ball, but she didn't want to lose what little control she had.

Wait.

Could she—could she stop their descent?

What am I thinking? I just got this power under control!

But you've controlled it before, back at the inn. You stopped that bullet from hitting Stephen.

But I lost control at the end.

Everyone is going to die if you don't do something.

I-I can't let that happen.

Kat balled her hands into two tight fists. *I* won't *let that happen. I am in control.* She closed her eyes. *I am in control.*

Cautiously, she felt inside for the coldness that surrounded her heart. With mental fingers, she expanded the cold ball, letting it slowly flow out to every part of her being. It wanted to rush, but she held it back.

She no longer felt the ship falling or Stephen's hands along her shoulders. She only felt the aching coldness inside her body, expanding until it connected with every particle around her.

Yes, they were falling. She could feel the ship cutting through the air toward the cold, dark waters of the Narrow Strait below. She didn't have much time. The ship was already exiting the clouds.

Kat grasped onto the matter beneath the airship and forced the particles together like a net. As the strands meshed, the *Lancelot* began to slow on the cushion of air.

She raised her hands, feeling the invisible strings that attached her to every particle around her. She could feel Stephen, the crew, the wood and metal from which the airship was made, the clouds, every particle of moisture. She could also feel the air, the water below, and . . .

Land. Just on the edge of her senses.

If she could use the air to push the airship in that direction, she might be able to land the ship.

Kat scrunched up her face. The cold ache throbbed inside her, but she was the one in control, barely. Her head began to pound as if ice picks were being driven into her skull.

She winced and moaned at the sensation, shutting her eyes against the pain, but kept her hands raised, tugging and pulling at the matter, willing the airship to move toward the land.

Something popped behind her eyes and an explosion of color filled her vision like fireworks. Her head throbbed even more and the coldness at the core of her being clawed outward toward her skin, fingers, and toes.

She didn't have much time. The monster was coming.

She reached out again toward the large landmass, but it was still too far away. However—she double-checked and confirmed—there was a smaller landmass. An island, not too far from the mainland. She could get the airship there. She *had* to get the airship there.

Sweat poured down the sides of her face and neck. Something hot and wet trickled from her right nostril, mingling with the water on her face.

Kat grit her teeth and moaned, her eyes still tightly shut. The throbbing inside her head was now a set of drums beating against her forehead. Nausea swam up her throat, riding on the column of frigidness taking over her body.

She curled her fingers and held them upward as if she held the airship in her very hands and guided it through the air. Down, down, toward that small bit of land—

Her knees gave out beneath her. Hands caught her and held her while voices shouted around her. She couldn't let them distract her. She had to finish this.

The airship touched the ground and her grip slipped around the air holding it up. It hit the earth with a thud, sending her back. Down she fell, her back and head hitting the deck. Another body fell on her, but she never opened her eyes.

The monster inside her roared in fury, and a smile slipped across her lips as she fell into the warm darkness inside her mind. She did it. She had controlled the power.

A chill spread over her as the darkness embraced her.

But at what price?

CHAPTER
11

STEPHEN'S STOMACH FLEW UP INTO HIS CHEST AS THE AIRSHIP plummeted through the dark clouds. One hand pressed against the mast, his other arm wrapped around Kat to keep her steady. Her eyes were shut, her face tense, but oddly so—more like concentration than fear.

He glanced toward the top deck, but it was too hard to see anything, let alone Robert at the helm. *Come on, Robert. I know you can do this. I've heard your stories. You've been through storms before. Pull up!*

Could they survive a crash in the water? Could the *Lancelot* even float?

Kat started to raise her hands, her eyes still tightly shut. The ship exited the clouds, plunging toward the water below—

And began to slow.

Stephen blinked and let out a breath. *Good job, Robert.*

Wait.

Kat's eyes opened and focused, but on what he couldn't tell. Her hands rose higher between them. With them tied together, her face was only inches from his own.

"Kat?" Stephen whispered, the word lost in the wind.

She didn't answer. It was as if she were seeing through him, watching something that no one else could see.

Maybe she was.

The ship continued to slow. Kat let out a long moan and her face scrunched up.

A solid ball formed in the middle of his gut, causing his mouth to go dry. It wasn't Robert who was slowing down the ship.

It was Kat.

The ship tilted downward, floating as if a hand were beneath it, guiding it toward the horizon ahead. They were free of the clouds now, but the rain still pounded down on them.

Kat gasped and sweat trickled down the sides of her face. She let out another moan, an anguished look crossing her face, her eyes now shut. A trickle of blood appeared beneath her right nostril.

"Kat!" Stephen yelled. He placed his hands on either side of her face. "Can you hear me? Don't do this! Don't—"

Kat collapsed. Stephen caught her beneath her arms as she fell. Her eyes rolled up into her head just as the ship crashed, sending them both flying back. The rope went taut, and pain shot through Stephen's waist and back.

Kat landed on the deck first. Stephen threw out his hands and knees, catching himself just before landing completely on top of her. She didn't seem to notice. In fact, he wasn't sure if she was conscious anymore.

The airship shifted, then went still. The rain had turned to a gentle drizzle across his back and head.

Stephen took in a deep breath and stared down at Kat. Men burst from the galley and started running toward them. From the opposite end of the ship, Robert used the handrails to vault down the stairs in one go. Stephen ignored them. "Kat?" He swept his thumb over her lip to remove the blood beneath her nostril. Her face was even more pale than usual. His gut clenched. How much had she exerted herself?

Robert was the first to arrive. He knelt down beside Stephen. "What the blazes just happened, Stephen?" he asked as he pulled out his dagger and began to saw away at the rope.

Stephen pressed his lips together and didn't answer. Robert's question confirmed his own thoughts. Kat had brought them down, not Robert.

"Was that her?" Robert whispered fiercely. The rope gave away. Stephen maneuvered to the side. "Did that woman really just land my airship? With just her mind? Is this the power you spoke of?"

"That was amazing, Captain!" someone shouted behind them.

Robert pressed his lips together, his one good eye burning furiously at Stephen.

"Spectacular landing!" another sailor called out.

Stephen shook his head slightly, his eyes pleading. *Don't tell them. Please.*

Robert stared at him a moment longer, then his shoulders slumped. "I won't say anything to the crew," he said quietly. "But we need to talk. Later."

Stephen nodded and turned back to Kat. He placed an arm beneath her head and another beneath her legs and stood up.

"Another story for the books," Anders said, beaming down on them. "And quick thinking on your part, Mr. Grey, tying yourself and the lady to the mast. When the rotor cut through the rope, I thought you were both goners."

Robert tucked his dagger into the sheath at his side and stood. He turned and faced the crew. "Thank you, men. However, though we might be on the ground, we are far from safe. Anders?"

Anders straightened. "Yes, Captain?"

"I need three groups of men. One to assess the damage. One to prepare for any enemies who might have followed us through the storm. And one to scout out the area where we landed."

"Aye, Captain."

Anders turned and started barking out commands to the sailors.

Robert wiped his face, his hand following his chin to the back of his neck.

Fitz came puffing up beside them. He bent over and placed his hands on his knees. "How is the lady?" he asked, turning his face upward.

Stephen glanced at Kat, now cradled in his arms. She was still out cold. "I'm not sure. I need to get Miss Bloodmayne away from this cold and rain."

Robert's face turned dark. He said something under his breath and Stephen was sure the words were not fit for polite company.

"Take her back to the captain's cabin. A few of the crew need stitching, but when I'm done, I'll come by with my medical box." Fitz stood and headed for the galley.

"All right." Stephen adjusted his hold on Kat. Even with the bulkhead gone, the cabin would at least provide shelter and privacy. As he stood, he was struck again by how small and light she was, and yet she had just landed an entire airship!

That kind of power had to affect her. Everything in life came with a price. They hadn't had a chance to talk, not since the incident in Covenshire, then the Tower, then getting away. But now that they had crashed who knows where, maybe they would finally have a chance to speak. Both of them.

Stephen lowered Kat onto the bed and took a step back. He couldn't leave her in those wet garments. Hesitating at first, he unlaced her boots and pulled them off, then stared at her corset. He shook his head. He didn't have a clue how to take the intricate garment off. She would just have to stay in her damp clothes.

He felt a presence behind him and looked back to find Robert standing in the doorway. Nearby, rain drizzled past the broken glass where the bulkhead used to be. Beyond, dune grass and boulders dotted the gray landscape.

"It's one thing to hear about such power, and another thing to experience it."

Stephen turned around. "Believe me, Robert, I know."

Robert crossed his arms and stared past Stephen. He shook his head. "And the Tower did this to her?"

"I don't know about the Tower, but I know her father had something to do with her being this way. I'm not sure to what extent, yet. We"—Stephen rubbed the back of his neck—"we haven't had a chance to speak."

"I'm not sure if I should be amazed or terrified. We were going down. I did everything I could to keep us afloat, but the *Lancelot* had taken too much damage and I couldn't control her. And then . . ." He raised his hand, palm up. "The ship just floated down and landed on the nearest island." He snapped his fingers. "Just like that."

Stephen nodded. He had watched Kat do it.

Robert rubbed the rim of his eye patch and brushed his hair back, then sighed. "I lost a good man, but considering the danger we were in, I'm thankful the rest of us are alive and in one piece."

"I'm sorry to hear that, Robert."

He shrugged, but Stephen could tell the loss weighed on his friend like a dark shroud. Abruptly, Robert met Stephen's eyes. "I don't like the fact that someone like Miss Bloodmayne exists. And that it was the Tower that created her"—he waved a dismissive hand as Stephen opened his mouth—"or near enough. She's a possible weapon in the hands of the city council. I know the council. I work for them. But I only do it for the gold, and for the people here, those fighting in Austrium. For our countrymen."

"What are you saying?"

Robert pressed his lips together. "If she was with anyone else but you, I would leave her right here and move on without a second thought. She is dangerous."

Stephen's face darkened. "So that's your decision."

"No, because you're with her, and there is a chance to cure her. And the fact that she *wants* to be cured. If she didn't, then . . ." He shrugged.

"Then you would maroon her."

"She's a monster. An abomination of nature."

"She's a scared young woman."

"And that is her saving grace." Robert raised a finger. "There is still some humanity left inside her. She hasn't become power hungry and used her power to attain more power. Perhaps we should be thankful that whatever the Tower did to her was performed on a woman like her, on someone who wishes to do good." He gave his friend a long, shrewd look. "But is it changing her, Stephen?"

Stephen glanced back. Kat looked so small in the bed, enveloped in the oversized coverlet. Only her head could be seen. His gut clenched. Yes, it was changing her. There existed two Kats, the smart, beautiful, kind Kat, and the scary Kat.

Robert sighed again. "Since I started running the blockade, I've been putting some pieces together. I'm not sure why, but it seems the city council instigated this war with Austrium."

Stephen frowned. "That's not how it was reported. The council said Austrium struck first."

"Yes, overtly they did. But something happened before, something that made Austrium retaliate. There's a story floating around with the other privateers that our council was responsible for that explosion in Emberworth."

"That's a serious accusation. Do you have any proof?"

"Nothing concrete, just bits and pieces I've overheard during my travels." Robert placed one arm across his middle and tapped his chin with his other hand. "The last thing this war needs is people who can do what Miss Bloodmayne can do. If she could land my airship, who's to say she couldn't tear an airship out of the sky? Or worse?"

Stephen swallowed. He hated to admit it, but Robert was right, and his friend didn't know half the things Kat could do. She would be a formidable force on the warfront, or on any front, for that matter. But could she be controlled? He'd watched her unleash that power. There was something primal about it, instinctive, and she said her abilities were somehow attached to her emotions.

"Anyway." Robert turned toward the door. "I should return to my men. It's going to take a couple days to repair the *Lancelot* enough to limp off this island. I appreciate what Miss Bloodmayne did. She saved my crew. That means a lot to me. And in return"—he let out a long breath—"I will do whatever I can to help you both."

The tension along Stephen's back gave way. "Thank you, Robert."

Robert gave him a firm nod and left.

Stephen turned back toward Kat. He wasn't sure how long she would be out this time. She had slept for hours after the Covenshire incident. Perhaps this time it would be no different. This power—whatever it was—took everything out of her.

He brushed her hair back and remembered her words on the deck as she'd hit his chest with her fists. *Why? Why did you leave me at the Tower?*

"We'll talk once you're awake," he said quietly. "And I hope you can forgive me."

CHAPTER

12

KAT FELT LIKE SHE HAD BEEN TRAMPLED BY A DOZEN HORSES. Every muscle hurt, every limb. Even opening her eyes caused her to wince. She coughed and slowly sat up, rubbing her eyes as she did so.

After taking a deep breath, she mentally took stock of her body. How much damage had her power done this time? She paused and massaged the area above her heart, pressing her fingers against her damp blouse. The numb area had expanded. Now it was an invisible fist-sized hole in her chest.

She pulled her legs up and wrapped her arms around her knees, her throat tight. Was she losing her soul? Was that what the numb area was? Nausea boiled up inside her. How much time did she have before her soul completely disappeared? What would become of her? Would the monster inside finally take over? Would she watch, helpless, as the creature lit the entire world on fire?

"Father, why did you do this to me? Why?" She curled her hand into a fist and held it against her breast. She didn't cry. Instead, she stared down at the scarlet bedspread. She recognized the coverlet. It was the one from the captain's cabin.

She glanced up. Sure enough, she was back in the cabin, only now the glass bulkhead was gone and a gentle wind blew through the jagged gap. Outside, light green dune grass waved along the breeze. The air smelled different. Smoky and salty.

Kat paused. Yes, she could hear the surf. Her mind flashed back to the storm. If they were on the ground, that meant she had succeeded in landing the airship on that bit of land she had sensed before passing out.

Well, at least one good thing had come from using that power. But it had cost her. She again fingered the area above her heart. Oh, yes, it had cost her.

It had cost her another part of her soul.

The door opened behind her.

Kat pulled the coverlet up over her legs and looked back.

Stephen stood in the darkened doorway. His eyes widened at the sight of her. "Kat, you're finally awake."

Kat didn't answer. Instead, she watched him cross the room toward the empty table nearby. She pressed her lips together. Her research was gone, along with the maps and navigation instruments. All of it had flown out the broken bulkhead during the storm. Only the table and chairs remained due to the hooks in the floor.

Stephen unhooked one of the chairs and pulled it up to the bed.

Kat stiffened at his nearness. Her emotions were a jumble inside her at the sight of him. One moment hurt, another anger, then joy. Sweet and bitter at the same time. How could that be possible? How could she still long to see Stephen, yet hurt at the very sight of him?

The rush made her dizzy.

Stephen sat down and leaned forward. "How are you feeling?"

Confused. Mad. Terrified. But she wasn't ready to share that yet, so she went with an easier answer. "Tired."

He nodded. "You've been unconscious for two days."

"Two days?"

"Yes."

Apparently her human body could not handle the power she unleashed. That meant she was still human, right?

"If you are up to it, I would like to answer the question you asked me during the storm."

Kat looked up, puzzled, until her memories caught up. During the storm she had pounded on Stephen's chest and asked him why he had left her at the Tower.

She sighed and tugged on the bedspread. Part of her wanted to dismiss Stephen. She wasn't sure she was ready yet. She had just come through an ordeal and still felt weak, not to mention distracted by the lingering fear over the numbness spreading across her body.

But she also wanted answers, and he was willing to give them to her now.

"Yes." She stilled her hand and looked up. "I would like that."

The confidence on Stephen's face melted away as he ran a hand along the back of his neck. "I don't know how much you know about my past, or how much you followed the *Herald* over the last few years."

Kat frowned. "The *Herald*?" She shook her head. "Not much. I rarely read it while I was at the academy."

Stephen nodded and dropped his hand. "I was engaged two years ago, to a socialite. Her name was Vanessa Wutherington."

She scrunched up her face. At the gala on that harrowing night Ms. Stuart had died, Marianne had said something about Stephen breaking off an engagement.

Stephen sat back and turned his attention to the dunes outside. "Just before the wedding, I found her with one of my colleagues, engaged in . . . intimate activities."

Her frown deepened. *Intimate . . . oh!* Heat raced across her face. Had the *Herald* written a story about that? Words jumbled up inside her mind, but none of them seemed like an appropriate response, so she remained quiet. But her heart was breached just a little by his vulnerable admission.

Stephen sighed, never turning to look at her. "Apparently the affair had been going on for a while. I was shocked . . . hurt . . . deeply." His hand clenched across the arm of the chair. "I broke off the engagement, left the police force, and became a bounty hunter.

"I lived alone for two years, going about my work, never truly realizing how much that event had colored my life. Then I met you at the gala, and the next day you approached me about a job. You're the first woman I've let into my life since Vanessa." He glanced at Kat from the corner of his eye.

She sat rigid on the bed, back straight, hands tightly held across her lap. When Stephen said he wanted to talk, she'd had no idea how much of his life he was going to share with her. This . . . this was deeply personal.

Stephen went on. "The moment we met, I slowly began to open up. I wanted to find out what had happened to my aunt. I also wanted to help you. You were different than most of the women I'd met. And then . . ."

A breeze blew through the missing bulkhead and a bird warbled outside.

"And then?" Kat said quietly, her cheeks still flushed.

"And then I saw what you did to Jake, Piers, and Rodger back at the inn in Covenshire."

Kat let out her breath. It all came back to that. The fact that she was different. No, not different. More than different. She gripped the coverlet tight between her fingers and savagely twisted the fabric. She was a monster.

"And I found out about the bounty on you."

Her fingers halted and her head shot up. "What? What bounty?"

"A bounty was placed on you. That's why Jake and the other bounty hunters were after you. When I found out about the contract, I assumed only one thing: that you had lied to me."

"Who set the bounty?" she asked, her throat tight.

"The World City Council. And . . . your father."

The flush disappeared from her face, leaving her light-headed. "What did the contract state?"

Stephen cleared his throat. "The warrant stated that you killed two young men."

She felt sick. "But Ms. Stuart said I didn't kill anyone." She looked down at her fingers and began twisting the coverlet again. "I-I burned someone when I—"

She had never told Stephen about that night. About Blaylock or the fire she had ignited at the gala.

"Stephen, I never lied. But I didn't tell you everything." Kat licked her lips, trying to work some moisture back into her mouth.

"Ms. Stuart—your aunt—instructed me never to tell anyone about this power inside me. I did do something that night at the gala. I—" She swallowed hard. It all came back to that night. Ms. Stuart would still be alive if she hadn't set the fire. And she wouldn't be on the run now.

She let out her breath slowly. "I lost control. I set one of the hallways on fire. There were young men there, men from the academy, and they were hurting my friend. I couldn't stand by and watch them do that to Marianne. But then it took over. The monster inside me."

She glanced at him from the corner of her eye. "Can you see why I didn't want to tell you about myself? About this power? About why I am searching for Dr. Latimer?" She watched him, half afraid of what she would see on his face. "I'm a monster."

Stephen leaned back and tugged at the bit of hair beneath his lip. He studied her as if coming to a conclusion inside his head. "No, Kat," he said a moment later. "You're wrong." He dropped his hand and leaned forward. "You're not a monster. A monster would not have saved this ship. A monster would not have saved me from that bullet back in Covenshire."

Kat shook her head. "That's not necessarily true. Maybe I saved you so that you could help me find Dr. Latimer. And saving the ship was simply self-preservation."

"Is that what you were thinking during those moments?"

Kat thought back. No. She cared about Stephen, so she had stopped the bullet. And she didn't want to see any more people die, so she had chosen to land the airship. She searched his face and realized he already knew the answer. Her lip began to quiver. Perhaps there had been a time when he had thought she was a monster, but no longer. At that realization, something shifted inside her heart, like a flower blossoming in the morning light.

He waved his hand. "No matter what you were, it doesn't excuse how I treated you. In my mind, you and Vanessa were the same. Vanessa lied to me, and therefore I thought you had lied as well when I heard about the bounty. I was angry, and in my anger, I chose to turn you in." He looked away, a pained expression across his face.

"I convinced myself that I was doing this for your good, that you would find help for your condition at the Tower. But deep down, I did it because of my hatred toward Vanessa. And that hatred tainted every part of my being until I could not see clearly: that you were, in fact, innocent."

"Stephen . . ." Kat whispered. One tear, then another rolled down her cheeks.

Stephen continued to look straight ahead, his face tight. "It was my assistant, Jerod, who forced me to realize what I had done, what I had become. I was bitter through and through. Once I realized this, what my bitterness had cost me, I couldn't leave you there at the Tower. I had to rescue you from the place I had sent you to, no matter the cost. And when I found you in that lab . . ." He clenched his hand and visibly swallowed. "What kind of man does that to his daughter?"

More tears flowed across her face. She wiped them away with the back of her hand. Stephen was right. What kind of man did that to his own daughter, even if she *was* a monster?

Stephen looked over. "Kat, I know I said this already, but I am sorry. I am so sorry for what I did to you." He reached over and held his hand above her clasped fingers. When she didn't move, he brushed the tops of her knuckles, then gently took her right hand and turned it over. "I cannot undo what I have done, but I aim to try. I will never let that happen to you again. I will protect you with everything I have, including my life." He ran a finger along the inside of her palm up to her fingertip.

A gentle breeze blew through the broken bulkhead, bringing with it a salty, sweet scent. How she wished they could stay like this. But Stephen couldn't make promises like that, not when he didn't know everything about her. About the darkness that lived inside her or the numbness taking over. Stephen wasn't the only tainted one. She pulled her hand away and held it to her chest. "But you don't know what I am, what *I* have done."

"Yes, I do. You just told me about the fire."

"But there is more. That wasn't the first time I lost control. One time . . . I almost hurt Ms. Stuart."

Stephen sat back, but didn't say anything, so Kat continued. He needed to know everything, even if it pained her to say it. "So far I've been able to pull back from the power inside me, or I've passed out from the overwhelming intensity of it. But there might come a point where I can't stop it. Someday this power might take over, and I fear what I will become." Her voice had dropped down to almost a whisper. "You saw what I did to those men back at the inn. I can do things—terrible things—more than just set fires and . . ."

"Remember when you walked into my office?"

Kat stopped and looked up.

Stephen gave her a serious look. "I said I would help you find Dr. Latimer. I stand by my word. Together we will find this doctor, and he will heal whatever it is your father did to you. In the meantime, I will help you control this . . . this . . . whatever this is."

Kat worked her jaw, her eyes shimmering with more tears. "I don't know if he can, Stephen. What was done to me was done before I was born. And now . . ." She looked away. "I think I'm dying. On the inside."

"We are all dying, all the time. That's part of growing old."

"No, not like that." Kat hesitated. She licked her lips as she stared at the wall ahead. She knew her soul was dying. And if it completely died before she reached Dr. Latimer, someone needed to know what was happening to her. "I-I need to show you something." Her fingers rose and she fumbled with the top button of her blouse.

Stephen frowned. "Kat, what are you doing?"

She ignored him and undid the next one. She did the third one, then pulled back the fabric above her corset. She pointed at her bare skin. "I can't feel my heart anymore."

His eyes went wide before he glanced away and swallowed, a red hue creeping up his neck.

Kat blushed, but she was determined to show him. So she removed the bedspread and swung her legs around. Thankfully she was still fully dressed, although damp, save for her boots, which were standing next to the bed. She made her way over to the broken glass near the bulkhead and picked up a shard, then walked back to the bed and sat down near Stephen.

"Here, let me show you."

Stephen looked back, his cheeks a dark hue.

Kat brought the shard up and ran the sharp point across her exposed skin.

"What the—" Stephen lunged forward. He grabbed her wrist and pulled her hand back. Blood trickled from the incision above her corset. "What in the blazes are you doing, Kat?"

Kat looked down at the wound. "I can't feel that. I can't feel anything. Ever since my time at the Tower, the area around my heart has become numb. It happened the other times I lost control, but feeling would come back. This time . . . it has not." Panic laced her voice. "And it's starting to affect my emotions as well. As if all of me is turning numb inside and out. I keep having these dreams where this voice tells me—" Her voice hitched and she dropped the glass shard. It hit the floor and shattered.

Stephen took a deep breath and brought her hand down, cradling it between both of his. "What does the voice say?"

Kat took a shaky breath. "It says I'm dying. It tells me that over and over again. Maybe I am?" She gave a small laugh, then a hiccup. "After all, my father was working on corpses, for what reason I know not. He said unlocking death would bring true power, and he said I was the culmination of his work. So maybe . . ." She shrugged.

His hand felt hot against her cold fingers. Stephen gently probed beneath her wrist and pressed between the tendons.

He paused, then looked up. "Maybe you can't feel your heart, but I can, right here." He rubbed the area with his fingers, then paused over her pulse again.

Kat let out a small laugh. "Of course I still have a beating heart, or else I wouldn't be alive." Or would she? Was she some kind of walking undead? She mentally shook her head at the image. "I just don't understand why I can't feel my heart here." She pulled her hand away from Stephen's and pressed her palm against the wound. "How can I not feel my own skin or this cut?"

Stephen let out a long breath. "I don't know. But hopefully this Dr. Latimer does. One step at a time, all right?"

She nodded. His eyes lowered to the blood on her chest. "And we should take care of that scratch."

Kat looked down and curled her fingers over the wound. "I'm afraid I was a bit impulsive." Her cheeks grew warm again. "But I wanted someone to know what's going on just in case . . ."

"Just in case what?"

"I don't know. This . . . thing . . . inside me, it's changing me. And if I change—if I don't remember who I am anymore, if I become someone completely different—I wanted to let you know so you can tell Dr. Latimer, if you find him. He will need to know everything if he is to help me. If—" She let out a long sigh. "If he can help me."

"Remember, one step at a time."

"One step. And Stephen?"

"Yes?"

If Stephen could have the courage to tell her he was sorry, then she could reciprocate. "I forgive you."

His eyebrows shot up.

"I forgive you for taking me to the Tower."

"I—" He sat back. "I don't know what to say."

"I say we start over. Fresh slates. All right?" Just by saying those words, a burden lifted from her shoulders. Somehow the jumbled knot of their relationship was loosened by those simple phrases. There was still work ahead for them, but they were on the right path again.

Stephen straightened and gave her a firm nod. "Yes, I would like that very much. Oh, and I have good news. Robert thinks he might know where Dr. Latimer could be."

Kat leaned forward, then realized her blouse was still unbuttoned. She turned away and clutched the front of her shirt. "Really?" she said as she worked the loops, her face as hot as a stove. Impulsive indeed.

"Yes. He's somewhere in Austrium serving with the World City military as a doctor."

Her shoulders slumped as she did the last button. Thankfully she had only scratched her skin with the glass shard, but she would need to see to the wound soon and do something about the stain. "Austrium is a big country. How will we find him?" Kat glanced back.

Stephen's face was firm. "I'm not sure yet, but it's more information than we had before. We will find him, Kat." He clenched his hand. "And we will find a cure for you."

A cure. Hope burgeoned inside of her like a small ray of light. Was it possible she might actually become normal? That was all she wanted. A chance to be normal. Kat closed her eyes. More and more she found herself petitioning God. Maybe he heard her, maybe he didn't. But she would ask anyway.

Please, God. Let us find a cure.

CHAPTER
13

AFTER STEPHEN LEFT, KAT USED A SMALL CLOTH TO COVER THE scratch, using her corset to keep it in place and cover up the stain, then pulled her hair back, straightened her clothing, and put her boots on. Her stomach gave a loud rumble, reminding her she had not eaten in two days. She pressed her hand against her abdomen and headed for the door behind her.

Bright sunlight pierced her vision the moment she stepped out onto the main deck, and the rays warmed her damp clothing. She held a hand to her eyes and glanced around. The sailors of the *Lancelot* had not been idle while she had been unconscious. The broken mast and rotor had been removed and most of the floor had been repaired with spare planks from the hold. There was still a hole near the middle of the deck, and rope had been secured around it so no one would fall through.

The sound of hammers filled the air. Kat looked around. Two sailors stood on the top deck, repairing the railing. Bright white clouds filled the sky above them.

Beyond the ship, she spotted more sailors in the distance and the wisps from a morning fire. Dunes and light green grass spread across the land to her left, and the Narrow Strait lapped against jagged rocks to her right. On closer inspection, she realized with relief that she had missed the rocks when she had landed the *Lancelot* on the

AWAKENED

dunes. Good thing, considering how much damage those serrated stone teeth could have done to the ship.

Her stomach rumbled again. Kat looked around. Where would Fitz be? Her gaze landed on the fire across the dunes. It was as good a place as any, and maybe she would find something to break her fast.

Kat found the opening along the railing and a rope ladder attached to the deck. She made her way down the side of the ship and jumped the last two feet onto the sandy shore.

A bang erupted to her right, followed by a shout and low growls and words. Captain Grim stood by the side of the ship, gripping one hand with his other one. At least she thought it was Captain Grim. A set of brass goggles with three lenses fanned out above the ocular lens and a set of gears on the side obscured much of his face. He glanced over, noticed Kat, and released his injured fingers. He twisted one of the gears, which moved a fourth lens, then pulled the goggles up from his face.

Soot and dirt covered his skin except where the goggles had been. As usual, a black patch covered his right eye, adding to the piebald effect, but any thought of amusement left Kat as she encountered his single icy blue gaze. They studied each other as seconds ticked by. Did the captain know what she had done? Of course he did. He would have noticed his ship miraculously landing itself instead of smashing to smithereens, and all without his guidance. That, and Stephen had probably told him.

He dropped his gaze and brushed his hands across his pants. "Looking for Stephen?"

It appeared he wasn't interested in talking about what happened. Kat let out a small breath. That suited her. "Actually, I'm looking for Fitz."

Grim nodded toward the curl of smoke. "Over by the fire."

He pulled his goggles down and went back to digging around in the gap in *Lancelot*'s hull. Conversation done.

Kat headed toward the fire, her boots occasionally slipping in the sand. As she drew closer, she caught the scent of porridge and her stomach gave another rumble, leaving her light-headed.

–89–

Fitz stood beside the fire, stirring the contents of a black pot that hung from a makeshift tripod over the flames. He looked up and smiled, beckoning with his hand for Kat to come over.

"Glad to see you up and about. That storm really took it out of you." He reached for a metal bowl from the stack at his side. "Hungry?"

"Very," Kat said, clutching her middle.

Fitz scooped out some of the grainy cereal and handed the bowl to her with a metal spoon. "Cooking outside for a change. The galley wasn't damaged, but sometimes a man needs to be outdoors." He closed his eyes and breathed in deeply. "Something about clean air."

Just then the wind shifted, wafting a puff of smoke Fitz's way and sending him into a fit of coughing. Kat laughed, then blew across the cereal and took a bite. "But isn't the air always clear up in the sky?"

Clearing his throat, Fitz sat down on one of the boulders nearby. "Depends on where we're sailing. The air above World City could choke a man to death."

That made sense, with all the factories and smokestacks. Kat continued to eat, watching Fitz as he enjoyed the morning sunshine, the light bouncing off his bald head.

As she scraped the bowl, Fitz opened his eyes. "Would you like some more?"

"Yes, thank you." She handed him the bowl and he refilled it, then handed it back. This time she ate slower.

"So how are you feeling? That was quite a fall you took during the storm."

Is that what they were saying happened to her? She held her spoon above her bowl. "Better, I believe."

"Good. You're lucky you survived. Mickey wasn't so lucky. Heard he fell from the ship during the storm." Fitz's shoulders drooped as he turned his attention to the black pot.

Mickey? Was he the sailor who'd come to help her? Kat remembered watching the skinny young man slip out the broken bulkhead and the terror on his face. A twinge of sadness stirred inside her, but nothing more.

Fitz removed the pot from the tripod with a set of thick mitts and placed it on the boulder he had been sitting on moments ago. "The repairs are almost done on the *Lancelot*. Enough to get us to our rendezvous point with our contacts in Austrium, at least. Hopefully there the captain can find a way to repair the main mast. I heard that you and Grey will be staying on here in Austrium."

Kat looked up. "We're in Austrium already?"

"Yep, landed on a small island close to the coast. That was some amazing flying on the part of the captain." Fitz eyed her. "Best flying he's ever done."

Did he suspect something?

Kat finished the last spoonful of porridge and placed her bowl and spoon down. Better if he didn't know. "What can you tell me about Austrium?" Funny enough, she hardly knew anything about the country they were fighting against.

Fitz sat down by the pot and wiped his forehead. "Well, in some ways they are similar to us. Advanced in technology, their industry is booming, and their food is excellent." He gave her a wink at that. "However, their country is three times the size of World City and the surrounding principalities. More farms and open space, whereas the World City population is confined to cities and the few spots along the coast."

"What about the people?"

Fitz shrugged. "Like most places, you have your good and your bad. They are more into fashion and the arts than World City. If you ever make it to Emberworth, you'll have to visit the Parthia Cathedral. The most amazing paintings you will ever find."

"You've been to Austrium?"

Fitz laughed. "Of course I have. We used to do a lot of business with Austrium before the war. That's one of the reasons Captain Grim hired on as a privateer for World City. He knows these skies better than most."

"Do you miss visiting Austrium?"

The smile faded from Fitz's face. "I do. This war makes no sense. There is very little for Austrium to gain by invading World City if it ever comes to that. In fact, I would say World City has more to gain. Especially land, the one thing we are lacking. Anyway"—he waved his hand—"I need to get the dishes washed and the salted beef soaking for dinner tonight."

"Would you like some help?" Kat had never done housework before. Ms. Stuart always took care of the household chores back home, and the hired maids handled all domestic affairs in the Tower dormitories. But she would do anything right now if it could keep her busy and her mind off her numbing heart. That, and she didn't want to be alone.

Fitz studied her, then nodded. "Sure, I could use some help. You are not like most genteel ladies I have met."

Kat gave him a winsome smile. He had no idea.

Stephen stood on the edge of the makeshift camp just beyond the airship, watching Kat and Fitz, whose backs were to him. She let out a throaty laugh, and Fitz answered with his own gruff chortle as he handed her a metal bowl, which she began to wipe with a white towel. Were they washing dishes?

Stephen snorted. Just when he had Kat figured out, she surprised him again. Vanessa would have never helped with such menial tasks. But Kat was different. Deep down, where it counted, she was pure gold.

He continued to watch them, studying Kat more than the old cook. The clothes Robert had provided for Kat were Austrium in style. He had briefly noticed during their time on the ship but never allowed himself to really look. Now he studied the lines, how the corset shaped her young figure, the long brown skirt partially hiked up on the right side and held in place with a buckle. And knee high boots, visible through the slit.

The schoolteacher look was gone. Instead, Kat looked like she was ready for an adventure.

A smile spread across his lips. He liked it.

Ever since their talk earlier, since the moment Kat had spoken those words he'd thought he would never hear—and certainly did not deserve—his heart had felt lighter, like he could tackle anything. Life had a new spark to it.

"What are you grinning about?"

Stephen glanced over and found Robert standing next to him, his face covered in soot except for the area around his eye and patch. A trickle of sweat ran down the side of his face, leaving a trail behind.

"If you could see yourself, you'd grin, too," Stephen said.

Using his sleeve to wipe his face—which only made things worse, leaving long streaks of soot where patches of clean skin had been—Robert looked at Fitz and Kat, then back at Stephen. "Horsefeathers. It's the lady." He smirked. "You, sir, are smitten."

Stephen folded his arms and continued to grin. "You know, I think I am."

Robert laughed. "It's nice to see the old Stephen back."

"It's nice to be back. We had a good talk this morning."

"And?"

Stephen turned toward Robert. "She forgave me."

Robert nodded thoughtfully. "You won't meet a lot of women who would forgive such a thing."

"You're right."

"I'd hang on to that one if I were you. Even with all the craziness around her."

"Hopefully Dr. Latimer will take care of that."

"So you're still planning to stay here in Austrium and look for the doctor?"

"Yes." Stephen remembered what Kat had shared this morning. There was more to it than her ability to release unearthly power when her emotions became intense. Whatever this was, it was changing her. Consuming her.

"Then I'll leave you both when I drop off the medical supplies at the rendezvous point. You can head back to the military base camp with our agents on this side of the strait."

"And what will you do?"

"I plan to head farther south and find a way to repair that

mast we lost during the storm, then go home." He gave Stephen a shrewd look. "And you? What are your plans after you find this Dr. Latimer?"

Stephen's gaze found Kat again as she pushed an errant curl back behind her ear and took another dish from Fitz. Robert was right. Kat was a woman he didn't want to lose again. Maybe when this was all over and Kat was cured, they could go back to World City and live a quiet life. Maybe—his heart gave a wistful twist at the thought—maybe even lead a normal life, one that involved proper courting.

Robert shook his head. "No need to answer; I can see it on your face. I wish you the best, my friend."

Stephen just smiled.

CHAPTER

14

JAKE RYDER RUBBED HIS CHIN AND STUDIED THE SHIP SITTING IN the port of Covenshire. She was smaller than the others tied to the pier, with two decks and one large smoke stack in the middle of the ship. Two pale cylinders, shaped and painted like seashells, hid the paddle wheels on either side. He and the other bounty hunters would be a little cramped on board, but Captain Harpur had assured him the trip to the coast of Austrium would take only five days. They could handle it. Time was of the essence now that they knew where Stephen had taken their bounty.

The city council had doubled the amount on the warrant for Miss Bloodmayne. With that kind of money, he could retire, or take the occasional contract if he wanted to. No more late nights, no more searching for criminals. He could enjoy an evening at home—his own home, not some rundown flat—with a bottle of scotch, a fire, and a good book. Maybe he would even get a dog.

Captain Harpur scurried down the side ladder of the boat and approached Jake, his boots clapping across the worn wooden planks. He was a short man, with thick dark hair and a face that looked like it hadn't been shaved in days. "So what do you think? Like I said, the *Calypso* isn't much to look at, but she's fast and small enough to avoid the Austrium blockade, especially if we head to the southernmost coast where the World City forces are based."

Jake nodded. "How soon can you leave?"

"Within the hour. I've already restocked her and the weather is perfect for a trip to Austrium."

"Then I'll let the other men know, and we'll meet back here at noon."

"Sounds good. I expect half of the payment when we leave, and the rest when I drop you off."

Jake narrowed his eyes. He wasn't sure how long it would take to find Miss Bloodmayne, but once they did, they would want fast transportation back. "I have an even better offer. I'll triple what we are paying you if you'll stay in Austrium and be ready to bring us back once we find who we're looking for. No questions asked," he said when Harpur opened his mouth.

The captain snapped his mouth shut and glanced back at the *Calypso*. Jake could almost see the wheels turning in the man's head. It was probably more money than the man made in a year. Of course, after they received the bounty, they could well afford to pay the man.

Harpur looked back. "It's nothing illegal, is it? I don't need any run-ins with the law."

Jake smiled. "I can assure you that our mission is quite legal and even sanctioned by the World City council."

Harpur whistled, a greedy gleam in his eyes. "The World City council, eh? I bet the council could afford to pay a bit more."

The smile slid from Jake's face and he casually moved his duster back, exposing the handle of his revolver at his side. "I should probably make one thing clear. I am not a man to be trifled with. I've made you a fair bargain. Take it or leave it." He let his duster fall back and began to roll up his sleeves. His multiple tattoos intimidated most civil men. "I'm sure I can find another captain who would like to earn that kind of money." He finished one sleeve and started with the other.

Harpur licked his lips, his eyes moving back and forth between Jake's arms. Barely a speck of flesh-tone remained across Jake's ink-covered skin. He was quite proud of the tattoos. He had one done after every job. They were his trophies. He had one spot left on his back. That was where he would put the last tattoo once he was done with this mission.

"So are you still asking for more money, or are you willing to take me up on my offer?"

Greed warred upon the captain's face. "Fine, it's a deal," he said and extended his hand.

Jake shook it. "One third now, one third once we reach Austrium, and one third when we arrive back in World City." He dropped Harpur's hand and stepped away. "I'll be back with the other two men at noon."

"I'll see you then." Harpur turned and headed back to his ship.

As he walked away, Jake ran through everything he would need before they left in the next hour. Piers and Rodger were waiting for him back at that dingy tavern they had found late last night along the pier. Just one more thing he wouldn't miss once they finished this job and he could retire: rat-infested inns.

Piers wrinkled his nose as he gazed at the *Calypso*, his monocle sinking into his cheek. "We're taking *that* across the Narrow Strait?"

Jake approached the ladder that led up to the ship. "She's all I could find on short notice. But she's fast, and the captain will wait for us in Austrium."

"Well, that's one consolation."

Rodger just grunted and grabbed the ladder behind Jake, his cannon-arm clunking against the metal side of the ship.

Once he reached the top, Jake looked around. The main deck wasn't much bigger than his flat back home. A couple feet away was a door that led to the quarters that he, Piers and Rodger would be sharing. He crossed the small space and popped the latch. Two pairs of hammocks hung on either side of a narrow walkway, one above the other. After a moment, Jake chose the lower hammock to the right and placed his bag down on the floor beneath it. Piers was small enough, he could have one of the top hammocks, and Rodger could have the other bottom one.

Jake left before Piers and Rodger entered the cabin. Behind him, Piers hollered about their sleeping quarters. He shrugged and continued toward the top deck. Piers would calm down. He always did.

As he reached the top deck, a large plume of steam shot from the smokestack with a loud whistle and a hiss. The *Calypso* began to move. The paddles on either side hit the water with a splash and started their rotation. Jake grabbed the railing to keep from falling. A smile spread across his face as he gazed out over the Narrow Strait. Finally, they were on their way and he could begin his hunt again for Miss Bloodmayne.

CHAPTER
15

THE *LANCELOT* GLIDED ALONG THE COAST OF AUSTRIUM, BUT FAR enough out to avoid detection. Stephen leaned against the railing on the topmost deck and watched the water beneath him. A bright and cheery sun shone above, and the water sparkled. The rotors filled the air with a soft hum as they propelled the airship forward.

A small part of him wished he could stay in this moment. Sure, he would miss World City, but there was something about being away from it all. Up here in the sky it was just him, the clouds and wind, and the gentle motion of the *Lancelot*. He could understand why Robert had left the city to pursue his father's line of work. There was a quiet thrill to the career of a privateer—when it wasn't flat out dangerous and terrifying.

Stephen laughed to himself. He was no privateer. Eventually he would be tempted back to the life of a bounty hunter, to the exhilaration of the hunt and the satisfaction of bringing justice to those who deserved it.

A bell rang behind him. Stephen glanced back. Robert stood at the helm, one hand on the wheel, the other cranking on a gear set along the side of the wooden box. A bell rang again.

Robert caught his eye and pointed to the left.

Stephen left his spot and headed toward the port bow just as the airship slowly turned at an angle and began to descend. He reached the railing and gripped the wooden bars.

The coast was lined with ragged cliffs overlooking the sea. Each wave struck the rocks and sprayed up like a geyser, sending plume after plume into the air. Between the cliffs was a small beach, and where the white sand met the rocky face of the cliffs, there appeared to be a cave.

The *Lancelot* angled for the beach. With an expert hand, Robert brought the ship closer until, right before the beach, he turned left. There, at the top of the cliff, was a single wooden walkway. As the *Lancelot* came about, another bell rang out with different tones. Stephen glanced back. Sailors scurried across the main deck and opened the large square hatch in the middle of the ship. Light colored fabric bloomed from the opening and spread out as gas filled the balloon. The rotor on top of the second main mast grew still as the balloon expanded and passed the metal blades.

The *Lancelot* slowed until it reached the walkway. By now the balloon had fully expanded, keeping the airship aloft. Robert slowed the ship to a stop near the walkway.

Anders unlatched the railing, hauled out a broad wooden plank, and banged it down between the airship and the walkway. Two sailors left the ship and split, one heading aft and one forward to catch the ropes flung to them by their fellows on board. As the men secured the thick coils around two large pegs stuck in the ground, the *Lancelot* jerked to the side, then settled into a hovering position next to the walkway.

Robert gave another gear a quick jerk, then walked away from the helm. "Welcome to Silver Cove, our rendezvous spot with military agents from World City."

"Beautiful place," Stephen said, glancing over the railing as they headed down to the main deck.

"Beautiful and out of the way. You can't spot the cave unless you are almost right on top of it. And the cliffs here make it easy to dock the *Lancelot*."

The men reached the main deck just as Kat stepped out from the galley.

Robert nodded toward Kat. "We won't be here long—too risky

with the tightened air security—so you should gather your belongings and be ready to disembark. I had a small satchel packed for each of you, and Fitz included some food."

"Thank you, Robert, for everything. I don't know what would have happened back at the Tower if you hadn't shown up, or how we would have found Dr. Latimer."

"You would have still escaped," Robert said, winking his one good eye. "You always had a knack for theatrical stunts, although running across the roof with a woman in your arms and climbing aboard my airship would be hard to beat."

Stephen snorted. "You make it sound like a penny dreadful."

"Reality is sometimes more interesting than fiction, my friend. Anyway, I need to meet with my informant, and you need to be ready to leave." Robert lifted a hand in farewell and walked toward the plank along with two of his crew.

Kat came to stand beside Stephen. "So this is it?"

"Yes. We will travel with the military back to their base and start our search."

Kat drew in a deep breath and nodded, a fist held against her middle.

"Nervous?"

She let out a shaky laugh. "We must be insane, venturing into a strange country at war to find a single person we have never met, hoping he can cure the bizarre problem I have before I turn into something abnormal and destroy the world."

He knew she was trying to make light of the situation, but the slight quiver of her lower lip gave away her fear. He wanted to grab her hand and reassure her, but now was not the time, certainly not in front of all these men. "You're not alone," he said quietly. "I'm here." He would not leave her again.

A shadow passed over the carefree moments from before. Stephen closed his eyes. He had no idea how Kat's condition fit into his understanding of the world, or of God. How did a human being come to have the power that she did?

He mentally shook his head. He didn't know. But one thing he did know, God could do anything. Including cure Kat's ailment, whatever it may be.

The moment Stephen, Kat, Grim, and his men stepped off the long flight of hidden stairs onto the white sandy beach below the docked *Lancelot*, a handful of soldiers emerged from the cave ahead.

"Captain Grim," one of the men called out, a short man with nut-brown hair and a full beard. "You're three days late. We were starting to wonder if you would show up."

"Sergeant Wilkins, my apologies. We ran into a band of wasps and bad weather. My ship was damaged and we had to land to make repairs."

Wilkins stopped a few feet away, his men behind him. They were all dressed in the olive green color the World City police wore, but the uniform itself was different. Brass buckles lined either side of the jacket, and golden tassels dangled from the the shoulders. The jacket split at the waist and hung on either side of the hip, exposing the men's revolvers. The pants were unadorned trousers in a matching olive green.

Kat stood behind Stephen, but his frame couldn't hide her from the eyes of the military men. Wilkins looked her direction and frowned. "When did you start traveling with a woman again, Captain?"

Instead of answering his question, Robert motioned toward the cave. "I have a favor to ask of you, but it is better that we discuss it in the cave while my men unload your cargo."

Wilkins raised one eyebrow, but nodded. Both men instructed their crew about unloading the ship, then started toward the cave. Stephen caught her eye and nodded for them to follow the men as well. Kat suddenly felt hot, even with the light blouse on. She should have realized there would hardly be any women here, that she would stand out.

The white sand squeaked beneath their boots as they made their way toward the cave. The entrance was not very big, about the size of a set of double doors. A couple charred logs and some fish bones bore witness to a recent fire just outside the entrance.

Wilkins led the way inside, followed by Grim, then Stephen and herself. Kat shivered and wrapped her arms across her body, the rapid heat from moments ago evaporating in the brisk sea air. Past the entrance, the cave opened into a vast cavern the size of the Tower's courtyard back home. To the right were crates and boxes stacked neatly in rows. To the left, makeshift beds lay on the ground and a couple barrels lined the far wall. Wilkins walked over to the nearest bed, grabbed a candle and matchstick from beside it, and lit the candle. He motioned for them to follow and headed to the middle of the cave where a long table and chairs were set up.

Wilkins headed toward the left side and pulled out a chair to his right. "For the lady," he said.

Kat glanced at Stephen before moving to take the proffered chair. Wilkins took the seat at the head of the table, and Stephen took the seat next to her. Robert went around and sat down on Wilkins's left.

"I would offer refreshments, but I'm afraid we haven't the time," Wilkins said as an apology to Kat while placing the candle on the table.

Kat dipped her head. "I appreciate the thought, but I understand."

Wilkins turned to Grim and the men briefly discussed the medical supplies Robert had brought, along with payment, and delivery of the next batch in a couple weeks.

"Now what is this favor you asked about?" Wilkins asked when their business was complete.

Robert gestured at Stephen. "First, introductions. The man across from me is a good friend and one of World City's best bounty hunters, Stephen Grey."

Stephen nodded in Wilkins' direction.

"Stephen Grey, eh? I've heard of you. Even over here we get the *Herald* once in a while."

Robert went on. "The lady next to Grey is Miss Bloodmayne."

Kat waited for Wilkins to respond, but apparently he did not recognize her surname or didn't see a reason to mention it. Her body relaxed and she let out a deep breath through her nose.

"Miss Bloodmayne." Wilkins tipped his head toward her.

"Miss Bloodmayne is a client of Stephen's. They are searching for a doctor. Recently I discovered this doctor is stationed over here with the military. We were hoping you could help them further their search."

"What is the doctor's name?" Wilkins asked.

"Dr. Latimer."

Wilkins sat back and pulled at the bottom of his beard. "Latimer, you say. You mean Dr. Joshua Latimer?"

Robert glanced at Stephen before responding. Stephen gave him a short nod. "Yes, that is the man."

Kat leaned forward, a fluttery, empty feeling in her stomach.

"Yes, I know him, or I know about him. I've never met the man myself. Heard he's done miracles with our soldiers on the front lines. Saved many men from death. Why are you looking for him?" Wilkins eyed Stephen.

Stephen folded his hands across the table. "It's personal, but I assure you, Dr. Latimer has committed no crime. My client is looking for information and believes Dr. Latimer can help her attain it."

Wilkins' mouth opened, then shut. He looked at Kat. "I see," he said a moment later. "And this information required you travel to Austrium? During a war?"

Kat straightened. "Yes, I'm afraid so. I need to see Dr. Latimer and talk to him myself."

Wilkins rubbed his eyebrow and sighed. "Well, the doctor's whereabouts are no secret, and since you travel with Captain Grim, whom I trust, I see no reason not to tell you. However, you will not be able to reach him at this time."

"Why not?" Kat asked before she could stop herself.

Wilkins frowned. "Because Dr. Latimer is stationed at Purvue, on the front lines."

"Oh." Kat sat back, the lightness inside her middle shrinking into a cold, hard ball.

"However, if he returns, he would most likely head to our main base at Ironguard, where the majority of our forces are. Perhaps we can help you get there."

It wasn't what she wanted, but it was better than not finding Dr. Latimer at all. "Yes, that would be nice."

"It will be a couple hours before we are ready for departure. I will send one of my men to fetch both of you when we are ready to leave."

Kat nodded, swallowing the lump inside her throat.

Stephen stood and held out his hand to Wilkins. "Thank you for your help."

Wilkins nodded and shook. "Now I must go. Make sure you're ready."

As the others stood, Wilkins licked his fingers and pinched out the candle flame, then turned and headed for the outside.

Stephen and Robert walked a short distance away and spoke in low tones

Kat remained at the table, now dim with the candlelight snuffed out, and brought a shaky hand to her forehead. Now that they were finally here, the idea of finding Dr. Latimer seemed daunting. How could they possibly talk to him if he was at the front lines? And could he really cure her?

She stared at her hands, hands that had flamed up days ago when the *Lancelot* was falling through the storm clouds. Hands that could crush a man's throat without even touching him. Just a mere pinch and—

Kat closed her eyes and clenched her fists. "God," she whispered, once again finding herself drawn toward the unfamiliar being. "You've brought us this far, farther than I thought we would ever come. Please continue to help us. Please"—she swallowed—"please help me."

CHAPTER

16

KAT RODE IN THE MIDDLE SEAT OF THE MOTORWAGON. THE VEHICLE reminded her of the steam-powered phaetons back home, only this one had an extended, covered bed where the crates full of medical supplies were stacked. Two more motorwagons followed behind.

For two days the caravan had bumped along the dirt roads that weaved through the hills of Austrium. Heat waves shimmered along the horizon as summer took hold of the country, turning what were once green fields into hills of gold. Tall oak trees dotted the landscape and lined the road, shading the motorwagons as they drove beneath.

Kat wiped her forehead, thankful for the Austrium-style clothing Captain Grim had provided for her. The calf-high skirt and loose blouse beneath the leather corset allowed the occasional breeze to cool her skin. For a moment, she wondered what Marianne would think of her attire. Marianne would probably laugh and want to try on the outfit herself, proclaiming it scandalous at the same time.

A sad smile crept across her face and her heart ached for her one-time friend. Could things ever be the same between them if Kat found the cure for this thing inside her? Or would Marianne always remember that night at the gala?

The wagon hit a bump and tossed her toward the seat ahead.

Stephen's arm shot out and caught her midsection. "Careful there."

Kat sat back and adjusted her skirt.

The motorwagon rumbled for a minute before Stephen turned to her and asked, "How are you doing today?" His voice was low enough so the driver could not hear him.

Kat glanced at him. Did he mean in general, or was he asking specifically about what she had shared days ago, about dying inside? "Nothing has changed," she said quietly. The area was still numb around her heart, but thankfully it had not expanded.

The road felt like they were driving over a washboard. Her teeth clacked with each bump and her backside grew sore.

Stephen leaned over again once the road smoothed. "Have you thought about what you'll do after this is all over?"

Kat placed a hand on the side of the wagon and watched the golden hills roll by. She had searched for a cure—and for Dr. Latimer—for so long, it had been some time since she'd thought about any life past that. Other women at the Tower had talked about their futures—to apprentice for the Tower, to work at the hospitals and perhaps even assist in the surgery theater, or to teach at secondary schools—and some had even secretly talked about marrying and raising a family.

But it had been a long time since Kat had let her mind—or her heart—go there. She tapped the metal railing. "I don't know. I enjoy teaching, Maybe I could find a job as a teacher or even a professor. I'm also interested in the medical field. A nursing school opened up just outside World City a couple months ago."

"What about a family?"

Kat jerked her head toward Stephen. Was he saying something? Her heart beat faster at the thought. She had no real experience with family herself. Her mother had died during childbirth and her father was barely home during her childhood. But she had read stories about families, about love, romance, and a lifelong bond. Sure, they had been penny novels, but still . . .

What would a life be like with Steph—

The field next to them exploded in a cloud of dirt and grass. The boom echoed between the trees and hills.

Stephen grabbed her and pulled her against his chest, shielding her. Another explosion sounded to their right.

Kat craned her neck to the side. "What's going on?"

Stephen shook his head, his face tight.

"Move it, move it!" their driver yelled. The motorwagon whined and jumped forward.

Kat pulled back and glanced outside the wagon, Stephen's arm still around her shoulder. More explosions popped up across fields.

"What's happening?" Stephen yelled toward the driver between blasts.

"Not sure," the driver shouted over his shoulder. "We are a little ways from the base. It must be under attack, and we're just a target of opportunity. Although I don't know how Austrium forces could penetrate this far onto our side."

The motorwagon roared as it flew down the dirt road. More explosions detonated all around them.

Kat looked back. The other two motorwagons were racing behind them, but as she watched, something small and metallic fell from the sky, hitting the last one.

Boom!

The motorwagon jumped into the air, then split into a dozen pieces, disappearing into a billow of smoke and licks of fire.

Kat turned away, her heart inside her throat. Time seemed to slow, and her mind continued to reconstruct the wagon blowing up, the look on the driver's face right before the explosion, over and over again, until her middle hurt. All it would take was one of those strange objects dropping on them and—

She shook her head, sucking in air. No, she couldn't go there. She pried open one eye. High above the wagon tiny brass objects zipped across the bright blue sky like flies. One flew near their motorwagon on Stephen's side and dropped a circular object—small and metallic, the size of a child's ball—a couple feet from the window.

"Kat!"

Stephen shoved her down onto the seat, covering her body with his as a loud boom went off. Ringing filled her ears as the wagon tilted to the side. Stephen's full weight pressed down on her until she could hardly breathe.

The wagon jerked upright with a shudder and smoke filled the air. Kat coughed and stared up at the canvas ceiling, her ears still ringing. Stephen's head rested just below her chin. "Stephen?" She pushed against his shoulders, but he didn't move. Something sticky trickled across her fingers. She drew her hand back. Blood. "Stephen!"

A scarlet trail trickled down the side of his neck and dripped onto her blouse.

The motorwagon rumbled beneath her as the driver started up the engine and the wagon lurched forward again.

"Stephen!" Kat shook his shoulders. Had he been hit by the blast? Where was the blood coming from?

She could hardly breathe under the weight of his body, his blood slowly dripping across her neck and chest. She sucked in another breath. "Stephen," she said in a choked whisper. "Don't be dead. Please."

The sky flew by outside the window as she struggled out from beneath him. Panting, she leaned against the back of the seat with Stephen's head across her lap. The blood was coming from somewhere behind his head.

Kat squeezed her eyes shut. *God, please help us!* He was up there, right? Maybe he didn't care about monsters like her, but Stephen was a good man. "Don't let him die, please, God. He's all I have left. If he dies, who will help me?"

Stephen groaned.

"Stephen?" Kat opened her eyes and coughed against the smoke.

Stephen placed a hand on the seat and pushed himself up. "Where am I—ugh!" He covered his face with his hand and his body trembled.

Kat pushed herself up farther, part of her skirt still trapped beneath his leg. "We're in Austrium, in a motorwagon."

His hand never left his face. "I don't feel well." The motorwagon turned a sharp corner, sending them both flying. Kat slid across the seat and hit the door. Stephen slammed into her a moment later. He let out another groan.

"You both all right back there?" the driver asked.

"No!" Kat helped Stephen back up. His eyes were wide and a sheen of sweat covered his forehead. "My companion is injured!"

"Don't panic. We're almost to the base."

Kat glanced up. Sure enough, nestled between two hills ahead were thousands of canvas tents. Smoke and fire dotted the camp. Seconds later, tiny metallic globes fell across the camp, followed by multiple booms and smoke.

The driver let out a curse and swerved out of the path of one of the metallic globes as it hit the dirt road ahead of them.

Boom!

Dirt, grass, and rocks flew into the air. Kat ducked down and covered her face. *I hate this. I hate this place. I hate these things!*

A hand brushed her head. Kat looked between her fingers. Stephen stroked her hair, his eyes slightly out of focus, like he'd had one too many drinks.

The wagon rumbled toward the outskirts of the base as a strange, motorized grinding noise filled the air. The sound grew louder and louder, punctuated by sharp, shrieking whistles every few seconds. From beyond the base's perimeter, brass machines the size of small carriages walked out on two frog-like legs. A small window encased the front of each where the driver sat. Steam rose from the pipe that ran up the backsides of the machines.

The machines' cannon-like arms rose and another set of high-pitched whistles filled the air as projectiles erupted from the end of the arms. Like arrows, the tiny missiles wove through the air and hit the brass contraptions zipping across the sky.

One of the flying contraptions fell near the road as the wagon sped through the opening to the base. Kat caught a glimpse of the machine—a brass dragonfly-like device with a metal globe clutched beneath its abdomen. One of the men from the checkpoint ran out and retrieved the contraption.

Once inside the perimeter, the driver of their motorwagon pulled back on a lever and the wagon swerved to a stop beyond the first row of tents. The other wagon rolled up next to them, and Wilkins hopped out of it before the driver turned off the engine.

"Anyone hurt?" he yelled over the shrill whistles. He came up to Kat's wagon and looked in. Stephen sat against the back of the seat, his eyes closed, his face pale.

"One of the passengers was hit by shrapnel." Their driver got out and opened the door on Stephen's side as another bipedal transport walked by, its cannon arms raised and ready to fire.

"And you, Miss Bloodmayne?"

Kat shook her head in a daze, distracted by the loud noise, the brass war machines lumbering by, and Stephen. She placed a hand on Stephen's shoulder. "No, I'm fine, but Stephen—"

"Will be taken directly to the medics."

Her shoulders sagged and she glanced back at Wilkins. "Thank you, Sergeant."

A few more blasts and whistles went off, but they were fewer in number and no longer in the base. The driver helped Stephen out of the wagon. Stephen wobbled as he placed his feet on the ground.

Kat held her skirt back and scrambled out behind them, her stomach knotted like a tangled ball of yarn.

Smoke billowed between the canvas tents. Shouts went up unseen. Soldiers in olive green uniforms scurried here and there, making the base look like a prodded ants' nest.

Wilkins approached their driver, and the two men assisted Stephen down the main dirt path. Kat quickly followed. From behind, she saw matted blood and hair around a large gash at the base of Stephen's head, and splotches of blood and torn fabric indicated multiple small lacerations across his shoulders and back.

She held a hand to her mouth. "Oh, God, please help him," she whispered.

A moment later, Stephen hunched over and heaved. The contents of his stomach came up and landed on the hardened dirt.

"We'll send someone to clean that up," Wilkins said, helping Stephen back up. "Right now we need to get him to a doctor."

Kat bypassed the mess and nodded, her throat so tight she couldn't talk even if she wanted to. She knew very little about head injuries, and had no idea how grave Stephen's was.

After a couple minutes, they approached a set of tents designated with a white star in the middle of a blue circle. At the end of the row stood the main tent with the medical symbol and a number one above the entrance. The men took Stephen there.

The interior of the tent was one cavernous room filled with four long rows of cots—a hundred at least—over half of which were occupied by injured men. The scent of blood and smoke filled the area.

Kat covered her nose and followed Wilkins and the driver as they lowered Stephen onto the nearest available cot. Women and men dressed in light blue uniforms with white aprons rushed between the rows. A couple women marked strips of cloth and tied them to the cots. Others bandaged up wounds or administered spoonfuls of what looked like laudanum.

In the back of the tent, tables were set up. A robust woman dressed in blue and two men dressed in white lab coats were talking and pointing around the tent.

"I'm sorry, miss, but we need to get back to the convoy."

Kat turned back and nodded to Wilkins. "Thank you for bringing us here."

"My pleasure. I will let Commander Powell know you are here. Usually civilians are required to check in, but with Mr. Grey injured, I'm sure he'll understand why I brought you both here instead. I can assure you Dr. Emmett and Matron Foskey will do all they can to help Mr. Grey. Until then . . ." Wilkins tipped his head and he and the driver left.

Kat stood there, her arms wrapped around her middle. Muffled moans and cries drifted around the tent. The man in the cot next to her began to cough up blood. Two soldiers entered with another man, his uniform singed and smelling of burnt flesh. They placed him in the cot across from her. Two nurses rushed down the row, one toward the man coughing, the other toward the burned man.

Kat collapsed at the end of Stephen's cot and held her face in her hands. Her head felt light, like her conscious self was drifting away from her body. All she had to do was let go, and she would no longer hear or smell or see the pain around her. She could drift along in the weightlessness of her mind—

She clenched one hand and looked up. *No. I need to stay here, for Stephen.*

She straightened and turned toward Stephen. His eyes were closed, his face still pale. She moved along the edge of the cot until she was sitting at his side, then reached over and took his hand and held it between her own. "I'm here, Stephen," she whispered. "Just hold on. Help is on the way."

CHAPTER
17

"Help is on the way."

Stephen relaxed at the sound of that voice. Like honey and sunshine across his pain-filled mind. Something warm held his hand. He wanted to open his eyes, but it hurt too much to even think about it. Instead, he slipped into the warm darkness . . .

"The cut isn't deep, but I cannot assess what the blow might have done to his brain. I'll have one of the nurses patch him up and we'll keep him overnight for observation."

A tenor voice. Neither harsh nor brassy. Not as soothing as the other voice. More voices hummed inside his head, like words heard underwater. The hum became a lull, gently pulling him along into the darkness again . . .

In. Out.

With each breath, Stephen drifted toward the pale light ahead.

In. Out.

He opened his eyes. He lay on a cot, his body molded to the dipping of the canvas. A wool blanket draped his body and chest, and his arms were tucked in on either side of him. A powerful thirst filled his being. Water! He needed water.

He sat up and his head twinged. Ugh, too fast. He pressed his hand to his face until the ache disappeared. At least he didn't feel dizzy anymore.

"Stephen?"

He glanced around. He was in some kind of tent, an enormous one, with dozens of cots in long rows. Lamps hung from the tent poles and cast warm pools of light down the middle of the area, leaving the perimeter in shadow.

A hand touched his shoulder. Stephen twisted his head even more and found Kat sitting nearby. The light from a nearby lantern lit her face. Another light glowed behind her, leaving a halo around her head. She looked like an angel, except for the dark circles beneath her eyes.

"Kat," he said in a hoarse voice. "You're here." His thirst grabbed him by the throat. "Water," he croaked.

She nodded and stood, the warmth of her hand disappearing from his shoulder. "I'll be right back."

He watched her move along the path between the cots, her tiny figure disappearing through the tent opening. The man in the next cot over stirred then settled down again.

Stephen frowned, slowly taking in the area for the second time. This place reminded him of a hospital. Was that were he was? A hospital? What happened to him? He remembered . . . a huge blast. And fear. Fear for Kat. Pushing her down and covering her with his own body. And . . .

Nothing.

He squeezed his eyes shut, searching his mind for anything after that. Nothing.

He brought his hand up and touched the skin across his shoulder where Kat's hand had been moments before.

Wait, his shirt was gone.

His eyes flew open and he looked down. His chest was wrapped in gauze, although the prickling of pain was located across his back and not his front. There was also a throbbing along the base of his head. He reached up and fingered the area. Instead of skin and hair, there was gauze. His fingers trailed the bumpy cloth, moving along his forehead, just above his eyebrows, and back down to the base of his skull.

The canvas flaps moved and Kat entered the tent. She made her way back to his cot, a tin cup in her hand.

"Here you go." She sat down in the chair next to his cot and held the cup to his lips.

Stephen let her assist him, gulping down the tepid, earthy water as if he would never be satisfied. After a couple seconds, Kat drew the empty cup away.

"Thank you." His whole body felt fatigued, like he had been running all day. Slowly he lay back down and stared up at the roof of the tent.

"How are you feeling?"

"Tired. And in a little pain." He glanced at Kat. Her eyes focused below his chin. The wool blanket had fallen to his waist and he hadn't pulled it back over his bare midsection.

She'd probably never seen a man without his shirt on.

Stephen grabbed the end of the blanket and pulled it up.

Kat's face grew red and she looked away.

A soft smile spread across his face. It was nice to know that, with everything going on with Kat, there was still an innocence to her. He tucked the blanket around his chest, leaving his arms free in the warm air. "So what happened to me?"

"You don't remember?" Kat glanced back, and, after observing he was covered again, brought her whole face around.

He almost shook his head, thought better of it, and said, "No. I remember we were in a motorwagon, and things dropping from the sky, and a lot of explosions."

"But you don't remember anything else?"

He scrunched up his face in thought. A blur of color, sound, and movement were all he had. "No."

Kat readjusted her hands on her lap. "Our convoy was hit. One of the motorwagons behind us exploded. We were also hit by a blast. You shielded me and took the brunt of the explosion. Something hit the back of your head and knocked you out. When you came to, you were groggy. We arrived at the base and brought you here. The doctor thinks you have a concussion."

"A con-what?"

"A concussion. An injury to the head."

Stephen felt the gauze again around his head. "How bad?"

"The gash itself was shallow. One of the nurses sewed it up. The doctor wasn't sure if there was internal damage, so he had you stay here overnight."

Stephen glanced around. "What time is it?"

Kat hid a yawn behind her hand. "Past midnight, I think."

Almost a whole day had past and he didn't remember any of it? Was that a result of the head injury? Kat yawned again and Stephen frowned. "Why are you here? Didn't they provide you with a place to stay?"

She cocked her head to the side. "Yes. But I wasn't about to leave you alone."

"But there are nurses here. This is a hospital after all, right?"

She paused and stared at him. "Do you think I would leave you after you saved my life?"

Stephen stared up into Kat's face, and something shifted violently inside his heart. He'd been a lone wolf for so long he had forgotten what it was like to have someone actually care about his welfare. His throat tightened. "Thank you, Kat."

A fire lit inside her eyes. "As long as you are here, I will be here as well."

"And how long will that be?"

Kat sat back and frowned. "I'm not sure. One of the doctors will want to see you in the morning. And while you were unconscious, I found out that Dr. Latimer is still stationed at the front lines." There was a tinge of disappointment in her voice.

"And when can we expect him back?" Stephen struggled up onto his elbows.

"One of the nurses said he should be back in a couple of weeks. Then his tour is over."

"A couple of weeks." Stephen lay back down. "I'm sorry, Kat. I wasn't expecting that."

She gave a small laugh. "I wasn't either. But it looks like we're going to have to wait."

He blinked a couple times, his mind turning over what they

would do next. He wasn't sure what the commander would think about a World City bounty hunter and young lady on his base. He'd have to check in with the commander the moment he was back up on his feet. That is, if the commander didn't come find him first.

But then what?

Stephen closed his eyes. Ever since his time on the *Lancelot*, and especially after his conversation with Kat, his heart had begun to open back up to God. Little prayers here and there now dotted his thoughts. Like now.

God.

What did he say next?

Thank you for saving me during that blast. The more he thought about it, the more he realized how fortunate he was. No, not fortunate. A little higher, a little faster, and whatever had hit him might have caused further damage, or even permanent damage.

Thank you for watching over Kat. Stephen hadn't really talked to Kat about what she believed, but he had a feeling her knowledge of God was limited or even non-existent given what he knew about Dr. Bloodmayne, unless his aunt had been able to share. But Kat would have said something, right?

Please help us reach Dr. Latimer. So far Kat hadn't had an episode, and scary Kat hadn't made an appearance, but she was changing, she had said so herself. How much longer did they have? And was there really a cure? Or would the scary Kat emerge permanently, and then what?

An image of World City filled his mind, red with flame and smoke. If Kat could throw men against the wall and land an airship with just her mind, was it possible there was no end to her power? And if scary Kat was in charge . . .

Stephen let his breath out his nose. No. He was not going to go there. They would focus on the here and now. At the moment, Kat was doing fine, minus the numb area around her heart, and Dr. Latimer would be coming back. They just had to wait. And God . . . well, God could do anything. Including heal Kat's soul.

CHAPTER

18

AFTER A RESTLESS NIGHT, KAT SAT UP IN THE CHAIR BESIDE Stephen's cot. Her head felt like it was full of wool and her muscles were sore from the hard wooden chair. Outside, the first rays of morning trickled through the tent flaps. Already the day promised to be a hot one.

Stephen, along with most of the other injured men, was still fast asleep. His chest rose and fell in a steady rhythm, and when she leaned close, she could hear the soft whoosh of his exhale. At this range, she could see a tiny white scar that ran through his eyebrow and the individual bristles of his three-day beard. The hardened façade he usually wore was gone, replaced with a younger, more carefree face. She wondered for a moment what Stephen had been like before he had caught his fiancée with another man. The time before he became a bounty hunter. Did he laugh? Enjoy life? Had there been a spark to his eye?

Kat let out a quiet sigh. She understood the heaviness of a dark past all too well. Her own circumstances had robbed her of the carefree life she had seen in others. Maybe when this was all over, they would both find a more peaceful future.

"I'll be back," she whispered. He never answered, just continued in serene slumber.

With a yawn and a long stretch, she stood and wandered to the back of the medical tent.

A handful of nurses were starting their morning routine. One swept the dirt floor, two more started their rounds, and a fourth brought in a tray of steaming bowls.

Kat slipped behind the tables near the canvas wall and watched the nurses work. The longer she stood there, the more out of place she felt. She turned away and wrapped her arms around herself. She had no business in a war camp. If only Dr. Latimer had been here. Instead, he would be at the front lines for a couple more weeks.

Kat squeezed her arms tighter across her middle. What if Doctor Latimer couldn't cure her? What if this whole trip had been in vain? Her hand stole to her throat, her stomach a nest of writhing snakes. What next? And what about Stephen? She glanced over her shoulder at the cot near the middle of the tent. A little bit higher, a little bit faster, and that debris would have killed him.

It's all my fault. Every person I'm around I place in danger. Maybe I should have never been born. My very being seems to destroy everyone around me.

A small piece of curled paper caught her attention. It was nailed to the last tent pole just above the table. The note was short, too short to be a list or a schedule. Kat leaned over the table and pulled the curled side back, exposing firm, bold handwriting.

Awake, O sleeper, rise up from the dead, and God will give you light.

She frowned and straightened. What an odd saying. Why was it posted here? Was it part of some poem? She glanced around, but no one was paying attention to her. She looked back at the note. What did it mean? Why had someone placed it here?

"I see you've found one of Dr. Latimer's famous postings."

Kat jumped and turned around, her heart beating fast against her ribcage. A young man stood a couple feet away, dark hair swept back, his face clean shaven. He wore a lab coat over a button up shirt and trousers. "Dr. Emmett." He gave her a short bow. "And you are?"

Kat worked her mouth. "Miss Bloodmayne."

His eyebrows flew up as he straightened. "Bloodmayne? As in Dr. Alexander Bloodmayne?"

Her face flushed. She shouldn't have given her name. "Yes," she said, the heat spreading along her hairline. "He is my father."

His eyes widened even farther. "What are you doing here in Austrium? This base is a long way from World City. Wait—" He held out his hand. "Are you one of the new nurses?"

Kat shook her head. "No, I'm here in search of someone." She gestured to the curled note. "Dr. Latimer, in fact."

"Ah." He shook his head. "I'm afraid he's not here. Did you come here by yourself?"

"No, with a bounty hunter. I hired him to help me track down the doctor."

"And where is this bounty hunter now?"

Kat looked back and pointed toward the cot where Stephen slept. "Our convoy was hit on our way here."

Dr. Emmett glanced in the direction Kat pointed. "During the bombing?"

"Yes. Mr. Grey was hit while protecting me."

Dr. Emmett started across the tent. "What kind of wound?"

Kat hurried to his side. "Head." She led him to Stephen's bed. "At the base of his skull. The medic said it wasn't bad and stitched it up, but wanted to him to stay for observation."

The doctor stopped beside the cot and rubbed his chin thoughtfully. "This man looks familiar. Grey, you said?"

"Yes, Stephen Grey."

"I've seen his picture in the *Herald*." He bent over and gently turned Stephen's head to the side and peeked under the wrap.

Stephen slowly blinked and opened his eyes.

Dr. Emmett placed the wrapping back and straightened. "Good morning, Mr. Grey. I am Dr. Emmett. How are you feeling?"

His gaze came into focus and he glanced at Kat, then at the doctor. "Tired. And the back of my head hurts."

"That is to be expected. Anything else? Nausea? Ringing in the ears?"

"No. I feel better than I did last night."

"That's good. I'll come by later this morning and do some tests. For now, just rest."

Stephen turned his attention to her. "Kat."

"Yes?" Kat noticed the doctor's reaction to Stephen's informal use of her name.

"Are you doing all right?"

She gave him a gentle smile. "Yes. They are taking good care of me."

Stephen yawned and closed his eyes. "Good. Very good." After a few seconds, his breathing evened out.

Dr. Emmett turned toward her. "From what I can see, I believe Mr. Grey will make a full recovery. He should be up and moving in a day or two. Have you had breakfast yet?"

Kat took her gaze from Stephen's face and blinked at the doctor. "Breakfast?"

"Yes. If you have not eaten, would you like to join me?" Dr. Emmett waited for her response, his hands held loosely behind his back.

"I—that is—yes, I will join you for breakfast."

Dr. Emmett smiled and extended his arm. "Then let me escort you to the mess hall."

"What did you mean when you called that scrap of paper one of Dr. Latimer's famous postings?"

Dr. Emmett sat back, the plate in front of him empty save for a couple of crumbs. A steady buzz of voices filled the enormous tent. Rows of tables filled the area, most of them filled with men in olive green uniforms. The smell of hot biscuits and fried salted pork filled the air. "Dr. Latimer is one of the most intelligent men I have met, but he is a bit eccentric. He's always scribbling down bits of Scripture from the Bible and posting them inside the medical tents. I'm not a religious man myself, but some of the verses are interesting."

"Do you know what that particular one means?" Kat asked.

Dr. Emmett shook his head. "No, but I find it comforting when attending those who are dying. The words sound like there is more to death than just the end of existence. I'm not sure what it really means."

Kat took a sip of tea. That was an interesting way of looking at it. In fact, the more she thought about it, the more she liked it. Almost like God was calling the one who had died back to life, but not just to life—to new life, to *light*. Did God really do that? Could he make a dead soul live? She brushed the top of her corset. Could he do that with her?

"Kathryn Bloodmayne."

She tilted her head, puzzled. "Yes?"

He smiled. "I'm sorry. Just putting two and two together. Your bounty hunter called you Kat. Now I remember—I read your name in the *Herald* when the Tower Academy accepted its first women students a couple years ago."

Kat brought her mind back to the present and nodded. "Yes. I was one of the first students and just recently graduated."

"If you don't mind, I would love to hear more about your time at the Tower. What was it like? How were you treated as a woman student?"

Kat took another sip and placed her cup down. As she shared about her classes, she found Dr. Emmett was easy to talk to, and they had similar interests in the sciences.

"I wanted to attend the Tower myself, but my family could not afford it." Dr. Emmett crossed his arms in a casual manner. "So I was trained instead by a local physician, joined the military, and here I am."

"Oh." Kat looked down at her almost empty cup. She had never really thought about how much her father's name and profession had given her. As much as her father had hurt her, the Bloodmayne name had provided her with an education most could only dream of. But it had come with a cost as well.

"Well, I should get back to work. Matron Foskey runs a tight schedule. Perhaps we can talk later about some of the things you learned during your time at the Tower." Dr. Emmett stood. "You know, we could use some help in the medical tents. I know you haven't been formally trained, but you do have some of the general knowledge of human anatomy and medicine. At least until Mr. Grey is better and you are needed elsewhere."

Kat's eyes widened. An opportunity to learn medicine first hand? "I would like that very much."

Dr. Emmett smiled. "Excellent. Then follow me. First I need to check with Commander Powell, then I will introduce you to Matron Foskey. "

CHAPTER

19

THE NEXT DAY STEPHEN TUCKED HIS BADGE INTO HIS FRONT pocket and gingerly touched the back of his head. The linen cloth was gone, but he could still feel the stitches that kept his wound closed and wondered if there would be a scar. He shrugged and left the commander's tent. It wouldn't be the first one.

Commander Powell had been surprised at his request to stay at the base until Dr. Latimer returned, but agreed after he saw Stephen's papers and badge. Even here in Austrium, his status as a World City bounty hunter held sway. Although how long that would last, he wasn't sure. With the city council corrupt and Dr. Bloodmayne after Kat, most likely his position—and the benefits it gave—would be revoked.

Better to make the best of it while he had the power.

Stephen headed down the rows of canvas tents. The base was more like a mobile city made of tents, motorwagons, and even the occasional airship. Commander Powell said they had been here for a year, but Austrium was pushing back and they might have to uproot the base. He could only imagine the kind of organization and stratagem it took to run this base, let alone move it.

Hopefully they would not be here long. Dr. Latimer was scheduled to be back in the next week or two. His tour was up and already he had plans to head back to World City. Perfect timing.

Stephen approached the grouping of tents marked by a blue circle with a white star within. Each tent was numbered, starting with number one, the main medical tent. He ducked through the flaps of the first tent. Only a handful of men remained now since the bombing, most having been discharged, housed in one of the smaller tents, or sent back to World City due to grievous injuries.

He still could not remember anything after the bombing, only vague images. However, he could well imagine what would have happened to Kat if he hadn't thrown himself across her. The projectile would have caught her directly in the face, marring or even killing her.

But then you would be free, a small voice whispered. *No more fear of that other Kat, no more wondering if she will lose control again—*

"No!"

Stephen stopped and glanced around to see if anyone had heard him. No one looked his way. He stuffed his hands into his pockets, his insides knotted up. He would do everything in his power to help Kat. He owed her that much. But what if Dr. Latimer couldn't cure her?

Then we'll find another way. And another. And another. We will keep on looking until we have pursued every possibility, and then we will still look.

Stephen approached one of the nurses and asked about Kat.

She glanced up from the list in her hand. "Miss Bloodmayne? The lady who came in with you? Tent four."

He thanked the nurse and headed back out. Tent four stood to the right a couple tents down. The flaps were tied back and a sharp, strange smell filled the air as he approached. Inside, he found Kat and the young doctor who had visited him yesterday. The doctor looked to be about his age, with thick dark hair and a clean-shaven face. His accent had marked him as from one of the villages north of World City.

The two stood beside a table laden with glass vials, pestles and mortars, glass tubes, large clear beakers, and some kind of slender metal cylinder with a flame at the top.

The doctor stepped away from the table. "I'll be back. In the meantime, continue with your work."

He left through the back exit without noticing Stephen.

A burning sensation flared inside his chest as he stared at the flap where the doctor had left. Seeing Kat with another man brought back all sorts of painful memories. Stephen closed his eyes and breathed in through his nose. No, he would not let his past cloud his present. Never again.

After a couple more breaths, he opened his eyes. Kat was so focused on the two liquids she mixed in a large glass tube that she hadn't noticed him.

Stephen opened his mouth to say something, then stopped and watched her.

When the liquids were mixed to her satisfaction, Kat grabbed a pair of metal tongs and used them to hold the tube above the small flame nearby.

He had never seen this side of Kat—the daughter of a renowned scientist and one of the first women to graduate from the Tower Academy. He watched the way her fingers steadied the tongs, the way she adjusted the flame on the metal cylinder with such precision, the way she focused on her work.

She was like no other woman he had ever met.

After half a minute, she withdrew the glass tube from the flame and turned off the cylinder. The flame went out with a pop as she placed the tube inside one of the holes drilled into a wooden stand.

"You're amazing." Stephen's voice broke the quiet inside the tent.

Kat dropped the tongs and looked up. "Stephen! I never heard you enter."

"I didn't want to interrupt."

She retrieved the tongs, a flush creeping across her face. She pushed back that tendril of hair that always seemed to come loose from her chignon. "I'm helping Dr. Emmett this morning. I don't know my father's formula for his healing serum, but I know a simple one from the Tower and offered to create a couple vials for the military's use." She settled the tongs on the end of the table.

Stephen shook his head. "Every woman I knew before you only knew how to play the pianoforte, or paint, or concerned themselves with the latest fashion. You're different."

The red deepened across her cheeks as she began to straighten the remaining empty vials into a single perfect row. "I was never much interested in those. I've always wanted to study science, ever since I was a little girl. I love how the world works. How mixing and combining elements can create both poison and medicine. How the human body is like a vastly complex machine. It all fascinates me."

She finally looked up, and Stephen knew he would never forget that look on her face. Her eyes glowed with excitement and wonder, and her face was flushed with passion. His stomach did a somersault. If he hadn't already fallen for Kat Bloodmayne, he would be on a crash course now. All the jumbled up feelings he had held inside cohered into a single emotion: he loved Kat. He had loved her since the moment he saw her, even when he left her at the Tower. He loved her now, and he would always love her.

"Stephen?"

Stephen swallowed the lump inside his throat, his blood racing throughout his body. "Yes?"

"Are you comfortable with a woman who thinks?"

He blinked at her blunt inquiry, then broke out in a laugh. "Yes, I am."

She nodded to herself as if answering an unasked question.

"Why do you ask?"

Kat paused, her hand on the last vial. "One of the young men from the academy said men were not interested in intelligent women."

Stephen sobered. "That might be true of some men." A woman like Kat would have intimidated many of the men back on the force. "But not me."

Dr. Emmett walked in and stopped when he spotted Stephen. "Mr. Grey. Is there something you need?"

Stephen waved his hand in a dismissive fashion. "I was simply checking on Miss Bloodmayne."

AWAKENED

Before the doctor could say more, Stephen turned and left the tent, a smile on his face and a fire inside his heart.

He spent the rest of the day wandering around the base. Most of the areas were closed to him, but there were still places he could walk and stretch his legs. As noon approached, the sun blazed down on the camp and heat waves rose above the tents and distant golden hills. Shots echoed on one side of the camp as new recruits trained. On the western end, rows of brass machines were lined up in single file.

He wasn't allowed to go near the machinery, but even at a distance he marveled at the vehicles. Each was the size of a small carriage set on two jointed legs that could bend. A small window encased in sheet metal marked the front where the driver sat. A long, thick pipe ran up the backside with a steam valve attached.

On either side of the window were two "arms" with cannons similar to the cannon-like arm the bounty hunter Rodger Glennan sported on his right side.

Stephen stopped.

A cold sweat broke out across his body. There was still a bounty on Kat, and that meant, sooner or later, Rodger—and Piers and Jake— would come. If what little Stephen knew about Dr. Bloodmayne was true, the man would stop at nothing to get his daughter back. To him, the Narrow Strait would be a mere hurdle to overcome. After all, the three bounty hunters knew the name of the ship he and Kat were on, and it wouldn't take much digging to find out what kind of work Robert did for the World City Council.

It was even possible the trail would lead them right to this base.

Stephen spun around. Why hadn't he thought of that before? He clenched his hands and hurried down the dirt path, away from the war machines and toward the medical tents. On the *Lancelot*, he had been too preoccupied with his guilt over what he had done to Kat. Then they had reconciled and all his thoughts had turned toward finding Dr. Latimer and a cure for Kat. Then the bombing occurred and—

Enough! I can't change the past, but I can prepare now.

His mind rushed through timetables and trajectories. How long would it have taken for Jake, Piers, and Rodger to figure out where he had taken Kat? How long before they found a ship to cross the Narrow Strait? He moved his fingers as he counted, then let out his breath. They still had time. There was no way the bounty hunters could already be in Austrium unless they flew, and even then no ship was as fast as the *Lancelot,* even after crashing for a couple days. At least none that he knew of.

But they needed to be ready just in case Jake and the other two men showed up. Hopefully Dr. Latimer would be back before then.

CHAPTER
20

THE *CALYPSO* PULLED INTO DUSKPORT IN THE LATE MORNING. After securing the small steamboat to the boardwalk, Captain Harpur extended the wooden plank and gestured toward Jake and the other two bounty hunters.

Jake slung his pack over his shoulder and started across the plank first. Between Piers' constant complaints about the filthiness of the ship, their tight living quarters, and Rodger's seasickness, he couldn't leave the ship fast enough.

Ahead, the small seaport of Duskport spread out before them, a collection of shabby buildings nestled along the shore. A couple fishing boats gently rocked in the harbor, their owners sitting on barrels on the dock, smoking pipes or cleaning nets.

He placed a foot on the pier and sighed in relief. Solid ground. Before he could take another step, Captain Harpur swung out a hand to stop him. Jake stopped short and narrowed his eyes.

"My payment," the captain said with a wiggle of his fingers.

Jake tightened his lips and reached inside his duster for the pouch he carried. He counted out the bills and thrust them into the captain's hand. "You'll receive your final payment if you're still here when we return."

Captain Harpur closed his hand around the bills with a gleam in his eye. "I'll be here, you can count on that."

"No matter how long our mission takes."

The captain waved him off. "Even if it takes you weeks."

"Good." Jake bypassed the captain and walked across the board-walk, his boots slapping against the wooden planks. Piers followed behind him, along with Rodger. The sooner they started their mission, the better.

He stepped onto the street and looked around. There wasn't much to the port. Just a bunch of run-down storefronts, weathered homes, and narrow streets. He tugged on the end of his mustache. Where to start? He dropped his hand. Taverns would be a good place to find out information.

Jake headed toward an old pipe-smoking fisherman sitting on a bench at the edge of the street. The man looked up and his eyes wandered over Jake's tattooed arms. With a puff of smoke, he pulled the pipe out. "Quite the colors you have there."

Jake folded his arms. "I like to think it means I've lived an interesting life."

"Sailor?"

"No. Not quite."

"Hmmph." The man took another long draw from the pipe. "So what brings you to Duskport?"

"Looking for someone."

"Here?"

"No. However, I would appreciate it if you could point me to the local tavern."

The man gestured with his pipe. "Just head down that street to the Laughing Gull. Can't miss it."

"Thank you."

"Sure, sure." The man settled back and continued with his pipe.

Jake started in the direction the fisherman had pointed. For being at war, Austrium seemed to be as laid back as rumors had portrayed the country to be.

Piers came up beside him. Even during the sea voyage, Piers had somehow managed to keep his white suit immaculate. Always the consummate gentleman, even if he was a bounty hunter. "So what is our plan?"

"Find information. The *Lancelot* was a blockade runner for World City, which means it ran supplies for the army. Find out where the bases are and start eliminating each one as a possible place for Miss Bloodmayne and Stephen Grey."

Piers nodded. "My thoughts as well. A woman in a military camp will be hard to miss."

"As long as we don't run into any problems with Austrium or the military crossing the country, we should find her in no time."

Piers waved his hand. "Keep a low profile, fit in with the locals, and we should be fine."

Jake glanced back. "Rodger might be a bit of an issue." Not to mention Piers' dapper outfit.

Piers glanced back as well. "Yes, but we'll be thankful to have him if we find ourselves in a fight."

"That's the only reason I brought him onto this job. That, and I didn't want that cannon of his trained on my back."

"Indeed." Piers adjusted his monocle, his sniper-cane clicking against the cobblestone.

Of course, neither did he want Piers' sniper skills tested against him. Fortunately, the bounty offered on Miss Bloodmayne was more than enough to share with each man, as long as they finished the job.

Find the lady, use the needles Dr. Bloodmayne sent with them on her, and ship her back to World City. Easy mission. Easy money. Then onto retirement. Jake smiled. Life couldn't be better.

"And what if we run into problems with the lady?"

Piers' words doused his happier thoughts. Miss Bloodmayne was not like any other quarry he had hunted before. Thought petite, she had thrown him and his men across the room back in Covenshire with just her mind. He didn't believe in much beyond what he could see, but even he couldn't deny that there was something odd about her. Something downright terrifying.

Piers must have caught the look on his face. "It's something we should be prepared for."

"You're right. And I've given it some thought."

"And?"

"We can't go head-to-head with her again. We will need to take her unawares, before she can do . . . well . . . whatever it is she did in Covenshire."

Piers sniffed quietly. "It's too bad we need to take the lady alive. If we had other options, I could take her out myself with just my sniper rifle."

"The council was adamant that she be taken alive. Too bad they didn't tell us about her 'special abilities.' We could have been better prepared."

Piers shrugged. "Well, now we know. So what's your idea?"

Jake stuffed his hands into his pockets as they walked along the street. "When we reach her, we scope out the area, then make a plan to catch her before she realizes we are there."

"Do you ever wonder if we should even be doing this?"

Jake glanced at Piers.

"What exactly is the Tower doing with a woman like her?"

"Since when did you develop a conscience, Piers?"

"I haven't. I just value my life. What if there are more like Miss Bloodmayne? Or what if the Tower is trying to create more?"

"I don't know and I don't care. All I know is when I'm done with this job and have the cash in hand, I'm leaving World City behind."

Piers clicked his tongue. "Perhaps you're right. World City is changing, and not for the better. Maybe it's time I found a new place to live. If it wasn't for this war, I would enjoy a chateau in Austrium."

Jake snorted. Piers would fit in just fine in Austrium, what with his smart clothes and high-class living. "Just keep the end in mind, Piers, and let's finish the job."

CHAPTER
21

SEVERAL DAYS AFTER SHE'D CAUGHT STEPHEN WATCHING HER work, Kat had just finished changing the bandages on one of the army cooks when she noticed a slow, faint buzzing noise outside the medical tent. Smiling, she tucked in the edge of the gauze. "There. Keep the area clean, and if the bandage falls off or becomes dirty, come back and we will place new salve and gauze over the wound."

The young man inspected the bandage and beamed up at her. Freckles covered most of his face and his ears stuck out on either side of his head. She narrowed her eyes. He couldn't be more than sixteen! How in the world had he ended up here?

"Thanks, Miss. Are you one of the new nurses?"

Kat shook her head, conscious of her Austrium attire. She had washed the outfit a couple of times since arriving at the base, but it certainly was not the most appropriate clothing for assisting in a medical ward. "No, just someone helping out."

The boy blurted out his thanks again and left. Kat watched him go, then turned her attention back to the strange noise as she dipped her hands into the bowl of water on a nearby table and washed up. The buzzing grew louder. She tilted her head to the side. It sounded like thousands of angry bees.

She wiped her hands, then placed the linen on the table and headed outside the tent, surprised at her own calm. It was late morning and clouds had gathered, blocking out the sun. Nurses, medics, and Dr. Emmett stepped out from the surrounding tents.

"Is it another attack?" one of the nurses asked.

"I don't know." Dr. Emmett frowned and looked up at the sky.

A slight chill touched her spine as Kat glanced up. She saw the wagon explode again in her mind, there one moment, a ball of fire and smoke the next. The memory seemed oddly distant, like something that had happened to someone else.

Tiny dots appeared in the sky above the horizon, rushing toward them in one writhing dark cloud. A bell near the middle of the base began to ring in frantic peals.

Faces paled and one of the nurses began to rock back and forth with hands clasped in front of her.

"What do we do, sir?" one of the medics asked, looking at Dr. Emmett, his voice rising in pitch. "The shelters aren't completed yet."

"Not another one." The nurse held a hand to her mouth as the bell continued to toll across the base. "We just finished patching up those wounded from the last atta—"

"Enough!" Dr. Emmett brought his hand down. "Focus. We have patients depending on us. We need to duck and cover. Find something solid like a table to crouch under. Assist patients to these areas if they can move, shield the rest with extra cots and blankets—anything you can find. Go, now!"

The crowd dispersed. Some of the nurses stumbled back toward the tents. One went from crying to hysterics. Dr. Emmett continued to shout out orders over the bedlam. The buzzing grew as the dark cloud of machines drew closer.

Kat stood rooted on the spot, mesmerized. She remembered the tiny dragonfly-contraptions buzzing around, dropping the metallic balls they held. Wind-up automatons, like the ones her mother used to invent. How could such beautiful little things be used for such devastation?

"Miss Bloodmayne! Move!"

Dr. Emmett's voice broke through her thoughts. Kat blinked and took in a deep breath. Move. Find shelter. Wait. No. Help others first. She turned and stumbled back toward the tent she had exited minutes ago. The cook she had bandaged was gone. The rest of the tent was empty. But there was a table that people could use.

Kat ran back out. "Here! She shouted, spotting a couple of people outside. "There's a table in here!" Two nurses headed her direction with a bandaged soldier between them. Kat held back the flaps. Another medic came by with a patient. She glanced inside. Between all five people, there was no room for her.

At the edge of camp, the bombing began.

Kat watched, a cold sweat spreading across her body, as reality pierced her numbness. The metallic globes fell like rain across the first row of tents, followed by explosions and fire and people dying. The metal-dragonflies drew closer.

Could she stop them? Her stomach twisted violently inside her as she watched the first wave approach. She hadn't accessed that power since she had lowered the *Lancelot*. But doing so had left a numb hole the size of a fist inside her. What would it do to her this time?

Dr. Emmett emerged from another tent. He spotted her and started running. "Miss Bloodmayne, what are you doing?"

Kat glanced at him, her mind frozen.

"Find shelter, now!"

The bombs reached them. Dr. Emmett shoved her away just as the ground exploded in front of her. Kat flew backward. She hit the dirt and the air left her lungs. She stared up at the sky, barely visible through the cloud of dust and smoke. More dark metal globes fell, but she no longer heard the explosions, only felt them in the vibration of the earth and air.

Within moments the bombing had moved on, but Kat could only look up. She couldn't think, couldn't move. It was as if she were stuck in that moment when the bombs fell around her.

The dust began to disperse.

Kat, move.

Something stirred inside her.

Move now!

Kat sat up. Her blood began to whoosh and her fingers tingled.

A flame flickered across her palm. She gasped and crushed her hand into a fist. The monster was awakening inside her, spurred by the shock paralyzing her body.

No, no!

She scrambled to her feet and her hearing returned in a wave that almost flattened her again. Horns blared across the base, adding to the desperate warning of the bell, punctuated by yells and the occasional scream. Smoke billowed up from the eastern side of camp in great dark funnels. Kat pressed shaking hands to her temples. The surrounding noise echoed inside her head. She plugged her ears with her fingers and closed her eyes. An image of Ms. Stuart appeared inside her mind.

"Calm down, Kathryn. Remember to breathe."

Right. Breathe.

Ms. Stuart morphed into Stephen.

"Focus, Kat. You're strong. You can do this."

I can do this.

But the blood still whooshed through her veins and her senses started to spread out. She could feel the matter around her, the broken tent poles and disturbed ground, the dust in the air, the tissue and skin damage of those closest to her. One was severely wounded, and she could feel his life force pulling away from his body.

Kat fell to her knees. "God, help me!" she cried. "If you are real, please help me." She looked up between her fingers. "Don't let me lose control!"

Awake, O sleeper, rise up from the dead, and God will give you light.

What? Why was she thinking of that scrap of paper now?

"Mi-Miss Bloomayne." Her name came out in a gargled voice.

She dropped her hands and looked back. Dr. Emmett lay on the ground a couple feet away, face up, his hands bloody and pressing against his abdomen. His face was pale and glistened with sweat.

Kat crawled on her knees toward the doctor.

"I've been hit."

She sat in the dirt, her gaze bouncing between his face and his wound. "How bad?"

He grimaced. "Bad." His eyes fluttered then rolled up into his head. His hand fell away from the wound. Blood spread across his white lab coat.

She stared at the stain as it covered him—the same color as the comforter in Captain Grim's cabin. Then she shook herself, faintly sickened, not by the wound, but by her own lack of emotions. How could she look at him and feel nothing?

Coming to her knees, she brushed the thought aside. There would be more wounded here on the base, and they were all going to need Dr. Emmett.

No, I can't do this. I should walk away now. She stood and turned. *No one would expect me to save him. He's too far gone, and the risk to myself is too great.*

Kat clenched her hand and held it to her chest. Even now, she could not feel the area below her blouse, the place where her soul was dying. If she accessed that power again, the numbness would grow and more of her would die.

She closed her eyes, her throat tight. Her whole body began to shake. *No.* She swallowed. *I have to save him. It's the right thing to do. I could never live with myself if I didn't try.*

With that, Kat spun back around and dropped to her knees. No one had appeared yet. It was just Dr. Emmett and her.

She held her hands over his body and bit her lip. It would take precise control of the matter in and around him. She pictured the human body from one of her textbooks—

Are you sure?

She pulled back. What if she couldn't stop her power and she went on to destroy the base?

The blood had spread. He had only minutes.

She pressed her lips together. She had to do it.

Kat closed her eyes and let her guard down. Sensation flooded back into her being. She gasped as she connected with the matter around her.

Focus.

She took a deep breath and directed her attention in front of her.

She could feel every part of Dr. Emmett. Every blood vessel, every nerve. She found the ruptured area and began to close it, starting with the organs and lining, working her way outward. Every part knit back together while she gathered the excess blood inside and moved it outward before closing the skin.

A laugh gurgled up her throat. How fragile the human body was! If she could close a hole, she could create a hole as well—

Kat clenched her teeth against the thought as she brought the last of his skin together.

The blood whooshed through her temples like a pounding train, each surge expanding her senses. Like a web, every particle connected to her. With a thought, she could do anything she wanted.

Abandoning Dr. Emmett, Kat rose to her feet. Why would she want to get rid of this? Her whole body pulsed with the power. With a twist of her wrist, she reached out toward the remaining buzzing bombers at the edge of the camp and crushed them like flies between her fingers. Down from the sky they fell, tearing into the tents below.

She laughed. She should have done that in the first place. Why waste her time healing when it was so much easier to destroy? And why stop there?

No, stop! The part of her that was still her cried out in panic. Kat took a step back and blinked. Her whole body felt like it was on fire, especially the area around her hand. Tent number four caught fire to her right.

The other Kat wanted to dance with glee. *Yes, yes! Let it all burn!* She flicked her fingers at the next tent. Tiny flames spread across the canvas

Stop, child. Turn back.

Both Kats paused, taken aback. This voice rose up from deep inside her mind, and it was neither of her. A voice completely different from the other, darker Kat and different from her own. A voice of light and compassion, of gentle, irresistible power.

Kat drew strength from it. *Yes, I need to stop this.*

Her thoughts felt heavy, as if she were physically trying to pull out from beneath something viscous and stifling. She strained against the thought-fog, clenching her hands as she did so. Her vision narrowed until all she could see were stars flashing across her eyes. Her head began to throb. She could no longer hear, no longer see. The strange voice forgotten, her entire being fought against the power inside of her, forcing it back to that deep place.

Nausea filled her belly. Something trickled down from her nostril. Just as the darkness closed in, she felt the click inside. The power was locked away once again. But it was the last time she could fight it. It had grown too strong. Her time was near. Either she found a cure . . .

Or she would become the monster.

CHAPTER

22

"I DON'T UNDERSTAND. WHAT'S WRONG WITH YOU?" A MAN MUR-mured as he bent to examine Kat, who lay on one of the cots in the back of a spare tent. The sun had set hours ago and the smell of smoke still hung in the air from the bombardment that morning. Only now had Stephen been permitted to see Kat.

"What do you mean?" Stephen asked as the tent flap fell closed behind him.

The man straightened and looked back. He wore a pair of dark trousers and a white shirt, his sleeves rolled up as if for work, though the cut and quality of clothing marked him as more than a work-man. His mustache and beard were neatly groomed and held a sprin-kling of gray. His dark eyes came to rest on Stephen.

Stephen stopped a couple feet away. "Who are you?" It was clear the man was not one of the medics. "And what are you doing here?"

The man extended his hand, glanced at it, then retracted it. "Forgive me. I have not had a chance to wash." He headed for the side table where a bowl and pitcher sat. "Nurse, soap please."

"Yes, doctor." A woman stepped away from the side of the tent, walked past Stephen, and headed out.

Doctor? Stephen narrowed his eyes. "I don't recall seeing you around the base."

"And you are not dressed in uniform, so I assume you are not part of the military." There was a trace of fear in the man's eyes, one Stephen was all too familiar with when hunting a bounty.

"The nurse referred to you as doctor. Doctor who?"

The man held his hands away from his body. There was a splotch of blood along his right side. "Dr. Latimer. I arrived with a convoy from the front lines an hour ago, apparently just in time to help out."

Stephen did a double take. Dr. Latimer? *The* Dr. Latimer?

"And who might you be?"

Before Stephen could answer, the nurse returned with a bar of soap.

Dr. Latimer took the bar with a nod and turned his back to Stephen. "I have found that cleanliness leads to better health. And you have yet to answer my question."

"Stephen Grey, from World City."

At the mention of his name, Dr. Latimer stiffened. Stephen narrowed his eyes. If he didn't know any better, he would think the doctor was a man on the run.

"And why are you here, Mr. Grey?" Dr. Latimer dried his hands on a nearby cloth and dumped it on the table before turning around.

"The woman you were checking is my client. She is under my protection."

Dr. Latimer glanced over at Kat, then at Stephen. One eyebrow crept up. "I see. What purpose brought you and the lady to a military base in Austrium, if I might ask?"

Stephen crossed his arms. "You. The lady hired me to find you."

"The lady, you say?" Dr. Latimer folded his hands in front of him. "That is not the answer I was expecting."

Stephen wondered what answer the doctor had been expecting. Was he running from something? It didn't matter. All that mattered was that he was the man Kat had been searching for. "We found out weeks ago you were here in Austrium, assisting with the war effort. We traveled all the way here and have been waiting for you. She needs your help. You might be the only one who can cure her."

"And what exactly ails the young lady?"

Stephen glanced at the nurse. "It's a personal matter that I will only speak to you about."

Dr. Latimer studied him for a moment before turning toward the nurse. "Nurse Eves, please step out for a bit and give us some privacy. I will find you if I need you."

"Yes, Dr. Latimer." The nurse turned and left via the side entrance.

When they had the tent to themselves, Dr. Latimer sat down on the empty cot nearest to Kat. "Forgive me. It's been a long day and I haven't had a chance to rest or eat. The lady there was to be my last patient before dinner."

Stephen lowered himself onto an adjacent cot and placed his elbows on his knees. "I'm sorry I'm keeping you from your meal, but this is important. Very important."

Dr. Latimer sighed and massaged his right temple. "I assumed as much. It's not every day I have the renowned Stephen Grey looking for me. Yes, I've heard of you. Although I will admit I thought you would be here for a different reason."

Well, that confirmed his suspicions. Dr. Latimer was wanted for something. He would inquire about that later, though.

"First, who is the lady?"

Stephen let out his breath. "Miss Kathryn Bloodmayne."

At the name Bloodmayne, Dr. Latimer's face darkened and his lip curled. "I see. I thought she looked familiar. Almost exactly like her mother. So why is Miss Bloodmayne looking for me? And does her father know?"

Now that the time had come, Stephen felt at a loss for words. How did he explain the strange power that Kat possessed when he hardly understood it himself?

Stephen sat up and rapped his fingers against his thigh. "Miss Bloodmayne came to me over a month ago with a strange request: to find you. Shortly after, I discovered my aunt—her housekeeper—had been murdered and Miss Bloodmayne was running from her killers. I helped her leave town, but eventually I learned a bounty had been placed on Miss Bloodmayne."

"By whom?"

"The city council. And her father."

"By her father? By Alexander Bloodmayne?"

"Yes."

"Odd," Dr. Latimer said under his breath. "Do they believe she murdered the housekeeper?"

"I'm not sure. The bounty was for something else—I'll get to that. What I do know is the Tower wants Miss Bloodmayne, and not for justice. She is . . . different."

Dr. Latimer's eyes narrowed. "How?"

Stephen's heart thudded inside his chest. He had never shared Kat's ability with anyone but Robert. However, the man before him was their one hopeful chance at finding a cure for Kat. If Dr. Latimer didn't believe him— "She can do things—control things—with her mind."

A queer change came over Dr. Latimer. He stood and began pacing alongside the cot, tapping his lips with two fingers. "It can't be. It's not possible. Did he really?" The doctor turned and started in the other direction. "But why involve his daughter?" Then he laughed sadly. "But then why not? Oh, Alexander, what have you done?"

Stephen stood as well and held out a hand to stop Dr. Latimer. "Wait. Do you know what is wrong with Kat?"

The doctor met his gaze. "I will need to know more. I will need to hear from Miss Bloodmayne about her own experiences." His shoulders sagged and he rubbed his forehead. "But if I am correct, then . . ."

"Then what?"

Dr. Latimer shook his head. "No. I will not decide until I know everything. First starting with what caused her to be in this condition now."

What did the doctor mean? Stephen's gut tightened as he walked over to Kat's side. There was talk around the base that some invisible force had crushed the remaining flying apparatuses near the end of the bombing. The moment he'd heard, he'd feared Kat had used her power again, but couldn't confirm it until now.

He let out a small gasp when he saw Kat's face. Tiny bruises marred her skin and there was a trickle of blood below her right nostril. "I don't know," he said, his voice tight. "Was she hit?" Blazes! Did her power do that to her?

"No, no. It appears some of her veins ruptured from tension, like she was concentrating on something so much it strained her veins. The nosebleed, however, could indicate something more. The fact is none of this could have happened from blunt force, at least not from what I can tell. There is no evidence of a strike."

"Kat," Stephen murmured. He brushed his fingers along her cheek. "What happened to you?"

"This woman means something to you. As more than a client." It was a statement, not a question.

"Yes. And she doesn't deserve what's happening to her."

Dr. Latimer let out a sigh. "I have found that it is good people who are inflicted with troubles, and those who deserve it remain unscathed. It seems Miss Bloodmayne is like her mother, Helen, in more than just looks."

Stephen looked over. "You knew her mother?"

"Yes. I knew both Bloodmaynes. Brilliant scientists. Helen was one of the premier inventors of automatons. Alexander excelled in everything else. However, I never knew their daughter."

Just then, Kat groaned and her eyes fluttered.

"Kat?"

She turned her head across the pillow and blinked again. "Stephen?"

"I'm here. What happened to you?"

"I—I don't know." She ran a hand across her face. "There was a buzzing sound . . . then people running . . . and smoke—"

Her eyes widened, and she gasped as she reached for the edge of her corset. "Stephen! I can't feel—" Her voice hitched and she struggled to sit. "It's worse! I can't feel anything!" She caught sight of Dr. Latimer and froze. Her hand dropped to her lap and her cheeks reddened. "I didn't realize someone was here." She looked around. "Where am I?"

"One of the spare medical tents, Miss Bloodmayne." Dr. Latimer came to her side. "What can't you feel?"

Her eyes darted from the doctor to Stephen. Her hair was disheveled and fell around her lightly bruised face. She looked small and vulnerable on the cot.

A fierce desire to protect her awoke inside Stephen, so strong it felt like a punch to the gut. He reached over and brushed the top of her knuckles. "It's all right, Kat. This"—he pointed at the man beside him—"is Dr. Latimer."

CHAPTER

23

KAT RAISED HER HAND, THEN PLACED IT BACK DOWN. SHE TRIED to speak, but her mind was a hazy fog of incoherent thoughts. Did Stephen say *Dr. Latimer*?

The man beside Stephen was older, with dark eyes and gray sprinkled throughout his beard and mustache. He wore a white button-up shirt, his sleeves rolled up and a splatter of blood across his right side. He watched her with a certain kind of curiosity. This was the man she had been searching for all this time? The man who wrote those articles about the body and the soul? The man who might know what was wrong with her?

"It's nice to make your acquaintance, Miss Bloodmayne."

He knew her name. Of course he did. Stephen had probably told him.

She dropped her head into her hands. Too much all at once. One moment she was fighting the monster within, the next moment she was repairing Dr. Emmett's body with that same power. And now— she gripped her face—the numbness had spread. Her entire chest, from the bottom of her ribcage to her collarbone, was dead inside.

But maybe that didn't matter, not if Dr. Latimer could cure her. Kat raised her head and her lips parted slightly. The dark clouds from moments before dissipated and she felt warm again, as if the sun had come out.

"How are you feeling?" Dr. Latimer asked as he held a cloth before her.

Kat tilted her head and frowned.

"Here." He shook the cloth. "For the blood on your face."

Her eyes widened and she took the small towel. "Where?"

"Beneath your nose."

Kat dabbed the area and pulled the cloth back. Sure enough, there was a crimson stain across the white fabric.

"Do you remember how you received those injuries?"

Kat glanced back. "What injuries?"

"There is some bruising across your face."

She touched her cheeks. She couldn't remember being hit by anything, but she did remember fighting the monster to the point where stars appeared across her vision. She shook her head. "No, I don't remember anything."

"Well, fortunately the bruises are small and will fade quickly. What about your head and nose? Any pain?"

Kat paused. "No."

Dr. Latimer grabbed the nearby cot and pulled it over. "I'll still want to keep an eye on you and for you to alert me to any changes. Now, if you are up to it, it seems you have been looking for me."

Kat lowered the cloth with tingling fingers. She still could hardly believe Dr. Latimer was finally here. "I have," she said breathlessly. "Ever since I read your articles about the soul and body in one of the journals from the Tower."

"The Tower?"

Kat took a deep breath. She would need to go all the way back to the beginning. The euphoria from moments ago bled into apprehension. What if he didn't believe her? Or worse, thought she was crazy and belonged in an asylum? No. She took a deep breath. She had come too far, been through too much to stop now. She would tell him everything.

Kat started from the beginning. With hesitant words, she told him about setting the nursery on fire and the time she moved the furniture and books during a strong emotional upheaval. "Every time I feel a strong emotion, something awakens inside of me, connecting me to every particle inside the room. I can feel everything, and move anything I want. I can make matter combust, or move it, or squeeze it together."

Dr. Latimer sat back and tapped his chin. "And what happens afterward?"

Kat looked down. "I lose control."

"What do you mean by that?"

"I can't explain it. Just this overbearing desire to light everything on fire. Or crush everything. Sometimes there is a voice urging me to do it. I've been able to hold back the impulse, or fight it once it has started. But I'm afraid someday I won't be able to stop."

"Have you ever hurt someone?"

Kat looked away. "Yes," she said in a small voice. Nausea swept over her and her face felt hot. "A month ago. A couple men were assaulting my friend. I grew angry. I threw two of them across the hall. Then I—"

Her throat closed. The memories came rushing back. Marianne's screams . . . smoke filling the hallway . . . the tendrils of fire creeping along the carpet. And Blaylock.

Even the thought of him now made something burn inside of her. Kat clenched her hands. But did he really deserve to be set on fire?

Yes.

Kat shook her head. *Wait. No.*

"Miss Bloodmayne?"

The tent came back into focus. Dr. Latimer watched her with a keen gaze.

"Yes, I hurt someone. I set Blaylock Sterling on fire."

Stephen's eyebrows flew up into his hairline. Kat swallowed. She had never told him whom she had set on fire that night.

"I see." Dr. Latimer smoothed his trouser leg. "And how do you feel about that?"

Kat shook her head. "I don't know. Most of the time I feel bad. But sometimes . . ." She felt guilty even thinking such thoughts. But they were true, and she couldn't deny them.

"Have you done anything else since that night?"

Kat rubbed her face. "Yes." Slowly she shared about saving Stephen from the bounty hunters and landing the airship.

"And has anything ever happened to you after using this power?"

"Yes," she whispered. "I'm growing numb inside. And the monster is growing stronger."

"Monster?"

"That voice. That other . . . me. The one that wants to burn everything. It's getting stronger. And as it does, the rest of me is growing numb." She jabbed a finger just below her collarbone. "I can't feel anything from here"—her hand moved to her bottom rib—"to here. And it's not just physical. It's my emotions too. I'm afraid that someday I will become numb all over and the monster inside will take over. And then . . ."

"And then?"

She shook her head vigorously. She would not say it aloud. She did not know the full extent of her power, but she could very well imagine. She could wipe out a room of people, or set the city on fire. Maybe even worse.

The nausea spread and black spots appeared across her vision. Her body trembled and she clasped her hands together. No. She would not access that dark power again, not even to save another person. It had been a mistake to save Dr. Emmett. Because of her actions, the monster was close now, hovering right below the surface of her consciousness.

Dr. Latimer stood and began to pace, pinching the bridge of his nose and shaking his head.

"So do you know what's wrong with her?" Stephen asked.

Dr. Latimer stopped. "Did your father ever say anything? Did he know what you could do?"

Kat shook her head. "No. Ms. Stuart told me never to tell him, and I never did. But he discovered it the night I burned Blaylock. He arranged my capture and had me brought to the Tower." She didn't look at Stephen. She had already forgiven him, even if the memory brought a dull ache with it.

"And what happened there?"

Her fingers grew cold. "He took me to his secret laboratory and strapped me to a metal table."

Dr. Latimer looked up, his face intent. "This room, describe it for me."

A chill spread across her body. "It was dark, except for a couple green lanterns. There were four tables and a strange electric contraption."

"Do you remember any smells? Or strange symbols?"

Kat shivered. "No, not that I can recall. I wasn't awake for most of it."

Dr. Latimer rubbed the back of his neck. "I know that room, and I know what experiments Alexander worked on in there. If what you are saying is true—the things you have done—then it is as I feared." He let out a long breath. "Alexander succeeded."

24

YOU ARE THE CULMINATION OF MY LIFE'S WORK.

Her father's words came back, ringing in Kat's ears. This thing—this monster inside of her—he was proud of it. He had succeeded at his ultimate goal.

"Succeeded at what?" Stephen asked. He sat on the cot across from Kat's and folded his arms.

Dr. Latimer dropped his hands and sighed. "To explain that, I will have to go back to the beginning. Dr. Alexander Bloodmayne was a brilliant young man, top of his class at the Tower, and immediately accepted into the science community upon graduation. I was one of his classmates. I also excelled in the sciences, but not like Alexander. He lived and breathed to learn. If Alexander had a god, it was knowledge, and he bowed to it every day.

"Then Helen came along. She was from the prestigious Steele family. She was intelligent in her own right and invented the most amazing automatons. Her understanding of mechanical techniques surpassed even that of Alexander, and he loved her for it."

Kat shifted on the bed. Father never talked about Mother. To hear Dr. Latimer speak of her with such respect made Kat wish more than ever that she had known her.

"They married and Alexander began pushing for the Tower to let women scientists work in the labs. After a couple years, the council finally relented when Alexander threatened to pull out altogether.

At the time, he was working on multiple experiments, one being the healing serum he is so famous for now. But what most people didn't know was that he wanted more. He wanted the power of life and death itself. And that's where I come in.

"I studied the human body. I have always been fascinated by how the human creature works, the intertwining of the physical, the mental, the emotional, and the spiritual. I started examining how interlinked all four parts were. At that time, and even now, humans are mainly viewed through the physical. We call ourselves enlightened, but we often deny the fact that there is more to us than our physical bodies. However, Alexander was an exception. He was interested in my studies and started asking me questions. At the time, I was as thirsty for knowledge as he was. We began to look outside normal scientific parameters and pushed the limits. What happened after death? How did life begin? Could such power be harnessed?

"We started with animals, small ones, using whatever means we could to extrapolate the power released upon death, but nothing worked. Then Alexander came in one day with a couple of books and old scrolls. They had nothing to do with actual science. Instead, they were old writings from hundreds of years ago. One would almost call them 'dark arts.'"

Dr. Latimer sat down and gripped his hands together. "That is when our fights began. I told him we were scientists and should use scientific methods for our research, not these mystic means."

Kat understood what he meant. She herself had been reluctant to look outside of science for a cure. That is, until her notes blew away through the shattered bulkhead during the storm.

"Alexander said I wasn't being open-minded. As the months went by, I grew more and more disturbed by what he was doing. My understanding of God and souls had grown in that time as well, cautioning me toward these experiments. I began to believe there are powers we are never meant to tamper with because of the destruction they could cause. We are humans, finite and frail. To unleash such power could possibly damage us, and to think we could harness such power was hubris.

"The experiments themselves . . ." Dr. Latimer lowered his head. Kat could almost see his thoughts swirling inside his mind. "I will not recount them here, only that I highly regret I was ever part of such activities." He pressed his fingers to his forehead. "May God forgive me the evil I committed."

Outside, crickets chirped in the dark stillness, and the occasional murmur of voices drifted in as people passed the medical tent. But inside, the atmosphere was cold and silent.

Dr. Latimer began again. "One night I found Alexander experimenting on himself, using the pagan rituals he had read about in the old texts. He had gone too far. I knew deep inside that what we were doing was breaking every corporeal law there was, and who knew what lay beyond. We were past the physical and into the spiritual, a place where we could potentially sever our souls."

Kat shivered and glanced at Stephen. He sat in the shadows, a dark, unreadable look on his face.

"I told Alexander to stop." Dr. Latimer held a hand to his face and spoke through his fingers. "I warned him that if he experimented with death, it could possibly taint his soul. Instead"—he glanced at Kat—"I believe he tainted yours."

Kat brushed her fingers along the base of her neck, but could not feel the sensation. "You think my soul is tainted?"

"Given everything you have told me so far, something happened that night with your father, and it was passed on to you. After that, Alexander and I drew apart. I heard Helen was with child months later, then passed away during childbirth. A year later I was expelled from the Tower and sworn never to reveal what I knew." He nodded toward Stephen. "Originally I thought the Tower had sent you to find me. Now I know better."

Stephen reciprocated the nod.

Dr. Latimer turned back to Kat. "I wandered from job to job, looking for work where I could find it. I found out my writings and journals had been expunged from the Tower library. Eventually I joined the military and have been with them ever since."

Kat gripped her throat. Her father had tainted her? Then it was just as he had told her in the Tower. "My father said the same thing."

Dr. Latimer looked up.

"While I was in the Tower, my father said that he had experimented on himself, and had unknowingly passed it on to me. But what I don't understand is *what* he did to me. What am I?" She flung her hands out and looked down. "Am I still human? Or . . . or . . ." She clenched her hands and looked at Dr. Latimer. "What is wrong with me? Do you know?"

Dr. Latimer shook his head. "I don't know. Not yet. But I have some ideas that I want to think on. I will need to delve into Alexander's thought process in order to deduce what he might have done." He sighed. "And that is not going to be easy for me. For now, I suggest we eat and rest."

But I want answers! No, I want to be free of this! Kat looked from Dr. Latimer to Stephen and pinched her lips together. The emotions inside churned into a giant upheaval. Her blood began to whoosh through her veins.

Kat scrunched up her face, the released the muscles. She took in a deep breath, willing herself to be calm. When she opened her eyes, she found Stephen watching her with an intent look. She had a feeling he knew what she was experiencing.

"He's right," Stephen said after a moment. "We have much to think about, and doing so with an empty stomach and tired mind will only muddle our thoughts. We're close, Kat. Only a little more time."

Kat wanted to hide her face in her hands and cry, but Stephen was right. By Dr. Latimer's own admission, he only had theories, not answers. She needed to give the doctor time to think. "All right." Her head throbbed just above her eyes. "A cup of tea would be nice."

She started to stand, but Stephen stopped her. "I'll bring you something back. In the meantime, rest."

"I agree with Mr. Grey. I will come back sometime tomorrow after I have finished my rounds. Until then . . ." Dr. Latimer dipped his head toward Kat, then left with Stephen.

Kat lay back on the cot, clutching the wool blanket between her fingers. She listened to the sounds of the camp and watched the flame flicker inside the lamp that hung from the tent pole. She replayed Dr. Latimer's words inside her mind. What kind of experiments had her father conducted? What rituals had he performed that scared Dr. Latimer? What did he do to her?

Stephen returned twenty minutes later with a steaming tin cup and a plate of mush with some kind of gray meat on the side. He handed them both to her. "It's not much, but with the whole base in disarray, it's all they had. At least I found some tea."

One look at the food and Kat's stomach turned over. "I think I'll just have the tea, thank you."

Stephen reached over and took the plate. "I thought as much. Still, it wouldn't be good to waste food." He scooped up the mash with a fork and took a bite. "Could be better." He ate all the mush and picked at the meat while Kat sipped the tea. The tin cup felt warm beneath her fingers and she clutched the cup close.

Stephen wiped his lips with his handkerchief and cast the plate of half-eaten food aside. "So"—he turned his attention to Kat—"how did you really get those bruises?"

Kat gingerly touched her face. "I'm not sure."

"Doctor Latimer said they were from intense strain. Did you use your power again?"

"Yes," she whispered.

"And?"

"I shouldn't have done it. I want to do good, I want to help people. But . . ." She closed her hand into a fist and held it against her heart. "This can never be used for good."

"What did you do?"

Kat let out her breath. "Dr. Emmett was hit during the bombardment. He had a gushing wound. I—I repaired it."

Stephen's eyebrows shot up. "You did? How?"

"When the power released, I could feel every part of his body. I found the ruptured organs, arteries, and skin, and pulled the wound closed after drawing out the excess blood that had pooled inside of him."

"Kat, that—that's amazing!"

She turned away and hugged her body. "I can feel the monster inside me now. It's here." She tapped the side of her head. "Constantly. I shouldn't have healed him. It made everything worse."

"You saved a man," Stephen said quietly.

Kat rounded on him. "At great cost! What if by saving one man, I turn around kill hundreds because I accessed that power and can no longer control it? I hate making these kinds of decisions." She held out her hands. "Do I save a life, or do I suppress the power? I can't do it anymore. I can't—" She gasped as flames popped up and surrounded her hands. "Stephen—help me!"

Stephen flew off the cot, his plate hitting the floor, and with two long steps was beside Kat. Sinking down beside her, he reached over and held her to his side. Slowly he stroked her hair and murmured something.

Kat tucked her head into his shoulder. Her heart raced and her fingers trembled. A red haze burned behind her eyes. She buried her face in the folds of his duster, allowing his scent of leather and soap to envelope her thoughts. "I don't want to be a monster anymore."

Stephen continued to run his hand across the top of her head. "You're not a monster. You are a woman confined within an invisible prison not of your making."

"I want to be free," she whispered. "If there is a way. Without crossing any more lines, physical or otherwise."

"And you will be. Soon."

Slowly, softly, Stephen began to pray over her. At least that's what it sounded like since he was addressing God. Kat held still, listening as he spoke with a solemn quietness that calmed her like nothing had before. He spoke to God as if he knew him. Did he know God? Stephen hadn't said much about his beliefs, but Ms. Stuart knew about God and when she had talked to him, it had sounded a lot like Stephen did now.

The red haze began to fade from her vision and her hands no

longer trembled. Kat sighed and remained where she was with her eyes closed. She didn't say anything, just listened to his simple words. If only she could stay like this forever. Stephen felt warm and comforting, and he drove the monster below the surface. But deep inside, she knew it wasn't enough. Someday, some hour, the monster would emerge, and there would be no stopping it.

CHAPTER

25

"You know I don't put much stock in faith or religion, but I believe . . ." Dr. Emmett's voice lowered to a hush. "I believe it was a miracle."

Kat looked up, the broom paused in her hands. The tiny purple pinpricks were already fading from her face. Stephen had brought her a mirror this morning, and in the dim light of her tent the marks had looked almost like freckles. That had been two hours ago, at least.

Now the morning sun shone through the flaps of tent one, the main medical tent. Matron Foskey stood beside Dr. Emmett at the table in the back.

Dr. Emmett's hair was brushed back and a trace of whiskers graced his jaw. "One moment, I was lying on the ground with a gouging wound along my midsection, and the next moment, it was gone."

"Gone? Like disappeared?" Matron Foskey folded her arms, her gray-streaked hair pulled back in a simple chignon under her white cap. Kat had heard that her cool thinking had saved seven men the day before. The woman was unflappable.

"No, more like healed. I don't know how to explain it. Like surgery, only no surgery took place. And there was someone bending over me, but I couldn't make out his or her face."

"And how do you know you weren't just hallucinating? Blunt trauma to the head can do that," Matron Foskey said with a sniff.

"There was still blood around the area, along the top of my skin and soaked into my shirt and lab coat."

"It could have been someone else's blood."

"And I have a scar along my waist, right where the wound was."

Kat looked away and started sweeping again.

"Well, if you ask me, it must have been a particular sort of miracle. Why didn't your 'angel' save any of the other men? Or Nurse Anne?"

Dr. Emmett rubbed the back of his neck. "I don't know. I wish I did. What I do know is that something—or someone—healed me. And I think it was God."

Kat huffed and swept more vigorously. Little did Dr. Emmett know it was an experiment gone wrong who had saved his life, not God.

She stopped and leaned against the broom, her head down. *No, I don't want to be bitter. It might have been a mistake, but by saving Dr. Emmett, I might just be helping others.*

She sighed and pressed three fingers to the base of her neck. She could feel nothing now from her neck down to her midsection. And the monster was there, in the back of her mind, like a seething dragon waiting to emerge from its lair.

She straightened and finished sweeping. No regrets. What was done was done. Perhaps Stephen was right. It was good to save one man, even at the expense of her own soul.

Later that afternoon Kat sat in the supply tent, marking medicine vials with a wax stick. Storm clouds were rolling in, announcing their arrival with distant booms and flashes of light.

Dr. Latimer ducked inside the tent. He wore a white lab coat with stains across the front. "Miss Bloodmayne, I'm glad I found you. Can you meet me later tonight in tent eight, after dinner?"

Kat gripped the glass vial she was holding and looked up, her heart beating faster. "Did you find something?"

"I think so." He turned to go, then glanced back. "And bring Mr. Grey with you. For propriety's sake."

"I will." She would have brought Stephen anyway. He had come this far with her, she was sure he would want to know what Dr. Latimer had found.

By the time she found Stephen after dinner, darkness had descended upon the camp and the rain was coming down in a deluge. They ran through the mud and puddles toward the tent with coats held above their heads. Once inside, they placed the drenched articles of clothing across two chairs and sat down on an empty cot. Dr. Latimer stood beside the small table. He held a leather-bound journal in one hand, his fingers trailing down the pages. More papers and journals lay on the small table before him. Rain pelted the canvas roof in a symphony of *thwaps*.

Kat glanced at Stephen. His hair was wet and slicked back and his shirt damp across the shoulders. He wasn't a very big man, not like some of the soldiers she had met here on the base. Rather, he possessed more of a lean strength and a keen eye. At that moment, his gaze turned on her and in the lantern light, she caught sight of the yellow specks in his hazel-green eyes.

He was one of the most handsome men she had ever known.

Kat ducked away, the thought slamming across her mind. She turned her gaze to Dr. Latimer, heat spreading throughout her body. How could she be thinking that at a time like this?

Even now, she could sense his closeness, only a foot away from her on the cot. The rain had also intensified his smell, that same smell from yesterday, of soap and leather and sweat.

What did he think of her? Once he had thought her a monster and left her at the Tower. Yesterday, he spoke of her as a woman trapped inside an invisible prison.

Kat clasped her cold, wet hands together. What she really wanted was for him to see her as a woman, the way a man saw a woman. She let out her breath. But that couldn't be. Not until she was whole again. If that ever happened.

Dr. Latimer turned, the leather-bound journal still in hand. "I've been thinking about Miss Bloodmayne's condition, and I think I know what caused it."

Kat looked up and gripped her hands tighter.

"Your father was performing experiments with death at the same time your life started. And I think somehow the two intertwined inside of you."

"Are you saying I'm dead inside?" The voice inside always said something similar. Could it possibly be true?

Dr. Latimer tilted his head to the side. "Well, yes and no. Obviously you are alive, but not in the same way we are. Somehow you were thrown out of the natural laws and physical principles that humans are confined to. You said that you are able to manipulate matter. I think only someone not completely bound to matter could do that."

He held his journal up and took a piece of paper from the table. "It's like this. Imagine my journal is life." He placed the piece of paper inside. "All things—humans, animals, insects—exist inside this sphere, and therefore are subject to the laws within. But you—" He picked up another piece of paper and laid it across the top of the journal. "You are on the outside of life. You are still human, feel human, act human, but your father's experiments threw you outside the world we live in. And being on the outside, you can change what's being done on the inside."

Kat looked from Stephen to Dr. Latimer. "But I see both of you. And this tent. And everything else."

"Yes, because you are still with this world, just not inside of it."

"But how does that explain what I can do?"

Dr. Latimer removed the paper and paced his hand on the journal. "A hand is a better example. I can open this journal, smooth the papers, and tear the paper out if I want because my hand is here on the outside. However, if my hand was locked inside the journal, I couldn't do those things."

"So," Kat said slowly, "because I exist outside of normal life, I can manipulate it?"

"Yes! That's it."

"So why is it changing me? Why can't I use this power for good?"

Dr. Latimer sighed and lowered his journal. "Because you were never meant to exist outside of life. Our souls and bodies are connected. Every time you tap into that ability, it kills a part of your soul. In fact, just existing in that limbo place damages you the longer you live."

A painful lump grew inside her throat. "So even if I never accessed this power again, it would eventually change me anyway."

"I'm afraid so."

All those years of controlling myself, all those times of fighting the monster inside, it was always a losing battle. She squeezed her eyes shut. *There is no hope.*

"Can you help her?" Stephen said sharply. "Is there any way to bring Kat back inside the book, er, life?"

Dr. Latimer took a deep breath and placed the journal down beside the papers and books. He steepled his fingers, his face downcast. "There is one possibility, but it comes with a huge risk."

"Any bigger than the one Kat is already living with?"

"Perhaps. She might actually die."

Silence fell across the tent, save for the soft tap of rain outside.

Stephen folded his arms and sat back. "What is it?"

"It is possible that, if we were able to restart Miss Bloodmayne's life, she would come back inside the laws of life."

"Restart? What does that mean?"

"If death is what tore her out of the norm, then perhaps death is what could bring her back."

Stephen sliced the air with his hand. "That makes no sense! How can she die and still live?"

Kat barely heard the exchange between Stephen and Dr. Latimer. Death had changed her. Her father's tests on death. No matter what she did to prevent the monster from emerging, her soul was still dying. All it took was for her to place her hand over her heart to know that. Soon the numbness would take over her entire body, or the monster would emerge permanently.

But was there any other way? How did one die, and yet not die? How much time did she have left? Perhaps Dr. Latimer could study her a little more before they took such drastic measures. Then again, it might be too late. This might be her only chance. And more than anything, she wanted to be normal again, with no fear of hurting others.

"Can you do it?" Kat lifted her chin and gazed steadily at Dr. Latimer. "If it comes down to it, do you believe you can restart my life?"

Stephen stood and threw his hands into the air. "This is crazy! No one has died and come back to life. Except for . . ." He ran a hand through his hair and turned around. "But he was God!"

Kat frowned. She had no idea what he was talking about. She looked back at Dr. Latimer. "Can you do it?" she asked again.

"I believe so."

"How?"

"I've been experimenting with electricity and the human heart. There might be a way to stop your heart, then restart it."

Fear clutched her insides. What did he mean? "How do you know doing something like this won't make my condition worse? How is it any different than what my father did to me?"

Dr. Latimer folded his arms. "I don't. In fact, it could exacerbate it. But it would not be like your father's experiments. I will be doing nothing outside of scientific parameters. I will not be dabbling with the mystic. I will not be using incantations or symbols to change you. I will simply be using the means God has already given me— the understanding of the physical human heart."

Kat licked her lips. "And you think it will work?"

"It's the best idea I have. I know of no other way to end your life then bring you back. Even then, this venture is highly risky. It is not a solution I came to lightly, but through deep thought and prayer. The choice, however, is up to you."

Potential death or potential freedom. Well, if Dr. Latimer was right, she was dying anyway. But what if it made her worse? "I have one condition."

"I'm listening."

Kat glanced at Stephen, then Dr. Latimer. "If it makes my condition worse, you end my life, permanently."

"Kat!" Stephen took a step toward her. "You can't—"

She held up her hand. "Those are my terms. I will not become a destructive force if this doesn't work."

Dr. Latimer leaned against the table. "So you're willing to go through with this?"

Kat tightened her fists. Stephen was right. This *was* crazy. Was she seriously thinking about letting Dr. Latimer stop her heart? Or letting her die if his theory didn't work? But what choice did she have? Every emotional outburst brought her that much closer to permanently unleashing the monster inside. It was worth the risk, even if she died in the process.

Kat let out her breath. "Yes. I've already hurt people. I'm afraid I might do more. And if what you said is true, then there is no stopping the force inside of me. Better to cure it or end it."

"Kat!"

Kat ignored Stephen's second outburst. Instead, she kept her gaze on Dr. Latimer.

Dr. Latimer studied her. After a moment, he nodded. "I will not end your life, but I will ensure you do not harm others. Is that a sufficient compromise?"

Kat pressed her lips together. She would rather he let her die, but that might be asking too much. "Yes."

Dr. Latimer straightened. "All right, then. First, we need to get back to World City. The machine I built might still be there, if the Tower did not destroy it."

"The Tower?" Her insides tightened. "How will we know if it's there? And how will we retrieve it?"

Dr. Latimer tapped his bottom lip in thought. "We'll figure something out. On our way back to World City, I will spend more time studying your condition. Perhaps there is another explanation, or another solution. If not, we will use my machine to stop your heart. Then, hopefully, I will restart it and you will be inserted back into our world. Like I said, it comes with great risk, and it might not even work."

Kat clutched a fist to her chest. "When do we leave?"

"My tour is finished at the end of this week. We can depart then."

Kat nodded, her mind racing through everything he had shared over the last two days. Every time her mind began to reason why she shouldn't do this, she suppressed it. There was no choice. She had faced dire situations before. She would face this one as well.

Dr. Latimer gathered his papers and journals. "Until then, I need to start my rounds."

"Of course," she murmured without looking up.

After Dr. Latimer left, the tent grew quiet. Even the rain had stopped.

"Kat, we should discuss this," Stephen said, breaking the silence. "We're talking about your life."

Kat stared at her hands. "I know." But no matter how much she explained to Stephen what was happening inside of her, he would not fully understand. For the first time, the monster was constantly there in the back of her mind. One more push and it might come to the forefront permanently, and she couldn't let that happen. She would not lose control again.

Even if it cost her her life.

Stephen reached over. His hand hovered above her own, then settled on top of hers. His warmth soaked into her cold skin." I lost you once, and it was my own fault. I was able to get you back, but where you are planning to go now, I can't go. There is no way I could save you."

Kat looked at him. The lamplight threw his face into sharp relief.

His eyes roved her face. "I don't want to lose you again." He pushed back her one small curl that always came loose. His face was only a foot away from hers, allowing her to see the concern in his eyes and something more.

Her throat went dry and a buzz started inside her head. Every nerve ending seemed arrested, like her whole body was holding its breath.

He hesitated, then lifted his hand away from hers and gently gripped her chin between his thumb and finger, tilting her head upward.

Blood whooshed through her veins, but in a very different way than when her power unleashed. "Stephen . . ."

He leaned forward until his lips brushed hers.

Heat swam over Kat's face and down her body. He cupped her other cheek and deepened the kiss.

Kat closed her eyes. This feeling was nothing like the power inside of her. It was exhilarating, uplifting.

A moment later Stephen drew back. "I don't want to lose you, Kat. I wish . . . I wish there was something I could do. I would do anything if it would help you. But I can't." He sighed. "I just wish there was another way, one that didn't involve harming you."

Kat nodded dumbly, her mind still on the kiss. He rubbed her cheek one more time with his thumb, then dropped his hands. She could still feel their imprint along her face.

Stephen stood. "Would you like me to walk you back to your tent?"

Kat tried to talk, but her mouth wouldn't move. Her mind had come to a grinding halt. She shook her head. She needed to breathe first and collect her thoughts.

"Are you sure?"

"Yes," she said breathlessly. "I just need some time alone."

He nodded. "Good night, Kat." Almost reluctantly, he turned and walked out.

Kat watched him leave, her body still pounding. A jumble of half-baked thoughts whizzed around inside her head.

Stephen had just kissed her. She touched her lips, remembering the feel. But . . . that wasn't supposed to happen! She pressed her fingers to her temple. They weren't even courting!

Then again, when had their relationship ever been normal?

And what did it mean? Did he love her?

Kat blinked, her mind finally moving like rusty cogs in an old watch. *What do I do now? Do I do anything? What happens next? Can anything even happen if there's a chance I will die?*

She sighed and dropped her hand. *Do you wish he had never done it?*

She knew her answer. *No.*

Kat stood and walked toward the tent opening. Light from the gas lamps reflected off the pools of water between the tents. No one else was about. She turned right and headed for the tents where the female nurses stayed, taking care to stay out of the puddles.

She didn't know how much Stephen meant by the kiss, but it did mean something. He wouldn't have done it otherwise. If there was one thing she knew about Stephen, it was that he would not trifle with a woman's affections. Especially not hers.

Did this change her decision?

No. In fact, it reinforced it. If there was any chance she could be cured and lead a normal life, she had to take it.

As minutes passed by, the euphoria slowly vanished, leaving behind an empty feeling in her gut. Puzzled by the strange reaction, Kat finally stopped and placed a hand on her midsection. She recalled Stephen's face again . . . and felt nothing.

A slight shiver ran down her spine. Was that supposed to happen? Did people feel something intense when it came to love, only to have it fade away when the one they loved left? That didn't seem right.

What if . . . what if her feelings for Stephen were being sucked into this numbing vortex inside of her?

Would she eventually stop loving him?

Kat pulled her hand away and stared at her palm as if it held the answer. Her mind flew back over the last few weeks.

This wasn't the first time.

She shook her head and took a step back, but the truth of that revelation blazed across her mind. She had barely felt anything when that sailor fell from the airship. And she'd almost walked away from Dr. Emmett as he lay dying on the ground.

Her hand began to shake and her breath came in fast spurts. The change inside her had grown without her even realizing it. There was no choice now. Even if she lived, what good would that life be if she could not feel love or joy or peace? She would simply be an organic automaton.

She closed her hand into a fist and breathed through her nose to calm herself. They had a plan. It had its share of danger, but it was a plan. Kat straightened her shoulders and looked up.

She would follow through with it. No matter what.

CHAPTER
26

JAKE WALKED UP TO THE SECURITY TENT THAT LED INTO THE Ironguard base. After three bases, this had to be the one where Miss Bloodmayne was located. It was the only one left besides the smaller units, and he doubted the military would allow a woman civilian along the front lines.

Steam rose from the mud-covered ground as the summer sun dried out the rain-drenched landscape. A gentle wind blew from the south.

"Halt!" A man in olive green uniform stepped out from the tent. From the corner of his eye, Jake saw at least three rifles trained on him and his comrades, probably more out of sight. "What business do you have here?"

Jake held out the documents the city council had given him.

The man looked suspicious before he walked over and took the papers. He studied the documents, the frown on his face deepening. "You're looking for a woman fugitive?" he said finally, looking up. "On a military base?"

"We have reason to believe she came here on one of the blockade runner airships."

The soldier slowly shook his head. "The only women here on the base are nurses—wait." He tapped the sheaf of papers against his hand. "There is one woman who came in on a supply convoy. I don't know much about her or what she is doing here." He folded up the documents and handed them back to Jake. "You'll have to check in with Commander Powell before you can search the base."

"I understand." Jake took the papers and placed them in his front pocket. "Please take me to your commander."

"Follow me." The man turned and started for the opening that led into the base.

Piers and Rodger joined Jake as he followed the young man. The base looked like it had seen better days. A hint of smoke filled the air and many of the tents showed evidence of fire, with charred sides and broken poles.

"Was there some kind of attack recently?"

The soldier looked back. "Yes."

"Casualties?"

The soldier never answered, just kept walking through the base.

Piers came up to Jake's side, his monocle fog-covered from the moisture in the air. "If Miss Bloodmayne is here, hopefully she was not one of the causalities."

"Agreed," Jake said, his shoulders tightening at the thought. That would make their mission a bit difficult since the bounty required the woman alive.

The soldier led them between the canvas tents toward a large one near the middle of the base. He ducked inside, and the three men followed.

The soldier stopped just inside the flaps. "Commander Powell."

A large man stood beside a table that took up most of the tent. His gray hair was parted to the side and he sported a thick mustache beneath a bulbous nose. Two other men stood beside him, all three dressed in olive green uniforms.

"Yes, corporal?"

"There are some men here from World City. They have documents from the city council concerning a woman."

"A woman?" Commander Powell straightened, his gaze landing on Jake, then Piers and Rodger. His gaze narrowed. "Let me see those documents."

Jake pulled them out and handed them over. He waited quietly as the commander perused the creased papers.

"I don't understand." Commander Powell placed the papers on the table and looked at the three bounty hunters. "Another bounty hunter came here over a week ago with the woman, seeking Dr. Latimer. Are you saying the city council wants this woman? On what charges?"

"Murder," Jake replied, hands behind his back.

"Murder? Her? It can't be possible. Have you met the woman?"

The three bounty hunters glanced at each other. Jake would never forget the way Miss Bloodmayne had thrown him against the wall with an invisible force, and the way she had laughed afterward. "She is more dangerous than you realize."

Commander Powell laughed in disbelief.

"In any case, you are to hand her over to us. Our orders supersede any others you have received concerning the woman, including Stephen Grey's request."

Commander Powell looked up. "I didn't say the woman was with Stephen Grey."

"We know who she came with. Now, about the woman . . ."

Commander Powell ran a hand through his thinning hair while his two officers looked on. He finally sighed and picked up the papers again. "I don't understand what's going on, but I recognize the seal on these documents. Are you sure Miss Bloodmayne is the right woman? I know her name is on this warrant, but still . . ."

"We are positive. And we sincerely hope you will comply with the World City council's demands."

Commander Powell's face darkened. "There is no need for threats, gentlemen. I understand the chain of command better than most. The woman you're looking for is with the medical unit. The corporal here will escort you. Take her quietly. I don't want a ruckus on my base."

"Thank you, Commander."

"And no shooting."

Jake nodded and turned, although he wasn't going to promise

anything. If Stephen tried to stop them, they would stop him first. "Where do we find the medical tents?" he asked the corporal.

"Follow me."

Jake glanced at the other two bounty hunters. "Let's go, men."

Piers nodded and Rodger answered with a grunt, his cannon-arm ready, though not yet armed.

Outside, the three bounty hunters followed the corporal around the command tent and north toward the tents marked with the blue circle and white star of the medical corps. Sunlight poured down on them. Jake readjusted his collar and wiped the sweat from his face.

A few soldiers glanced their direction, their eyes lingering longer than Jake felt comfortable with. He, Piers, and Rodger stood out amongst the sea of olive-colored uniforms. The faster they retrieved Miss Bloodmayne, the better.

The corporal stopped just beyond the first medical tent. "Wait here while I find Miss Bloodmayne." He left before Jake had a chance to answer.

Jake scowled at the corporal's back. Like blazes he was going to wait! Not when there was a chance she would run or perform that black magic on them again like last time. They need to catch her and sedate her before she knew anything was happening.

He looked around. As far as he could see, the area was empty, at least outside. "All right." He eyed Piers and Rodger. "Here's the plan. We're not going to wait for the corporal to bring Miss Bloodmayne to us. We need to catch her off guard, and that means finding her ourselves. Silently search the tents and try not to be seen. Once you locate Miss Bloodmayne, meet back here and we will retrieve her together."

"And what if the corporal finds her first and brings her here?" Piers asked, adjusting his monocle.

"Then have Dr. Bloodmayne's injection ready. We won't have much time to react and we don't need her going off again."

Piers patted the small satchel at his side and nodded, his face almost as pale as his white suit. Apparently they were both remembering their last encounter with Miss Bloodmayne. Rodger, however, seemed untroubled.

"Now go."

Rodger went to the left and Piers to the right. Jake walked behind the tents, peeking inside each one, lingering only long enough to glance inside and move on.

At the third tent, he found her.

Miss Bloodmayne stood behind a table, her back to him, mixing an assortment of liquids from small glass vials into one large one. The rest of the tent was filled with crates. His heart gave a long, hard beat at the sight of her. Petite and pretty, but he knew better. That woman was a monster, and the sooner they took her back to World City, the better. The trick was getting to her before she could turn her magic on them.

Jake headed back to the rendezvous point.

"I found her," he said quietly once Piers and Rodger arrived. He pointed down the row. "That way, three tents down. Piers, do you have the needle ready?"

Piers pulled a glass syringe from his satchel and checked it. "I hope this does what Dr. Bloodmayne says it does."

"Don't we all?" Jake mopped more sweat from his forehead. "Rodger and I will grab her. You'll administer the liquid. All right?" He peered at both men. They nodded back. "Good. Let's go, before the corporal shows up."

The three men made their way to the tent. The closer they drew, the faster Jake's heart beat. They needed to grab her fast and insert the needle. If they didn't . . .

His stomach twisted and he breathed in quietly. He was confident that whatever the reason the Tower—and the city council— wanted her, it had to do with what she did to them that morning in Covenshire. Was the Tower creating humans with some kind of magical power? Was Piers right? Should they even be helping the Tower?

Just focus on the bounty. He took another deep breath. It wasn't his problem. Soon he would have the cash in hand, and he would be gone from World City.

They stopped outside the tent. Jake motioned toward himself and Rodger, then mouthed, "*Ready?*"

Rodger nodded, his face grim like usual.

Jake held up a fist, then lifted a finger with each number. One. Two. Three.

The men rushed into the tent.

Miss Bloodmayne turned. Her eyes went wide and her mouth opened. The glass vial she had been holding fell to the ground and spilled out. "What are you— How did you find . . . ?"

Faster than Jake could blink, she spun and went for the other side of the tent. Blazes! He tore across the ground, caught the back of her corset, and yanked. Before she could yell, he wrapped his other arm around her neck and choked out her fledgling scream.

"Now, Piers!

Piers was already at his side, thrusting the needle into the side of her neck.

She shook her head and fought his hold.

"Come on," Jake breathed as her face began to change. Her lips curled into a snarl and a fire lit inside her eyes. "Work!"

She went stiff. Her eyes returned to their normal color and rolled up into her head. Jake caught her as she began to fall. "There we go." He looked around. That was a close one. "Now let's get her out of here."

"I don't think so," said a cold, hard voice.

Jake grit his teeth and turned. Of all the people he didn't want to run into.

Stephen Grey.

CHAPTER
27

STEPHEN'S HAND SHOOK AS HE POINTED ONE REVOLVER AT JAKE and the other one at Piers. Rodger already had his cannon arm trained on him. His heart thudded madly inside his chest. How the blazes had Jake and the others found Kat so quickly without him knowing? If he had been a couple minutes later . . .

He licked his lips and forced his mind to concentrate. If he shot now, Rodger would pulverize him with that cannon-arm of his. On the other hand . . . "I won't let you take her."

Jake eyed the revolver pointed at his head. Both men knew Stephen was the better shot and wouldn't miss at this distance. "You don't have a choice, Stephen," Jake said in a calm voice, but the pallor of his face said otherwise. "We've already presented the city council's papers to the base commander. He knows we are here and why." He adjusted his hold on Kat. Just seeing her unconscious body sag against Jake made Stephen want to forget any self-restraint and shoot.

"What did you do to her?" Stephen steadied his hands as sweat trickled down the side of his face. "Why is she like that?"

"We knocked her out."

"How?"

"Something Dr. Bloodmayne gave us. You know what she can do. You saw it in Covenshire. There was no way we were going to take a chance this time."

Out of the corner of his eye, Stephen caught Piers pressing down on a button near the top of his cane. There was a whirr of clicks, and seconds later, the additional sniper mechanisms emerged from the sides of the cane. "Don't think about it, Piers."

"Just being proactive, Grey. I don't want to be the only one without a gun if this turns into a party."

"There won't be a party if you just leave the lady here."

"Why are you protecting her, Stephen?" Jake asked, his own hand creeping toward the revolver at his side.

Stephen snorted. He knew this was just a delaying tactic on Jake's part. Still, perhaps he should let the three bounty hunters in on the Tower's dirty little secret. "She needs help. She's sick, and there's a doctor here who might be able to cure her. Trust me, if you take her back to World City, Doctor Bloodmayne and the city council have no plans to cure her. They just want to take what she can do and multiply it."

Jake shrugged and held up his own gun. "Not our problem. We just want the money. And you know you can't stop us."

"Maybe not all of you. But I'd rather try than let you take her back to those monsters."

"What in the blazes are you doing?" a man yelled behind him.

Stephen glanced back to find an officer standing in the tent opening.

The officer pointed at Jake. "The commander said no shooting!"

Jake glared back at the man. "Does it look like I'm shooting? I'm just holding my gun."

"You were supposed to wait for me!"

"We found the woman and took her. Now, corporal, if you would escort us from the base . . ." Jake swung Kat up over his shoulder like a sack of flour and started for the entrance, his gun still trained on Stephen.

Stephen's fingers itched to pull the trigger, but he kept them out of the trigger guards. *God, what do I do? How do I save Kat?* If he shot, there was no going back. He couldn't just disable Jake and Piers—too risky. He would have to go for a kill shot each. Rodger

AWAKENED

would fire back, and if he actually lived through Rodger's cannon blast, he would be arrested for shooting on the base.

But he couldn't let them take Kat, could he?

His mind raced through different scenarios, dismissing each one as fast as it came. He had no jurisdiction here. Jake had signed papers from the World City council demanding Kat's capture. Even the commander would not stop them. And if he shot them, he would be arrested. It was a no-win situation.

Jake was right. He had no choice.

With his heart in his throat, Stephen lowered his revolvers.

"Good choice, Grey," Rodger said with a grunt as he followed the others outside the tent.

Stephen's shoulders slumped. Hope shattered inside him. He listened as their footsteps faded away from the tent. No matter what he did, he couldn't save Kat. Even with his guns in hand, he had been unable to stop Jake and the others.

He fell to his knees and his arms sagged at his sides. A part of him still wanted to chase after Jake and use whatever means necessary to get Kat back. But his rational side stopped him. He couldn't shoot Jake, not on a military base. It would not end well.

A lump swelled inside of his throat. Last night he had all but confessed his love to her, and now . . .

I couldn't save her. It felt like the Tower all over again, after he'd left Kat there. Only this time he had no idea how he would find her. He didn't even know if they would take her back to the Tower, or somewhere else she couldn't be found.

What do I do, God? You know what will happen to her once they take her back to World City. This time her father might actually transform her into a monster.

Stephen dipped his head, his insides as tight as a coiled spring. A memory from another time and another place filled his mind. Him, on his knees, head bowed, staring at the wooden floor as Aunt Milly stood nearby. It was the night the caretaker had come to take his parents' bodies away.

"How do I go on, Aunt Milly? A part of me doesn't want to ever move again."

Her hand had rested on his shoulder. "You just do it. You get up, and you take a step. This is the first of many trials you will face in your life, Stephen. You can either let them break you, or you let them make you stronger. And remember, you're not alone."

Stephen swallowed. Aunt Milly wasn't here now to tell him to get up. She was gone, just like everyone else in his life.

No, that wasn't true.

He took a deep breath and looked up. He still had God. God had never left him, even when he had walked away years ago.

God, he breathed. Slowly, quietly, strength trickled back into his body, spreading across his chest and limbs. Aunt Milly had been right. There had been many trials in his life since the day his parents had died, and at one point, he'd almost let them break him. But not this time. He was stronger now, and he wasn't alone. He had never been alone.

God, all I ask for is the strength to stand again and find Kat. Let me find her one more time. I can't save her from the monster inside of her, but I can rescue her from those who would do evil to her. Let what is dying inside of her live again, let her soul be awakened. By your power . . .

Stephen took one more cleansing breath, then pushed up from the ground. A fire relit inside his chest. It wasn't over yet. He stood and holstered his revolvers. He couldn't rescue Kat here at the base, but that didn't mean he couldn't follow Jake, Piers, and Rodger outside its confines. And if he couldn't catch them before they left for World City, he would pursue them there.

As long as God gave him breath, he wouldn't stop until he found Kat.

CHAPTER
28

"WELL, WELL, GREY. WE MEET AGAIN."

"Robert." Stephen stepped onto the deck of the *Lancelot* three days later. "You have no idea how glad I am to see you." He dropped his pack and clasped forearms with the airship pirate. Dr. Latimer came aboard behind him. "If there's someone I trust to get us to World City fast, it's you."

Robert let his arms fall and took a step back. "You're lucky I received the message from the base. I had just finished repairs and was about to head back to World City when I received the telegram. You did not send any details." Robert glanced behind Stephen. "And where is the lovely lady?"

"That's what we need to talk about."

Robert's gaze came back and he gave Stephen a firm nod. "To my quarters. Anders!"

The tall sailor came to Robert's side. "Yes, Captain?"

"Take us out. Head to World City along the new coordinates. We shouldn't have any problems with Austrium wasps this time."

"Yes, Captain." Anders turned and started shouting orders to the other sailors. The gangplank was withdrawn and the opening closed. A handful of sailors were already deflating the large balloon that kept the *Lancelot* afloat while more were readying the rotor engines.

"This way," Robert said and turned around.

Stephen grabbed his pack and followed, Dr. Latimer close

behind. There was still evidence of the air fight from a couple weeks ago, places where the wooden planks had been patched, and a new wooden tower to which the fallen main rotor was now attached. A patchwork of the old ship and new materials.

Robert led them to the door beneath the top deck and stepped inside. Down the dark hall they went while outside the rotors began to hum in preparation for takeoff. He opened the door and ushered them into his quarters, his gaze lingering on Dr. Latimer.

The ship lurched as the rotors took over. Steadying himself against the doorway, Grim gestured to the room. "Gentlemen, take a seat."

Stephen went directly to the large metal table in front of the wall of windows, which sparkled with new glass and fresh paint.

Dr. Latimer still stood inside the doorway, his eyes wide as he looked around. "This is quite a ship."

Robert flashed him a roguish smile. "One of the finest you'll find in the skies. I'm afraid I did not catch your name."

Dr. Latimer looked back. "Dr. Joshua Latimer."

Recognition dawned on Robert's face. "Ah, yes. It's nice to finally meet you, Dr. Latimer. You were not an easy man to track down."

Dr. Latimer frowned and glanced at Stephen.

"Captain Grim was the one who helped me find you."

"I see." Dr. Latimer crossed the room and took a seat next to Stephen. There was a wariness in his gaze now, but his eyes still lit up as he glanced around the room.

The rotors reached a new pitch, and the ship started moving. Outside the window, the Austrium coast began to pull away.

Robert took a seat opposite of them. He placed his elbows on the table and leaned forward. "So where is Miss Bloodmayne?"

Stephen let out a long breath. "They captured her."

"Who?"

"The Tower."

Robert scowled, his eye patch digging into his eyebrow. "How did they do that?"

"The bounty hunters Jake Ryder, Piers Mahon, and Rodger Glennan caught up with us at Ironguard Base."

Robert sat back and crossed his arms. "Well, considering they knew you escaped by my airship, and the city council knew where I was heading, it's not surprising. The council must want the woman bad to send those three across the Narrow Strait. I'd be curious to know how much the bounty is."

"It's quite a bit," Stephen said, remembering the contract. "More than enough to allow all three men to live comfortably for the rest of their lives."

Robert whistled, his eyes widening. "Yes, that kind of money would send those three anywhere. I'm almost tempted myself."

Stephen scowled.

Robert shrugged. "I'm a pirate. However, I do have principles. And taking that lovely lady back to the Tower would cross those lines."

"Good to know," Stephen said.

"So have you thought about what you're going to do next when we arrive in World City?"

"Yes." Stephen folded his hands across the table. "First find where they took Kat. Then go from there."

Dr. Latimer cleared his throat. "We will also want to retrieve my electrical stimulus device from the Tower. I have a feeling Alexander is not going to waste any time with Miss Bloodmayne once he has her, which could worsen her condition."

Stephen went cold all over as Robert asked who Alexander was. An image of Kat appeared in his mind, laughing with that insane look in her eyes, standing in the middle of World City, her hands spread out as she set the city on fire.

"Like what?" he heard Robert ask, bringing him back to the conversation.

"Alexander will try to figure out how to trigger Miss Bloodmayne's power, then how to harness it. Eventually he'll want to replicate it."

"To what end? Is the council planning to build some kind of human weapon for the war? Or do they want that power for themselves?"

"I'm not sure. It could be any number of things." Dr. Latimer frowned. "However, I have a feeling there might another motive, at least where Alexander is concerned. Something dark and covert. Miss Bloodmayne looks almost exactly like her mother. I imagine it would be hard for Alexander to experiment on a person that looks like his beloved dead wife. It would go against his very being. There is something driving him, something more than just knowledge and power."

"And what do you think that is?" Stephen asked, fearing the answer.

Dr. Latimer shook his head. "I don't know. And that worries me."

CHAPTER
29

DR. BLOODMAYNE LEANED ACROSS HIS DESK AND REACHED FOR the stack of notes to the right. Books lay open on the left, piled atop each other like a paper pyramid. Rain pounded the window behind him. A pungent smell lingered from the lab next door. At least the moans had stopped.

He didn't bother to turn on the gas lamp on the wall nearby. Instead, he held his notes up to the weak light filtering through the window. He preferred rainy days to sunshine. He seemed to get more done, and the rain soothed his mind.

He glanced at his latest scribbles, thoughts that had come to him last night. All this time he had thought that Kathryn's power was triggered by will or thought. But what if that wasn't the case? What if it was more primal?

He lowered the paper and tapped his chin. When he had her in his lab, she said she couldn't control the power inside her, that it was somehow triggered but she never said how.

What if—what if it was triggered by emotion?

"Yes," he said softly and placed the notes down on the desk. He stood and turned toward the window. "That would make sense." Rain pelted the panes with a steady tap. Heavy, dark clouds hung over World City, leaving the city looking like one of those Goth paintings that hung in the Capitol building. A couple of Tower scientists ran across the street below with newspapers held over their heads.

Death, life, matter, they were the fundamentals of reality. The building blocks of everything that existed. Of course the kind of power that controlled them would not be directed by higher thought. It would be controlled by instinct, by emotion. Until the mind learned how to control it.

"But is the flesh strong enough? Can a human direct that kind of power without consequence?" Dr. Bloodmayne slammed the side of his fist against the window and bowed his head. "I need to know." *Why did you leave, Kathryn? I offered you everything!*

He twisted around and grabbed the back of his chair. No matter. She would be found, and soon he would know how much Kathryn could take. And this time he would try a different approach. He would find her emotional triggers and see the power for himself.

The door on the other side of the room opened. Miss Nicola glanced in, her auburn hair a shade darker in the shadows of his office. "Pardon my interruption, Dr. Bloodmayne, but there is a telegram for you. The sender wrote that it is urgent and for your eyes only."

Dr. Bloodmayne waved her in.

Miss Nicola opened the door the rest of the way and crossed the room. Her lab coat was pristine and wrinkle free, her hair piled up fashionably on her head. She gave him a debonair smile as she placed the telegram on his desk and took a step back. She reminded him of a cat with that suave, confident gait and look of a feline who knew it owned the room.

"Thank you, Miss Nicola." He picked up the telegram, the paper smooth and cool between his fingers. "I need you to check on the specimen in the next room. It has finally quieted down enough so we can begin the initial round of injections."

Her smile widened, and that same eager look he felt when he worked filled her eyes. Yes, he had found an apprentice after his own heart. Why couldn't Kathryn have been more like Nicola?

She gave him a small nod and took a step back. "I will start right away, Dr. Bloodmayne." Instead of exiting through the door she had come through, Nicola went right and headed into one of his secret labs. A low moan escaped the room when she opened the door, and the pungent smell grew strong again.

Dr. Bloodmayne withdrew his handkerchief from his pocket and held it to his nose. If only there was a way to work without that death-like stench.

Nicola closed the door behind her. Dr. Bloodmayne thrust his thumb under the crease of the telegram, forcing it open. The message was short.

FOUND HER IN AUSTRIUM. BRINGING HER BACK BY SHIP. WILL ARRIVE IN FIVE DAYS.

He read the telegram again and placed it on the desk. The date on the telegram was yesterday, which meant the bounty hunters would be here in three more days.

Excellent. He knew if the bounty were high enough, his daughter would be found and brought back. In the end, the price was worth it. The council would be pleased to know that he would shortly be resuming his studies on matter. And even more importantly . . .

He crossed his office toward the bookcase to the left. He reached for a single book bound in dark red leather and pulled. Instead of releasing the book, the entire bookcase swung open with a subtle groan, revealing a small, dark room beyond.

Dr. Bloodmayne reached inside to his right and felt for a small lever. With a flip of his finger, the gas lamp within lit with a quiet hum. As he entered, the bookcase closed behind him.

The air was cold in here, as if it were an icehouse, but there was no ice present. Just a single brass box against the wall. The rest of the room was empty. No tables, no chairs, no bookshelves.

Another, lower hum emitted from the brass box, which stood as tall as a man and three feet wide, with tubes and wires surrounding the outside save for a circular glass window near the top.

He stopped before the box and reached for the circular glass. "Helen," he whispered, his fingers stopping just shy of the glass that separated him from his wife. She looked exactly the same as she did almost twenty years ago. The same beautiful face. The same thick, dark hair. And if he could see them, her eyes would be the same color as coffee. "How I've missed you."

A deep longing filled his being, so full and thick it almost hurt physically. She was the only thing he had loved more than his work, and since her death, he had thrown himself even deeper into his studies. No knowledge was taboo, no risk too great, if it could bring Helen back.

His hand dropped slightly. But what about their daughter?

His lips turned downward and he thrust his hands into his pockets. Kathryn was a means to an end. She was not Helen. If only she had been cooperative when he had first brought her to the Tower, or if he had known that his experiments had changed her, giving her the power he had desired for so long, then he might have Helen now, at his side, instead of in that cold mechanical box before him.

"I just want you back," he said as he gazed at his wife. "Just to talk to you again." He tightened his hands into fists inside his pockets. "And I will. Soon."

CHAPTER
30

THE TRAIN CHUGGED INTO WORLD CITY LATE THAT MORNING. Jake frowned as he looked out the window of their private car. An unusual dense fog hung over the city like a funeral shroud. Strange weather, considering it was still summer.

The train zipped by factories and three-story flats as it made its way to the central station. The *Calypso* had made excellent time across the Narrow Strait, clipping off a day and allowing them to arrive early into Covenshire. Captain Harpur had been more than eager to take the rest of his payment and be on his way once they'd arrived in the harbor. Jake felt the same way. The sooner they dropped off Miss Bloodmayne at the Tower, the better.

Rodger sat across from him on the dull velvet seat, cleaning his cannon-arm with a rag and a small can of grease. Piers sat beside him, eyes closed, his head against the window, a small snore escaping his lips. And Miss Bloodmayne . . .

Jake looked to his left. The petite woman lay across the bench, her body tucked in between their packs and the wall. True enough, the clear liquid inside the needles Dr. Bloodmayne had provided had kept her sedated almost the entire trip, minus the times they fed her or allowed her to use the loo. Fortunately, she had been too incoherent to display those sensibilities women usually employed at the thought of such private functions. All in all, an easy trip and, in the end, a rewarding one.

The carriage Jake had ordered waited for them outside the station. Between himself and Piers, they covered Miss Bloodmayne with a cloak and moved her to the carriage. Rodger followed, his mere presence enough to deter anyone who might have questioned them.

It took half an hour for the carriage to make its way to the Tower. The sky never changed from its dull gray and the sun never appeared. The air smelled of smoke and rot even more than usual. Just another thing he wasn't going to miss once he had the cash for Miss Bloodmayne's contract and could leave World City behind.

At the front of the Tower, the carriage stopped. The iron gates were open, leaving the way clear to the front double doors. Good. Hopefully that meant Dr. Bloodmayne had received their message about arriving into port early.

Jake paid the driver double to keep him quiet, then helped Rodger situate Miss Bloodmayne over his shoulder. No one greeted them at the door, and they found the halls inside empty. Even better. Dr. Bloodmayne had probably cleared the Tower so as not to arouse suspicion. That or the fact that it was Sunday.

They took the first staircase they found and headed up. The interior was dark, the only light weak daylight coming from the windows placed on each floor. The Tower reminded Jake of an asylum he'd visited years ago during one of his missions. Dark, bleak, and unwelcoming. And the screams that came from the hidden rooms—

Jake shook his head and focused on the next set of stairs. This was not an asylum. This was the Tower, one of the most prestigious places in all of World City.

After five floors, Rodger huffed. "How far up are we going?"

"Dr. Bloodmayne's office. Tenth floor."

When they reached the eighth floor, Rodger leaned against the wall, his face glistening. Here the configuration of the stairs changed. They must be at the actual tower part of the building. Next to the narrower staircase was a sign: "Private Tower Labs. No Trespassing."

"Almost there," Jake said, looking back at his comrades.

They entered the stairway and headed up. As they neared the

ninth floor, a ghastly smell enveloped Jake's nostrils. He gagged and buried his face in the crook of his arm.

Rodger swore behind him. "What is that awful smell?"

Piers coughed. "Smells like the old cemetery next to the church in Roxsford where I grew up. Sometimes when the place flooded, the coffins would surface and split open. The whole village would smell like this."

Jake gagged again at the thought of open coffins and decayed bodies. Rotting corpses were about the only thing that made him queasy. They quickly passed the ninth floor and headed toward the tenth. At the top, they found a row of doors. The tainted smell still lingered here, but not as strongly. Strange green light seeped out beneath the last two doors. A faint light shone through the first door. The dingy window at the end of the short hall did little to light up the place.

"Let's get this over with," Rodger said.

A long moan came from the nearest door with the green light.

A cold sweat broke out across Jake's body, and his heartbeat hammered inside his ears. He couldn't agree more. He moved across the hall toward the door with the faint light and knocked.

There was a rustle behind the door, then it opened with a creak. Dr. Bloodmayne stood in the doorway, his silver hair slightly disheveled and three dark stains across his white lab coat. His hawkish eyes took in the three men, then settled on his unconscious daughter. His thin lips stretched into a wide smile. "Good. I'll show you where to place her."

Dr. Bloodmayne stepped into the hallway, leaving what looked like his office behind. He bypassed the doors until he reached the last one with the green light. "In here," he said, unlocking the door.

Jake entered first. His eyes adjusted to the dim green light coming from lamps set around the room. A single metal table stood in the middle, bathed in the sickly glow. Black tubes hung from the ceiling. On the floor were white chalk marks, drawn in precise lines and curves. This did not look like a place of science at all—more like a pagan ritual scene from hundreds of years ago.

"Place her on the table. Gently."

Everything inside Jake screamed for him to leave and take the woman with him.

Just think about the money, he chanted inside his head, drowning out the other voice. It didn't take long. He'd learned a long time ago not to ask questions about his bounties. Turn them in and take the money, that was his policy. The habit helped him now.

Rodger laid the young woman on the table. The green light made her look otherworldly, eerie. Like he was catching a glimpse of the woman from Covenshire who had picked them up with her mind and thrown them across the room.

Jake twisted around and held out his hand. "The bounty, if you would." His palms were sweaty, and adrenaline rushed through his veins. Piers frowned as he looked around the room. Jake grit his teeth. *Now is not the time to become moral*, he thought toward the dapper bounty hunter. Rodger didn't seem to care as much.

Dr. Bloodmayne ignored him and walked toward his daughter. "Did you have any issues with her during the trip?"

"No, the needles you gave us kept her sedated." Jake kept his hand out.

"Good, good," Dr. Bloodmayne said under his breath. His eyes glistened as he looked over the woman, much like a raven might look over a carcass.

Jake felt that rush again to grab Miss Bloodmayne and run. What kind of man was Dr. Bloodmayne? And what was this place really? This was not at all how the *Herald* portrayed the Tower.

He closed his eyes and pictured an overstuffed chair next to a roaring fire. And a dog—a hound of some kind—sitting at his feet while he held a glass of brandy. With that image in mind, Jake looked at Dr. Bloodmayne. "Our money, Dr. Bloodmayne. Or we leave and take the lady with us."

That seemed to wake up the old man. He straightened and glanced at them. Piers looked a bit pale in the green light. Even Rodger now had a wariness to his being.

"I have your bounty back in my office. Follow me." Dr. Bloodmayne bypassed the men and headed back into the hallway. As they passed the other door with the green light, another moan drifted into the hallway. Jake walked faster, his throat dry.

Dr. Bloodmayne entered the door at the end of the hall where they had first found him. Unlike the dark and morbid room they had just left, this one was warm in a sterile, intellectual sort of way. A single gas lamp was lit along the left wall, casting its yellow light across a large wooden desk and chair. Behind the desk was a wide window that overlooked World City. Gloomy gray clouds continued to hang low over the cityscape. Bookcases lined the walls, filled from top to bottom with countless leather-bound books, many of them very old.

Dr. Bloodmayne went around the desk, pulled open the drawer, and retrieved a thick sealed envelope. "Your bounty."

Before the other men could move, Jake crossed the room and took the envelope. They would divvy it up once they were away from the Tower.

Piers and Rodger followed him as he left the office without another word. The faster he left this place, the better. And he never wanted to return.

Down the stairs they flew until they reached the bottom floor. The hall was empty and silent. The only sound was their breathing.

"Wait." Piers grabbed Jake's arm and pulled him to a stop. "Are you sure about this?"

What the blazes? Jake spun around. "What are you talking about, Piers?"

Piers dropped his hand. "Leaving the woman here. You saw that room. That's not a normal room. And those were definitely not normal markings on the floor."

Jake glanced around as if expecting something to jump out from the shadows. "Now is not the time to develop a conscience."

"But what if by leaving the woman here, we've done something heinous?"

"I'm sure we've all turned in bounties that we didn't agree with."

"This is different. And we all know it."

Piers was right. What if by leaving the woman here, they

enabled the Tower to eventually create even more people like Miss Bloodmayne? What would become of World City? The world itself? Is that why Stephen had come back for her?

No.

Jake clenched his teeth. Stephen came back because he'd grown soft. Maybe he was even infatuated with the lady. Jake had no such compunctions. What the Tower did was not his business. His only job was to find bounties and turn them in. Whatever happened afterward was not his problem. Stephen had become involved, and that's where he'd gone wrong.

"It was a job, just like any other job. We may not like what the client does, but that's not our concern. We find the bounty, we get paid. That's it. So what'll it be, Piers? Do you want to go back for the lady? Or"—Jake held up the envelope—"do you want the money?"

Piers glanced at the stairs, then stared at the envelope with a pensive expression. "I'll take my cut. However, before we leave, we should make sure the money is in there."

Jake paused. He glanced at Piers, then at Rodger. They had come this far together, but who was to say if, at the sight of the bills, the men would turn on each other? He had no desire to fight for the cash, not here at least. He just wanted his share and to leave this place.

"What are you waiting for?" Rodger asked in a gruff voice. His eyes narrowed as he slowly reached for one of the weapons strapped to his chest.

"Equal shares, right?" Jake asked, pinning Rodger with his gaze.

"Yes, that is what we agreed upon. Unless you're having second thoughts." Piers tilted his head to the side as if studying Jake.

"No, I'm not. I just wanted to make sure."

Piers folded his arms. "Make sure of what?"

Instead of answering, Jake opened the envelope. It seemed Rodger and Piers just wanted their money as well. The bills were in the largest denomination and—he counted them quickly—all there. He recounted and divided the cash into three equal shares.

Piers and Rodger took their shares with suspicious gazes.

"It's all there. You watched me count it." Jake glared at the two men. "I don't think any of us want any trouble. But—" He drew his gun out so fast that Piers and Rodger were still blinking as he pointed the weapon at one man, then the other.

A muffled scream echoed from somewhere upstairs.

The hair rose along Jake's neck and arms. That sounded like a woman—No. He wasn't going back up there. "I say we take our money and get the blazes out of here."

Piers looked up at the ceiling, then back at Jake. "Agreed."

Good. Piers had come back to his senses.

Piers placed the bills in his breast pocket and turned around. He headed toward the front doors, his cane clicking against the floor, his white attire pale in the dark hallway. However, Jake knew Piers was watching his back, even if his demeanor looked nonchalant. Given how his hand was tucked up by his chest, he was probably fingering his small pistol.

Jake swung his revolver at the other bounty hunter. "Rodger?"

Rodger grunted. He had already put his money away. "Good working with you, Jake." Rodger gave him a firm nod and followed Piers down the hall.

After a couple seconds, Jake let his breath out, and his shoulders sagged. It had been a risk to work with them, but in the end, it had paid off. Another scream came from deep within the Tower. He looked at the ceiling. Nope, not his business. He tucked the envelope into the inner pocket of his vest and started for the door, his revolver in hand. He wasn't about to stick around to find out what Dr. Bloodmayne had planned for his daughter.

CHAPTER

31

KAT WAS DROWNING AGAIN IN THAT DARK, DEEP OCEAN OF HER dreams. Every time she rose above the water, something grabbed her by the ankles and pulled her back under.

She gulped in a mouthful of water and choked. Her arms and legs ached from the exertion of keeping her face above the waterline. She couldn't keep this up much longer. Soon her body would give out and she would sink into the dark, murky water. Why keep fighting the inevitable? Her body felt so heavy, so tired.

Yes, yes. Let go, whispered that insidious voice.

Kat stopped treading and let her body slip beneath the water. She watched the surface draw farther and farther away.

No! I can't give up. Not yet! She kicked out and reached for the surface—

Her eyes flew open. She breathed rapidly, searching the room around her. Everything was dark save for a single gas lamp against the wall to her right. In moments, her eyes adjusted. She saw no windows or doors. The air was cold, like a winter's night, and smelled like dust.

Kat sat up and brushed her hair back. Nausea crept up her throat, and stars popped across her vision. She could still feel the effects of whatever medication had been injected into her, and the point where the needle had been repeatedly inserted into her neck.

She pressed a cold hand to her heated face and swallowed. Her heart continued to thump rapidly inside her chest, but not as fast as it had a moment ago.

She was no longer drowning in a dark ocean. But where was she? She glanced again at the gas lamp on the wall. The bare hint of a doorway stood beside it. And in the corner to the left—

Kat gasped and pulled back. The area around her vision darkened.

A rectangular brass box the size of small bed stood near the gas lamp. Tubing and wires wound around the contraption and near the very top was a round piece of glass, faintly lit.

Inside the glass window . . . was her mother's face.

The scream tore from her throat before she could stop it. Kat held a hand to her mouth and screamed again. She would know that face anywhere, even though her mother had died at her birth. For hours she had stared at the painting of Helen Bloodmayne in the hallway back home, looking for traces of herself in her mother's image.

Only to see it now in the flesh.

Kat turned away and squeezed her eyes shut, her hand still pressed to her mouth. It couldn't be! She was hallucinating. Yes. The medication was interfering with her mind.

She glanced back at the metal box. Her mother's face was still in the glass, her eyes closed as if she were asleep. What looked like frost surrounded the glass.

Kat slowly lowered her trembling fingers. Was it possible?

She did a sweep of the rest of the room. There was nothing else. Just the gas lamp and the metal box.

Kat slowly stood, her body drenched in sweat. She felt like at any moment her mother's eyes would open. But as she cautiously walked toward the metal container, nothing happened. A faint humming sound emanated from the tubes and wires. Kat stared at her mother as another shudder rippled through her body. Every detail was exactly like the portrait back home, down to the small beauty mark on her left cheek.

She hesitated, then reached out and touched the glass. Instantly she pulled back. Her fingers burned from the intense chill. She looked at her fingers, then back at the glass. Whatever this contraption was, it was colder than ice. Colder than anything she had ever experienced before.

The longer she stood there, staring at the face inside the glass, the more she knew that the woman inside the box was indeed her mother.

"How is this possible?" she whispered. She had visited her mother's gravesite many times with Ms. Stuart. How could it be she was here? Unless . . .

Her mother had never been buried in the first place.

Her stomach doubled over. She held a hand to her mouth again, afraid she was going to retch. What was going on here? This room. She spun around. What was it? *Where* was it?

Only one place would hold such an advanced piece of technology. Only one place her father—if he was involved, and she was sure he was—would have kept her mother.

The Tower.

Kat took a couple steps back before she fell to her knees. *When did I get here?* She could only remember bits and pieces of the last few days. Those men, those bounty hunters, must have brought her back to World City. And here she was again, back in her father's clutches.

She gripped her face, gouging her skin with her fingers. Why was her mother here? Why had she not been put to rest? What did father hope to accomplish with her? Was he experimenting on her like he was on other corpses?

Kat gagged on that last thought. If he were, then her father was truly vile.

The door opened beside the gas lamp, sending a beam of light into the room. Kat looked up and blinked.

"Hmm. You weren't supposed to wake up for a few more hours."

Father.

A burst of hatred welled up inside of her, burning away the terror from the last few minutes. She brought her full gaze on him and struggled to her feet. "Why is mother here?" She pointed at him, her finger shaking. "*Why is she here?*"

Her blood burst into fire inside her veins. The wind began to whip around her, pulling her skirt tight around her legs. Her hair flew back away from her face.

Her father stood in the doorway, a satisfied look on his face. "So I was right. Emotion *is* what triggers your power."

Wait, what? Kat brought her hand up. Flames licked her fingers and palms. For one moment she wanted to thrust her hands out, choke her father, and watch his eyes bulge as she forced every bit of life out of that arrogant head.

She took a step back. The darkness inside her was overwhelming, almost as if she were drowning again. *No.* She shook her head and looked down. *No. I will not be like him.* She closed her hands into two tight fists, quenching the flames. She breathed in through her nose. *I will not kill. I cannot give into the darkness.*

But it felt like it was up to her neck, sucking her into its fiery embrace. Only barely was she maintaining control.

Father walked into the room, seemingly oblivious to the struggle inside her. He reached out a hand and caressed the side of the box. "Yes, this is your mother. Sweet, beautiful Helen. I had her body preserved in special cryo unit I invented myself."

Cryo? That explained the intense cold. And why her mother looked perfectly preserved. "So who's buried in St. Lucias?"

Her father shrugged and looked at Kat. "The coffin is empty. But I couldn't have Helen's body disappear. The *Herald* needed a burial to write about, so I gave them one, while keeping Helen for myself."

Kat looked at him in shock. He was insane! Keeping the dead body of her mother? What did he expect? To bring her back to—

Kat froze. Dizziness swept over her. That was exactly it. All this talk about power and matter, life and death. It led to one thing. Her father wanted to bring her mother back to life. In a small way, she could actually understand. He had loved her mother more than anything in the world. Perhaps she would have done the same in his place.

He turned back toward the brass box, his hand near the circular glass. If he could, she was sure he would cup her mother's face. How his fingers were not burned by the cold, she didn't know.

"I never wanted you, you know." His voice, even and smooth, struck her like a whip, and any pity she'd felt for him vanished. "Helen was my life. And you took her away from me." He turned around, his face cold. "Then I found out what you could do and I thought we could be partners. That we could forge a relationship, and through our work, bring your mother back. However, you turned me down."

He'd never wanted her. Father had always been cold toward her, but to actually hear him say those words . . . Kat felt like she was going to collapse. Only strength of will kept her on her feet. She would not show such weakness in front of him.

"But I will have Helen back, one way or another." He walked toward her, his hands in his lab coat pockets. "I do not need you, I just need what is inside of you. And the council wants their share of your power as well. All I had to do was figure out what brought that power out, and now I know. Emotions. I just have to push you far enough, and the power comes out."

Kat took a step back. That's why he had her in here. He knew seeing her mother, especially in that brass box, would trigger her. And it had worked. Almost. Even now she could feel the monster roaring deep inside her chest, demanding to be let loose.

"Now I just need to find a way to harness and replicate it. And when that happens, I won't need you anymore."

His hand came flying from his pocket. Kat raised her hands, the fire erupting toward her fingertips, but the needle was already plunging into her neck.

"I'm sorry, dear." For one brief moment as she struggled for breath, she thought her father actually looked remorseful. "You woke up before I was ready." Then he took a step back and pocketed the glass syringe.

"Father . . ." She raised her hands again, the dark power a flurry inside of her, but the medication was already taking effect. The room grew hazy and a hum started inside her head. "Please don't . . ."

"I can't have you lighting this room on fire or throwing me against the wall. That wouldn't do at all. But at least now I know how to coax that power out."

Kat slipped to the floor. Her father knelt down beside her. "That's right. Go to sleep. The next time we meet, I want to see your power in full force. Until then . . ."

She closed her eyes and fell back into the inky darkness.

"Wake up, Kathryn."

Kat barely heard the words as she blinked against the dim green light and shifted her head. There was something inside her ears, like cotton, but not soft the way cotton would be. More like tiny metal balls covered in rubber. They were connected to thin metal rods that ran along either side of her face down to her chin, where they merged into a thick wire that draped across her torso.

Kat shifted, then gasped. Her whole body ached, like a thousand needles had been pressed into every inch of her, except for her chest. As before, she could feel nothing around her heart, not even her heartbeat.

Her father stepped back and wrote something across the board he carried. "Experiment seven. This time we will try a different kind of fear." He turned and walked toward a doorway to the right.

Her body stiffened on the cold metal table as the memories of the last few hours—or days—came back. First the test, something to push her emotions to the brink. Sometimes it was a hallucinogenic drug. Other times it was something real. No matter how she fought to stay calm, eventually she would react. Then came the high-pitched whistle delivered through the gadgets inside her ears, paralyzing her mind. Then sedation by needle. Over and over again.

Metal bands wrapped around her wrists and ankles, trapping her against the flat surface. The door shut, leaving her in silence. It was starting once again.

Kat licked her lips. Time had blurred into one long line of green light, heady incense, terror, piercing shrills, then darkness. With each experiment, she fought the monster inside her, barely reining it in. During the last trial, she had picked up the tables and lamps around the room and pulled them around her in defense before the earphones delivered a paralyzing whistle and a needle pricked her neck.

Sweat trickled down the side of her head. She couldn't keep this up much longer. Each experiment tore away what little strength she had left to fight the monster, and the numbness around her heart was spreading.

She swallowed. That's what Father wanted. He wanted her to lose control. He wanted her to access that power. He was testing her limits, and how to stop her, all so he could control her.

As if sensing her thoughts, the monster shifted beneath her physical being, waiting to be let loose again. Her lip began to tremble. What would her father do this time? What would *she* do this time?

The metallic smell of blood filled her nose, mixing with the ever-increasing scent of incense. Kat froze. Was it her blood, or someone else's?

One by one, the green lamps went out except for one, leaving the room in almost darkness. Kat looked to the left, then to the right. She couldn't see or hear anything.

There was a muffled creak, then a click, as if a door had opened and closed somewhere nearby. She wanted to tear the earphones out so she could hear better, but the piercing whistle helped her quell the monster inside her. Her cheeks burned at the thought. Just what Father wanted.

Kat lay still, every normal sense stretched out. The urge to expand her power almost overwhelmed her, but she held it at bay, instead using her limited hearing and sight.

Something skittered to her left. She twisted her head toward the sound, but could see nothing. Another scurrying sound. Like tiny claws clacking across a marble floor. Every hair stood on end. More skittering, closer, closer . . .

With a shriek, Kat pulled on the metal bands, reopening the wounds around her wrists and ankles. The table beneath her moved slightly, like something was climbing it.

She gasped, her eyes wide but seeing little. She jerked her head left and right, trying to catch a glimpse of whatever was out there.

Something wet touched her calf. Another creature crawled onto her midsection, just below the numb area.

Kat screamed.

Dark power filled her being, exploding across her body with the fury of a gale, blasting away everything touching her. The air filled with squeaks and thuds as the creatures hit the wall and floor. A moment later there was a rush of clacks.

They were coming back.

She sank deep into the dark power until she could feel everything in the room. Dozens of rodents were rushing toward her. With one thought, she gripped them in the air.

Her hands caught fire, their orange glow surpassing the green light inside the room.

Kat grit her teeth, her mind teetering on the abyss of fear. She twisted her wrists until her palms were up and spread her fingers wide. She would not let those creatures touch her again!

A dozen screams and squeals ricocheted across the room as every rodent popped into flames. The smell of burnt hair and flesh filled the air.

Kat turned and looked to her right, her senses expanding past the walls. Beyond the room were five people. She bared her teeth and squeezed her hands.

"Now, now!" Someone shouted. "Now before—"

There was a gurgling sound.

Stop!

Kat gasped and opened her hand.

This is not you. Fight it—

"I can't!" she screamed at the ceiling. "I can't keep doing this! I can't keep fight—"

A high-pitched whistle filled her mind until her eyes watered and she thought she was going to retch. The familiar sting entered her neck. The shriek faded, but her mind still pulsed with the sound as her whole body shivered from the coldness spreading through every vein in her body. With one last effort, Kat forced the monster back inside.

"She is ready," her father said nearby. "The council is demanding a demonstration. I think we can safely give them one."

A tear slipped down her check, her body relaxing of its own accord. She could still feel each rat die inside her head. She never wanted to kill anything, even creatures such as those. Yet her father was driving her to do things she would have never done.

Her body grew cold and her hands came to rest at her sides. Only a sliver of her soul remained. She could feel it deep inside her, like the last ember of a dying fire.

Did her father not realize what was going to happen once that ember went out? He thought he was controlling her with the earphones and sedatives, but the truth was they only helped her control herself. She was the one stopping her power each time. But she couldn't do it much longer. Soon, the monster would be unleashed and it would envelope her and consume her soul.

Then she would be the monster. And there would be no stopping her.

Another tear slipped down her cheek. Someone walked by and turned the green lamps back on.

She grasped at one last thought at the medicine took effect. *God, if you are real, don't let them do this to me. Don't let them turn me into a monster.*

CHAPTER

32

STEPHEN STOOD ON THE PROW OF THE *LANCELOT* AS THE WIND whipped through his hair and duster. The airship coasted just above a sea of dark clouds and misty air rushed across his face and knuckles. He leaned forward as if that act would make the *Lancelot* fly faster. He had to get to World City in time. He had to get there before . . .

How much time had passed? He ran a hand through his windswept hair. A week at least. Depending on Jake and the others' mode of transportation, Kat had already been in World City for a couple of days, if not longer, locked in the Tower, experiencing who knew what experiments performed on her.

She was already on the edge. Would her father push her past the point of no return? Would the other Kat emerge permanently? And if so, what could they do?

He slammed a fist on the railing. He had promised to keep Kat safe. But what could he have done? Should he have started a gunfight right there in a military base?

Yes. He sighed. *No. Blazes, I don't know!* Every time he saw Jake in his mind's eye, hauling Kat out of the medical tent, he wanted to draw his gun. But it was too late now. And deep down, he knew he had made the only choice he could have if he wanted to be free to pursue Kat at the present.

But what if he had to make another choice between breaking the law and saving Kat? That just might be what he had to do to save her. Break into the Tower, shoot people, and go against everything he believed in as a lawman. And what if he was too late? What if Kat was already gone?

Stephen pinched the bridge of his nose, his throat tight. Would he have to shoot Kat in order to save World City?

God, don't let that happen. Please don't make me have to choose. Please save Kat. Heal whatever is wrong inside her. Don't let her father destroy her.

"Watching for World City?"

Stephen opened his eyes and looked to the right. Dr. Latimer stood beside him, his eyes shaded by his hand, his gaze forward.

"Yes. Grim said we are close."

Dr. Latimer nodded, then grabbed the railing when, as if in answer, the airship dipped down below the cloud cover. Minutes later, World City spread out below them, a sea of buildings, factories, and smokestacks with the Meandre River running through the middle. On the other side of the river stood the Tower, like a finger thrust toward the sky, and the Capitol building to the left, its glass dome reflecting the dark gray skies above.

Minutes later the *Lancelet* banked to the left. A sky tower stood near the edge of the city with multiple platforms. It was as close as Grim could take them.

Stephen's heart squeezed tightly inside his chest. Somewhere down there was Kat. But where? His gaze settled on the Tower. His best bet was there. And that's where that electric machine Dr. Latimer needed was located. But how in the blazes was he going to break into the Tower again? They knew who he was, probably had a warrant out on him.

He closed his hand into a fist. It didn't matter. He would find a way in, one way or another.

Stephen stared out the smudged window as the motorwagon raced through the dirty streets of Southbrook, away from the sky tower and toward the Tower. It felt odd to be back in World City. Nothing had changed. People still rushed to the factories or home, newsies stood on the corners pushing their papers, and smoke covered the city like a thin gauze. Yet it felt different. Like Stephen was seeing it through new eyes. He was a different man now. No longer broken. He still had cracks inside his soul, but they were filled. Repaired. Kat had forced him to see how broken he was, and his time on the *Lancelot* and in Austrium had given him time to heal.

The motorwagon bounced, sending a plume of steam into the air. Stephen caught the front seat and looked out. A ragtag cluster of kids raced across the street. The driver slammed on the brakes and yelled at them, shaking his fist.

Yes, World City was as busy as ever.

Stephen sat back and pulled at the hair below his lip as the motorwagon leaped back into drive. In the seat next to him, Dr. Latimer seemed lost in thought as well.

"It's been many years," Dr. Latimer murmured.

Stephen looked over.

"Many years since I set foot in those halls. There's a good chance no one remembers me. I've grown a beard since then, and I'm sure those who would recognize me will be in the labs or offices, not out wandering the halls."

"What are you saying?" Stephen asked.

"I might be able to walk in and grab my invention."

"Just how big is this invention of yours?"

Dr. Latimer held up his hands. "About a foot and a half tall, and half a foot wide. Not something I could conceal under a coat, but if I take the back stairs, there is less of a chance that I will meet someone."

"Except those who might know you."

He shrugged. "It's a risk no matter how we do it."

"What about Kat? Do you think they are holding her at the Tower?"

"I'm not sure. The Tower, the Bloodmayne residence, or perhaps the Capitol building itself."

"Blazes!" Stephen leaned forward and ran both hands through his hair. "How do we find out?"

"Let's start with retrieving my machine. Without it, it won't matter if we find Miss Bloodmayne. It is the only idea I've been able to come up with that might help her."

Stephen shook his head. "I don't like it, this 'might' business."

"Neither do I. Ideally, I could have studied her condition further, but we ran out of time." Dr. Latimer sighed. "Given what she shared, I'm not sure if she had much time left anyway."

Stephen sat back, his insides clenching until he felt like a wrung-out dishcloth. No matter what, whether it was her father or time, he would eventually lose Kat without a miracle.

A couple minutes later, the motorwagon pulled up to the Tower. The sky grumbled overhead, threatening to drench the city in a summer rain.

"Can't stay," the driver said, hopping out of the front seat and pulling his goggles up across his forehead. The grime from the motorwagon left his face covered in soot save for two circles around his eyes.

"Here, then." Stephen pulled out two bills. He was running low on funds and wasn't sure when he would be able to stop at his office.

"Thank ya kindly, sir." The man stuffed the bills into his front pocket, slapped the goggles back down, and with a grind and whine, the motorwagon started down the street. It certainly was not as elegant as a phaeton.

Stephen turned to find Dr. Latimer staring up at the Tower, a nostalgic expression on his face. The dark clouds made the Tower look more menacing and less like a place of academia. "I do miss this place, even after all that happened to me years ago. I once read that God has placed eternity in the hearts of men, that it is our prerogative to search out meaning and understanding. Only now I realize that means doing so with the Creator by our side. That in our exploration of the world around us, we come to understand God more. When we search for knowledge on our own, it only leads us to greed, not to glory."

Dr. Latimer stuffed his hands in his pockets and sighed. "What if Alexander had explored matter in the light of the God who made matter? What might he have accomplished?"

Stephen glanced away, imagining how Kat's life might have been different. Dr. Latimer placed a hand on his shoulder and gave him a wistful smile. "Come. We should be going. Please excuse the musings of an old man."

Stephen followed Dr. Latimer toward the entrance to the Tower. Was the doctor right? Did it matter how a person approached their understanding of the world? He shook his head. Science was not his strongest suit. But he did find some comfort in knowing that Dr. Latimer had a respect for God and that he would not be performing the procedure on Kat just for knowledge, but in the desire to save her.

A woman exited the double doors and hurried down the stairs, a stained lab coat over her blouse and skirt, and small wooden crate clutched in her hands. A glint of red hair showed from beneath the dark scarf she wore. Stephen stopped. He knew that woman.

He raised his hand and waved. "Miss! Wait!"

She turned and looked at him.

Yes, she was the woman he'd encountered in the Tower weeks ago, the one he'd run into on the top floor and who had recommended that he escape through the storage room.

Her face blanched at the sight of him.

He paused. Not a good sign.

She turned to leave, but Stephen ran up to her, his hand outstretched. "Please, wait. You work at the Tower, right?"

Her shoulders sagged and she turned around. "No. Today was my last day."

"Oh." Well that put a damper on the plan forming inside his head.

"Wait, I remember you. You were here weeks ago. You rescued Kat." A glint of life came back into her eyes. "How is Kat doing?" Then her face wrinkled. "And why are you here again? Are you here to stop the experiments?"

Dr. Latimer came up beside Stephen. "Did I hear right? You work here?"

The young lady glanced at Dr. Latimer and back to Stephen. "No, not any longer. The Tower and I did not agree on certain . . . methods they were employing."

"Then you and I have something in common." Dr. Latimer gave her a short bow. "Dr. Joshua Latimer, at your service. I was once a scientist here a long time ago. I also had issues with some of their—er—methods."

The lady looked at him with wide eyes. "I am so sorry to hear that. Then you also knew about the"—she looked around fearfully—"the experiments?"

"If you're asking what I think you're asking, then yes."

She staggered back and let out a slight moan.

Stephen grabbed her by the elbow, steadying her as Dr. Latimer took the crate from her hands. "Are you all right?"

She covered her mouth, closed her eyes, and nodded. "No one believed me." Her eyes popped open, a look of sorrow touched with indignation filling them. "Not even Papa. When the Tower found out I was asking around, I was called up to the head office and released from my apprenticeship. I came this morning to pick up the last of my belongings." She gestured at the box in Dr. Latimer's hands. It contained a photograph of herself with an older man and a small pile of books, along with a few beakers and glass tubes.

Stephen thought fast. He certainly could not enter the Tower, and there was the small chance someone would recognize Dr. Latimer. But what if this young woman went up to retrieve the device? True, she was no longer a part of the Tower, but she still had access.

"Are you here to stop them?" she asked. "After all, you were once a policeman. Aren't you supposed to stop things like this?"

Stephen rubbed the back of his neck with his other hand. "It's a bit more complicated than that." That was an understatement. He had been trying to bring these accounts to light for years. "But there is something you can do, something that might help us toward that goal."

She nodded, her face serious. "Anything."

Stephen glanced at Dr. Latimer. "Tell her."

Dr. Latimer studied her with a downturned mouth. "I need an instrument that I invented years ago retrieved from within the Tower. There is a possibility that it was disposed of, but considering Dr. Bloodmayne's fascination with the machine, I am doubtful."

Her brow furrowed. "What kind of machine? What does it look like?"

"It's a cylinder, a foot and a half tall, half a foot wide. It emits electrical arcs, like lightning, around its surface."

Her eyes widened. "Yes, I know of a machine like that. Dr. Bloodmayne keeps it in one of his private laboratories. But it will not be easy to retrieve. Why do you need it?"

Stephen let out his breath. "Because it might be the only thing that can cure Miss Bloodmayne."

She sucked in a breath. "Cure her? You mean it can stop that— that power of hers?"

"I believe so," Dr. Latimer said.

The woman grabbed Stephen's hand. "Where is she? Where is Kat?"

Stephen took a step back and gently detached the lady's hand from his. "We're not sure. We believe she is back under the control of Dr. Bloodmayne."

"Back with her father?" The young lady's face paled again. Now bereft of Stephen's hand, she began to wring her own. "That's not good, not good at all— Wait." Her hands stilled. "Dr. Bloodmayne and some of the Tower scientists are at the Capitol building today to present a new invention to the city council in hopes of gaining more money for the Tower. That's not Kat, is it?"

Stephen's face hardened. "It's possible." *I'm almost certain of it.*

The young woman stood there for a moment, mouth open. Then she snapped her jaw shut and straightened her shoulders as if casting aside the frightened, overexcited persona from moments ago. There was strength now in her face and in her posture. "Then I will go get that machine of yours. If asked, I will say that it is one of my belongings and I am taking with me."

Stephen held up his hand as the woman turned. "Wait. What's your name?"

The woman glanced over her shoulder. "Fealy. Miss Marianne Fealy. I was a longtime friend of Kat's, and if there is anything I can do to help her, I will."

CHAPTER
33

THE GENTLE MUSIC OF A STRING QUARTET FLOATED THROUGH KAT'S ears. Stephen appeared inside her mind, a gentle smile on his lips, his hazel-green eyes on her. He wore his usual leather duster and revolvers, but they didn't seem out of place. He extended a hand toward her in supplication for a dance.

Without hesitating, she took it, and he moved her to the dance floor.

Women dressed in brilliant colors and men in dark suits waltzed around them, but they were only periphery. She had eyes only for Stephen.

He held her close as they danced around the ballroom. Chandeliers twinkled overhead, and the marble floor was smooth beneath their shoes. His hand was firm around her middle while his other hand clasped hers.

The room began to darken. Stephen pulled away. Kat reached for him, but he disappeared at the edge of the room. So did all the other people until, finally, she stood alone in the ballroom. Then the chandeliers went out.

The warmth inside her disappeared, but the music continued to filter through her ears. A cold breeze swept across her body, and she shivered. Cold bands pressed against her wrists and ankles, and something hard pressed against her back.

Kat shifted her head and opened her eyes. She blinked as the room came into view. Windows lined the far wall, filled with green foliage beneath a gray cloud-laden sky.

She blinked again. This was not the room she had been in the last few days. Or was that weeks? How long had her father kept her in the Tower, experimenting on her?

She looked around again. The room was bare and small, its only notable feature the row of windows across from her.

Glancing down, she found herself dressed in a light white gown, the type that patients were usually dressed in before surgery. Metal bands held her wrists against a tilted table. She tried to move her legs, but they were also bound to the table with only a small shelf on which she could stand.

An airship slipped across the upmost part of the windows, blocking the sky for a moment.

She wasn't in the Tower anymore but somewhere on ground level. Where?

The door opened to her right. A young woman walked in with auburn hair piled on top of her head and a pristine white lab coat over her dress.

Kat did a double take. Nicola? Her old schoolmate and rival?

Nicola stopped in front of Kat. She looked every inch like Dr. Bloodmayne's apprentice, contrasting sharply with Kat's own situation and appearance. Nicola continued to stare at her, her gaze trailing over Kat's body until Kat wanted to curl up into a ball to hide. Instead, she lay on the table with her hands and ankles bound, and her cheeks flushed.

"So you're Dr. Bloodmayne's special presentation for the World City council." Nicola let out a quiet laugh. "I must admit I'm a bit surprised. There wasn't much to you at the academy. To think that during all that time you were something special." She tapped her lower lip with a perfect finger. "I look forward to seeing what you can do today."

Special presentation? Kat balled her hands into two tight fists as her heart beat faster. "What do you mean?"

Nicola smiled that not-so-nice smile. "Why, you're the guest of honor for the private exhibition the Tower is holding for the World City council. Not since Dr. Bloodmayne presented the healing serum has the council been this excited about the Tower's research." Kat recoiled as she remembered her father's last words. *She is ready.* Did he mean to push her to her limits in front of the council? Did he really think he had mastered her power?

"Nicola, you can't let him do this!"

A scowl soured Nicola's expression. "Please! My father has no idea what he is doing!" Leaning forward until her face was inches from Kat's, Nicola spoke in a low, confident voice. "I know exactly what kind of man Dr. Bloodmayne is, something you never seemed to realize. He is a genius. The fact that he was able to break the barriers surrounding matter and unlock the power of the universe only proves it. Pity that power was wasted on you."

Kat lunged forward as far as her binds would let her and felt a flicker of satisfaction when Nicola took a hasty step back. "That power you speak of? That power will be his undoing! I have held back as long as I could, but it almost has me. Don't you understand? One more push and I will crack. You do not want to see what lies inside of me!"

Nicola's face grew hard. "You were always dense, Kathryn. Too thick to see beyond the simple science we were taught at the academy. There is so much more out there, but antiquated morality always held us back. Until now. At least Dr. Bloodmayne had the courage to test the limits."

"Some lines should never be crossed!"

"That's what you think. But you will see."

"You don't understand! If Father unleashes the power inside of me, I might . . ."

"Might what?"

Kat swallowed, an image of a large room filled with people going up in blazes filling her mind. It would happen, she knew it. "I might kill everyone here."

Nicola laughed. "No, I don't think so. Do you think Dr.

Bloodmayne is a fool? He has precautions set up. And I heard he stopped you every time at the Tower."

"Don't you understand? I helped! He never stopped the power fully. I did that!"

Nicola crossed her arms. "You do not have enough faith in your father. I do. That is one reason he chose me to work with him, not you."

"Is the specimen ready?" a gruff voice asked behind Kat. She craned her neck to look back, but could see only the edge of the metal table to which she was strapped.

"Yes," Nicola uncrossed her arms, almost purring as she gave Kat a long look. "Dr. Bloodmayne will be pleased. She is already moving toward the emotional state."

A figure came around the table.

Kat felt like she had been dumped into an icy river. That couldn't be Blaylock Sterling! But she knew it was. Those familiar blue eyes, those high cheekbones, that blond hair. Only now rearranged in a grotesque way to cover the ruin of his face.

His eyes lit on her and the blue color turned to a wintery chill. "Kathryn Bloodmayne. I wondered what it would be like to see you again."

"Blaylock Sterling," she whispered, unable to take her eyes off the damaged right side of his face. As if the skin had melted off, leaving behind mottled, distorted flesh. She'd done that to him, the night of the gala. She had burned half his face off.

Kat's hands began to shake. She couldn't stop the growing power inside her any more than she could that night. More people were going to burn. More people were going to look like Blaylock if someone didn't stop this madness.

"Blaylock, I'm sorr—"

He grabbed her by the throat, choking off her words. "Don't say those words to me! Don't you *dare* say those words to me! The only conciliation I have is that you are already paying for what you did." A grin spread across his face, with terrifying effect, as it only let the left side of his face and lips turn upward. "I've enjoyed watching

Dr. Bloodmayne experiment on you. Every cry, every scream—" He stroked her jaw with his thumb. Kat turned away, revolted by his touch. "Almost as if I were the one eliciting them from you."

The shaking moved from her hands to the rest of her body. He moved in closer, his smell a mixture of decaying flesh and antiseptic. "Make sure you show the city council what you can do. Dr. Bloodmayne needs the funding so he can start on me next."

Kat stared at Blaylock, a cold chill erupting across her body. He couldn't be serious. At least she fought the power every time it rose up. Blaylock would do no such thing.

Something like muffled applause came through the walls. Blaylock stepped back and looked beyond her. "It sounds like the council is ready."

"Then let's prepare the patient," Nicola said, pulling out a long white cloth. "We can't have you screaming and disturbing the council, not when Dr. Bloodmayne needs them to allocate more funds for the Tower."

As Nicola leaned over, Kat jerked her head back and forth and yelled.

"Blaylock! Hold her still!" Nicola barked.

Blaylock came around and gripped her cheeks, digging his fingers into her skin. Kat yelled again as Nicola thrust the cloth into her mouth. Blaylock pulled her head forward and Nicola yanked the cloth so tight around her head Kat felt like her jaw would be dislocated.

"There." Nicola stepped back and admired her as if pleased with a painting. "Now the earphones."

Blaylock reached behind the table and a moment later, held up a steel rod shaped like wishbone with small, rubber-covered metal balls at the end of each branch. Kat watched with wide eyes as he placed the device beneath her chin and inserted the balls into her ears.

Nicola nodded, and her voice sounded muffled. "She's ready."

Blaylock stepped back and the two of them disappeared around the metal table. A moment later the table jolted, then began to move.

The wheels beneath gave a muffled creak as they turned her toward the exit. Blaylock reached over and opened the door.

Beyond the door stood about thirty men gathered in a large hall beneath a two-story glass dome. Pillars stood throughout the room, supporting the crisscross of beams two stories up. Leafy plants were stationed beside the pillars. String music played a soft melody on the other side of the room. The outer walls were lined with a handful of guards dressed in dark navy suits with long metal batons and pistols strapped to their sides. A strange scent filled the air, the same one from her father's secret labs back at the Tower. A smoky, sweet scent that seemed to be coming from the long, thin candles set across the front of the platform.

If it were any other time or place, she would have been awed by the architecture of the meeting hall inside the Capitol building. Even in an age of emerging equality, very few women were privy to the inside dealings of the ruling council of World City.

A dozen heads turned her direction. She only recognized a few of the men. John Ashdown, the head councilman, William Sterling, Blaylock's father. A couple more from pictures in the *Herald*.

There was no unease on their faces at the sight of her strapped to a table, no propriety or turning away. Instead, the men studied her with outright curiosity and intellectual aloofness as Nicola and Blaylock wheeled her past them.

Black spots appeared across her vision. No, there was no one here who would help her, no one who would stand up for her. It was like a nightmare, the kind where she couldn't move, couldn't run away. All she could do was watch images unfold while hoping to wake up.

Only this was not a dream, and there was no waking up.

Past the crowd of men was a raised platform on which stood her father and two other men dressed in lab coats. Her father wore his deep green Tower uniform trimmed in gold threading, something he only wore on special occasions. His hair was brushed back in that perfect manner she always remembered. His eyes glowed and a hint of a smile touched his lips as he looked over the men. This was his crowning moment. She could almost read it across his face, and it made her sick.

As Nicola and Blaylock wheeled her around the platform, her father stepped forward. "Welcome, councilmen of World City."

His words were muffled by the earphones, but Kat had no trouble making them out.

"Not too long ago I stood before you and revealed my latest invention, the healing serum. As you know, this serum has already saved many of our soldiers on the battlefield. But what if I told you we could end the war permanently and bring our people back?"

There were whispers among the men. Blaylock and Nicola stopped the table beside Father and his other assistants.

Kat ducked her head, wishing with all her might that she could hide. Instead, she was on display for the elite of World City to see. Her bottom lip trembled beneath the gag and her body broke out in uncontrollable shuddering.

"As some of you know, I've spent over twenty years looking for a way to unlock the power to control matter. Some of you even gave me private funding because you understood what that kind of power could do for World City. No longer would we need factory workers. A handful of people could accomplish what it takes a hundred to do now. We could power our factories simply by moving or combusting matter. Fewer people would mean less labor costs and less coal would mean less smoke hanging over World City.

"Beyond our borders, we could end the war with Austrium. Yes," he said with a nod, "with this kind of power, we could pull airships from the air or crush the enemy lines by manipulating the matter around them. Within days, we could see Austrium retreat and a final victory for World City.

"But let's talk about how this would benefit you personally," he said, raising his hands as a few men starting clapping. "We could change the medical frontier. We could heal bodies by expunging harmful germs or heal broken bones with a thought. Who knows—"

He raised his other hand, passion in his voice. "We might even be able to bring the dead back to life."

"So what exactly is this matter you speak of, and how does it work?" one of the men near the front asked, his arms folded.

Father lowered his hands. "Everything around us is made of matter—the air, this building, even our own bodies. Whoever controls matter controls one of the greatest powers in our world. And whoever controls the controller, well . . ." He laughed and motioned toward Kat. "I think a demonstration is worth more than a thousand words, so let me show you."

He stepped back, his face still toward the crowd. "This woman is my first success in controlling matter."

"Why is she strapped to the table? And gagged?"

Her father glanced back at her. Kat tried to swallow but the cloth stopped her. Sweat beaded her temples, and a cold wave washed over her body. *Please, Father, don't do this!*

"We are still working out some of the complications that come with controlling this kind of power. The woman you see here is strapped to the table for her own safety, but don't be alarmed, we have safeguards ready. The contraption around her head helps us keep her under control, along with the medicine I brought with me." He motioned behind him. "She is the proof I will show you today that a human can possess power over matter, and if I am given more funding, I have more volunteers ready to undergo the treatment . . ."

Kat swerved her head and looked toward the back of the stage. She could barely see the table that stood behind them. The light from a nearby gas lamp glinted off several rows of glass syringes.

The sedatives. Or were they the hallucinogens?

She breathed through her nose as a red haze spread across her vision, almost obscuring the councilmen and all but silencing her father's speech. How could these men be a part of this? How could they let her father do this to her?

Because they didn't see her as human.

They were here for a means to an end. They had goals for this city, and, if her father were right, what he revealed today would help them further their agenda, including the war with Austrium. As long as it didn't hurt them personally, they were willing to do anything—expend anyone—to achieve those goals.

Her humiliation began to morph into something darker. The coldness from moments before disappeared in the sudden heat that surged through her body. She uncurled her fingers, her breath coming fast. If it was a show they wanted . . .

Her palms began to burn.

A hush spread over the crowd. Kat glanced to her right. Small flames flickered around her hand. She could do it. She could just let go and show them what she could really do—

She closed her eyes, barely holding back the dark power erupting inside of her. She panted against the gag and closed her hand into a fist, willing the fire to disappear.

"As you can see, igniting matter is but one of her abilities," Father said above her.

"That wasn't much of a demonstration," one of the men called out.

Kat opened her eyes and glared at the councilman who had spoken. She could feel her connection to every cell in his body, could feel his blood pumping, almost hear his every thought. All she had to do was close off that small gap inside his throat, pull the cells together and block off the air—

The man fell to his knees, his hands around his throat. The other men around him took a couple hasty steps back.

"That's enough, Kathryn."

Kat barely heard her father as she gasped at her own action. *No, I can't go there!* She squeezed her eyes shut. She heard the man take in deep draughts of air and stumble across the floor.

"As you can see, with the power of matter under her control, she can ignite things, tamper with the human body, or move things with her mind."

"And how will you control her? What stops her from doing that to all of us?"

"I'll show you. Kathryn, please move something."

Kat turned away and stared up at the glass dome. She felt like she was in those deep, dark waters, drowning again. If she let go and sank beneath, would Father really be able to stop her? Deep inside, she knew the answer. No. The power was too strong.

"Don't do it, Father," she whispered, her words coming out muffled through the gag. An airship moved across the glass, blocking the sky for a couple of seconds. She had to delay as long as possible, keep the monster trapped inside of her, at least until she blacked out like she had in the past.

But something told her it wouldn't happen this time. The monster had grown too strong under her father's experiments.

Something pinched her arm. She glanced to the side and caught sight of a needle withdrawing from her upper arm. A hallucinogen.

"You'll do it, one way or another, Kathryn," Father said quietly as he pulled away. "I need you to do this."

"Father, please . . ."

Her vision darkened. She stood in a dim corridor with windows lined up along one side. Rain pelted against the glass. Paintings hung along the other wall. Paintings of the Bloodmayne family. The door opened at the far end, and a figure walked in.

"Kathryn Bloodmayne." Blaylock's voice sent a shiver down her back.

The figure shambled along the runner toward her. His face came into view along the farthest window. "I've never kissed a smart girl before." His deformed lips turned upward and the skin below his right eye crinkled into a gruesome display.

"It's not real," she whispered.

Blaylock made his way down the hall toward her.

"Wake up, Kat!" she said breathlessly. "Father injected you with something. Just wake—"

Blaylock stretched out his hand.

Kat screamed. The paintings trembled, then shook harder. The first one shot across the room, right in front of Blaylock. Another one followed, and another, until Kat had pulled every single one from the walls, using them to block Blaylock from her view.

The corridor faded. So did the windows, and the paintings. A painful coldness rushed through her veins, forcing the images away. Kat blinked her eyes. There was a loud clatter in front of her. Glancing down, she found a pile of paintings, with their ornate golden frames, in a heap on the platform.

"Good, very good." Her father stood beside her, his face toward the audience. "What you just witnessed is the subject controlling the matter in this room. Remember, all things are made of matter, even the air. With just her mind, she was able to pull the paintings from the walls and place them here. Think of what our men could do if they had that kind of power. They could stop a motorwagon, ignite a platoon, or even pull an airship from the sky."

Kat barely heard her father's words. Her breath halted and her eyes flew open. Something cracked inside of her. The power she had held back for so long rushed through her, lifting her from the table. It burned away the coldness, pumping her veins with a heat so intense she cried out in pain.

Her father turned toward her as Nicola sidled up beside him. "Dr. Bloodmayne, do you want a syringe?"

He held up his hand. "Let me talk to her first. I'm not ready to halt the presentation yet. We need at least one more display." He approached her. "Kathryn, stop now."

Kat slipped beneath the dark waves of her mind and a different voice emerged from her mouth. It laughed that cold, hard laugh.

"Kathryn," her father said as he held up a small rectangular box. The cable emerging from the box was the same black and thickness as the one attached to the earphones around her head. His finger hovered over a metal switch. "I will stop you if I have to."

She glared back. The power connected her to every particle in the room and continued to expand. She could feel the Capitol building, every brick, every ounce of mortar, every heart beating. And the power continued to expand. Farther, farther. She could feel it all. Every single particle within World City.

A crackle erupted inside the earphones, followed by the familiar high-pitched whistle. This time she was ready for it.

The monster roared and extended its claws beneath her arms and legs. With a powered thrust, it broke the metal manacles that held her to the table and ripped the earphones off.

Her father took a step back and dropped the box. "Bring me the syringes. Now!"

"Yes, doctor." Nicola raced across the platform while snapping orders to the assistants nearby.

Kat raised herself off the platform and stepped down from the small ledge as another laugh bubbled up her throat. With one hard thrust, she tore the gag from her mouth. They were mistaken if they thought they could take her now.

The lab assistants hurried across the floor with syringes in hand while Blaylock hovered nearby, his gaze dancing between her and her father.

"Kathryn, I'm warning you!"

Kat waved her hand and the syringes flew from the assistants' hands and against the wall, hitting first with the needle, and quivering at that point. Her lips curled into a smile as she gazed back at the table full of needles. With another wave, all the syringes rose into the air and shot across the room, hitting the wall with a dozen pings, leaving them trembling like darts.

She turned her attention back to her father, then to the crowd. "You want to see power? You want to see what I can do?" She raised her hands and flicked her fingers wide open. Flames erupted around her palms. "Then I'll show you!"

CHAPTER
34

"I THOUGHT YOU SAID YOU COULD CONTROL HER!" ONE OF THE councilmen yelled.

"Emerson, Blaylock, get those syringes!"

The panic in her father's voice sent a shiver of delight through Kat. She turned her attention to the assistants. "I don't think so." Kat clenched her right hand into a fist. Emerson and Blaylock froze in mid-run.

John Ashdown raised his hand and pointed at her. "Shoot her!"

Around the room, the guards drew their guns and shot. Without releasing her hand, Kat arrested every bullet in midair. She laughed at the incredulous looks on the councilmen's faces. "Aren't you impressed? After all, this is what you wanted, isn't it? Someone with power like this—"

She sent the bullets toward the syringes. With loud pops, the glass vials exploded, splattering their clear liquid against the wall and floor.

More shots erupted around the room. Bullets hurtled toward her, but it was as if she were watching leaves float in the breeze. She caught each one and sent them toward the walls.

"Kathryn, stop now!"

A shudder went up her spine and anger burst inside her. Kat swirled around. She glared at her father. "There is an old story Ms. Stuart once read to me about a man who wished to create the ultimate person. Instead, he created a monster, and that monster burned him alive. Moral of the story?: Be careful what you create, or you might awaken a monster."

Dr. Bloodmayne raised his hands in a placating gesture. "Now just calm down, Kathryn."

Kat sneered. "Did you tell these men why you really created me? Do they know about my mother's body you have preserved back at the Tower? Or you—" She looked at John Ashdown and the other council members. "I know the real reason you want this power. You started the war with Austrium." A couple of them turned and looked at each other. "Yes, I see your minds, like electrical impulses, and I can read each one. How many people did you send across the Narrow Strait? How many people have died so you could expand your little empire?"

The blood whooshed inside her veins at dizzying speed. Faces flashed across her mind: Captain Grim, Dr. Emmett, the soldiers at the base. Stephen. Each one affected or hurt by the war. The flames grew around her hands until it looked like she was holding two balls of fire. She glared at the men. "You were hoping to use this power inside me to accomplish your goals, but you cannot control me. No one can control me!" She laughed and raised her hands.

"God help us!" William Sterling yelled. "The woman's gone crazy!"

The monster hesitated, and the real Kat emerged. She looked around the room then glanced at her hands. Shock filled her being. She could almost see the claws of the monster extending beyond her own fingers. "Yes," she whispered, horrified. "God, help m—"

She gasped as the monster pulled her back under.

"Kathryn, this is not you!"

She swung her head toward her father. "What do you know about me? You were never there! And that Kat you think you know? Soon she will longer exist! You killed her! With every experiment, with every day you were absent from her life." She raised her hands again. "Now only I exist. Isn't that what you wanted, Father? Power? Shame you never treated the other Kat better. Maybe she would have shared it with you. Then again"—she gazed at her hands—"Maybe not. I think I shall use fire. I do like igniting things . . ."

She turned toward the drapes that framed the windows surrounding the hall. One by one they burst into flames. The men shouted and started for the doors, but Kat raised her hand and a wall of fire appeared in front of each exit. She laughed.

Her father stared at her with a disapproving frown. Her lips twisted into a snarl and she brought her hands up in front of her. All she had ever wanted was for him to look at her and see her. Now that desire was gone. He no longer mattered. Father would never hold her captive again. He would never disappoint her.

A vortex of flame began to swirl around her. She would take him out. She would take them all out. Smoke billowed through the room as the smell of burnt fabric filled the air. The men rushed toward the middle of the hall as the flames grew along the perimeter.

Kat gathered all the matter inside the room, then shot her hands into the air. The glass dome above exploded into a thousand shards. The debris rained down on the screaming men. She would destroy them first, then the building.

Then she would set all of World City on fire.

CHAPTER

35

Lightning flashed overhead. Stephen drew up the collar of his duster and gazed up at the topmost part of the Tower. It had been a half hour, and still Miss Fealy had not returned. Had something gone wrong? Had she been caught? Could she not find Dr. Latimer's machine?

A horse-drawn carriage rode by, followed by a sleek phaeton. Across the street, a man emerged from the Tower, dressed in the standard lab coat. He headed for one of the outlying buildings.

As the sky grew darker, lights appeared in the windows along the multi-stories, all except for the very top. Those windows remained dark.

Dr. Latimer coughed beside him and readjusted his coat. Neither man spoke.

Boom!

Stephen whipped his head around, searching for the explosion. His eyes traveled from building to building to the left, then up along the rooftops. There. A plume of smoke, darker than the clouds overhead, churned toward the sky.

"That's not good," Dr. Latimer muttered beside him. "If I'm not mistaken, that smoke is coming from somewhere near the Capitol building."

Explosion. Smoke. Possible fire. All near the Capitol building.

Kat.

Blazes! Were they too late?

Another figure appeared in the doorway of the Tower just as lightning flashed above. Stephen let out a long breath as Miss Fealy scurried across the courtyard with something wrapped in a dark cloth in her arms. He stepped toward the street curb and hailed her. After looking both ways, she darted across the street.

"Here you are," Miss Fealy said, panting. "I had to wait until the floor was empty, then I had to find the switch that turned off the device."

Dr. Latimer took the contraption from Miss Fealy and peered under the dark cloth. "Yes, this is it. Thank you."

Stephen turned in the direction of the Capitol building. "Our apologies, Miss Fealy, but we need to leave now."

"I'm coming with you."

What the—Stephen swung around. "We don't have time."

"I still have my Tower pass. It might help get you into the private exhibit."

Stephen and Dr. Latimer glanced at each other. If that explosion had indeed come from Kat, getting into the exhibit probably wouldn't be a problem. But they couldn't waste any more time. Besides, police and firefighters were sure to start showing up and asking questions. Her pass could come in handy then.

"All right. But keep up." Without waiting, Stephen took off down the block at a brisk pace. He would be running right now, but he doubted Dr. Latimer could jog with that device of his, and Miss Fealy was likely to trip in her long skirt.

The three made their way along the street. Minutes later the sky opened up in sheets of rain. Stephen wiped the water from his face and continued. Bells started clanging in the distance. Each blare made his stomach tighten until it was a firm knot inside his middle.

They turned after three blocks and headed north. Ahead, wreathed in smoke and steam, stood the Capitol building in all its architectural glory. Two stories high, with lavish molding and circular metal designs along the railings and windows, it rivaled the Tower as one of the most spectacular buildings in World City. A wide case of stairs, the length of the façade, let up to the grand portico itself. Rain pounded the stairs, and a river of rainwater ran along either side. The entrance was empty. Not surprising given the downpour. No fire engines yet either, or one of the older water carts. Or any policemen.

Stephen nodded. Good. The last thing they needed was an audience witnessing scary-Kat going all-powerful.

Stephen reached the steps and took them two at a time until he reached the massive set of oak double doors. No guards greeted them at the entryway. He paused. There should be someone here admitting people inside.

Lightning flashed behind him and thunder rolled across the city seconds later. Stephen wiped his face again and looked around, then pressed down on the metal handle on the right.

Dr. Latimer came up beside him, panting and clutching his awkward bundle. "Where are the guards?"

"I don't know, but I don't like it"

Stephen pushed the door open. A long marble hallway greeted them. The ceiling above consisted of interlaced metal rods and glass. A light haze of smoke diffused the pale light in the hallway, creating an otherworldly glow, and the sound of rain pelting the window-panes echoed throughout the empty corridor.

"Where is everybody?" Miss Fealy asked, her soprano voice reverberating through the hallway.

Stephen shook his head, but his senses screamed that something wasn't right. The Capitol building should be bustling with activity, even on a stormy day like this. Unless the council had dismissed everyone for the private exhibit.

Maybe they had.

He stepped inside and drew out one of his guns. The air was tainted with smoke. He squinted and stared down the corridor. The light haze was thicker at the end near the set of double doors that led into the dome area. On closer inspection, he spotted more smoke, darker, seeping through the crack below the doors.

He started down the hall, dread weighing in his stomach. The closer he drew to the doors, the more the silence pressed in on him. If there were an exhibit going on inside the dome, there should be an announcer or conversation or applause. Anything.

Halfway down the hall lightning streaked over the glass ceiling, followed closely by a deafening crack of thunder. Stephen jumped, Miss Fealy gasped, and Dr. Latimer glared up at the sky.

Stephen took a couple deep breaths through his nose and steadied himself. This weather was not helping the mood.

Once he reached the doors, he paused. He stared at the smooth wood, his heart racing inside his chest. Images of what he might find flashed across his mind. Kat being experimented on for a room full of councilmen. Kat losing control and shooting fire everywhere. Kat throwing the men and guards against the walls.

He swallowed, an empty feeling in the pit of his stomach. Time to find out.

Stephen opened the door, his gun ready.

CHAPTER

36

SMOKE BILLOWED OUT OF THE DOOR THE MOMENT HE OPENED IT. Stephen coughed and stepped back. His eyes watered from the noxious fumes. Moments later, the air cleared a little, but the meeting room was still full of the dark haze. There were no gas lamps lit and no lights. His sense of foreboding skyrocketed.

He tucked his head inside his elbow and proceeded forward. It was more terrible than anything he had pictured. Just inside, the scent of burnt flesh and fragrant incense filled his nostrils. Stephen gagged against his leather duster. It was like that rotten-meat smell from the secret labs up in the Tower, only worse. Much worse.

Someone retched behind him, and there was more coughing.

Stephen blinked and looked ahead, keeping his nose firmly pressed into his elbow. Smoke filled the cavernous room and flames still burned around the perimeter. He couldn't see past the first set of columns toward the middle where the assembly would be.

"I don't like the look of this," Dr. Latimer said as he came up beside Stephen, his voice muffled behind the handkerchief he held to his nose, his face pale. "And I recognize that scent. Not the"—he swallowed—"burnt smell, but the other. It's the mixture of herbs Alexander would burn during his most contemptible experiments."

There was a gasp behind him. Stephen glanced back. "Miss Fealy, I think you should stay there for now."

She nodded, holding a lace handkerchief to her face.

Stephen grimaced, his mouth dry. He felt the same way he did that one time he'd had to investigate a brutal murder down in Southbrook. That nauseous, chilly feeling.

He forced himself to move forward. *Just get it over with, Grey. Best to find out what happened and deal with it.*

As the smoke cleared, he could see ahead. A pile of dark lumps lay in a mound below the remains of the glass dome. Rain poured down from the broken glass above.

As he drew closer, the lumps began to take shape, with small spirals of smoke and steam rising from the pile.

They were—he recoiled.

They were bodies.

His hand began to shake and he glanced this way and that. Where was Kat? A wave of dizziness rushed over him. He stopped until the spell passed and his vision cleared. His heart beat with heavy thuds. Did she do this?

There were more bodies scattered on the other side of the circle of pillars, and a couple more on a platform that had been set up. An angled metal table stood on the platform with metal bands where a person's wrists and ankles could be secured, only the metal bands looked as if they had been melted away.

Stephen glanced at the bodies. They were burned so badly there was no indication as to who was who. Just charred human figures. But he could wager who they were. The World City council.

Dr. Latimer came and stood silently beside him. The rain sizzled as it fell upon the bodies. "I had no idea . . ." He shook his head. "No one deserves this. Not even them."

Stephen stiffened. He wasn't so sure about that. These men had poked and prodded Kat like she was something less than human until they finally unleashed the monster inside her. Did they really think they could let loose something so powerful and not be scathed?

He looked up. "Kat?" he said quietly. A fire popped and fizzled nearby. He stepped out into the open and around the bodies. The rain had turned into a gentle drizzle. "Kat?"

Something stirred just off the edge of the platform. Stephen brought his gun up.

"What do you want?" It was Kat's voice, but in a tone he had never heard before. The figure staggered past the platform into the circle of light shaped by the glass dome above. It was Kat all right, but the wrong Kat. Her long dark hair hung in wild tendrils around her face and past her shoulders. She was dressed in a simple white gown that resembled a pillowcase with holes for the arms and legs. Her skin was pale, like a ghost. "Why are you here?"

"Kat, it's me, Stephen."

"I don't want to be around people right now."

She started to turn. Stephen holstered his weapon and stepped toward her.

She spun around, a ball of fire forming around her palm. "I said leave me alone!"

"Do you remember me?" Stephen slowly took one step toward her, then another.

Her face crinkled, almost like a lost child's. Then it morphed back into that hard look. "No. Now leave."

His heart thundered inside his chest. He had seen what this Kat could do. But he had to get through to her—find the other Kat inside. "I won't leave you. I promised myself I would never leave you again."

That same lost look came back, and it broke something inside of him.

"Gently," Dr. Latimer whispered behind him. "We don't want to provoke her, not if we hope to help her."

Stephen nodded slightly, his eyes fixed on Kat. He had broken through to her once before back on the *Lancelot* when the airship was going down. Maybe he could do it again if there was any part of her old self left.

He continued toward Kat. She lifted her hand, the flames growing around her palm, and snarled at him. "I said *leave!*"

"No." Only a few more steps. "Kat, I know you're in there. You can fight this."

She growled and extended her hand. "That Kat is dead. I killed her!"

"I don't believe you." Stephen reached past her flaming hand and cupped her cheeks with both hands. The fire from her palm singed his elbow, causing his leather duster to smell like burning hair. "Kat, look at me."

Fierce dark eyes stared back.

Please, God, let her still be in there.

The air began to churn around them and the fire blazed up from her palm. He could feel the heat, like a furnace along his left side.

"Kat," he whispered.

Her pupils dilated. Her brow furrowed. A spark of recognition flashed across her eyes. "Stephen?"

"Yes." His body exploded in adrenaline, shoving aside the burning throb of his burnt elbow. "I'm here."

Her face crinkled. "I—I'm almost gone. I can't feel anything anymore. My soul—it's barely alive." She grabbed his forearms. "You need to do it. You need to shoot me before . . ." Her eyes went wide as she glanced past his face. A look of horror spread across her features. She let go of his arms. "What have I—" She clawed at her cheeks. "God, what have I done?"

She let out a gurgled scream and her eyes rolled up into her head. Her back arched, her head shot up, and her hands fell to her sides.

"Quick!" Dr. Latimer appeared beside Stephen with the device in his hands. "We need to do it now, before she goes back under!"

"Tell me what to do."

"Place her on the floor." Dr. Latimer looked back. "Miss Fealy, I will need your assistance."

Stephen placed his hand on Kat's back, his other on her midsection, intending to lower her to the ground. Instead, he found her as stiff as a board. Her eyes continued to roll inside their sockets and a trickle of blood appeared below her left nostril.

He switched tactics and scooped her up. Her body would not bend, but at least he could get her to the floor.

"Wait," Dr. Latimer said. He looked around at the puddles that had formed everywhere under the missing dome, as if seeing them for the first time. "Over there." He pointed to a dry area along the perimeter.

"What the blazes difference does it make?"

"There is no time to waste, Mr. Grey!"

Exasperated, Stephen did as the man asked and set Kat on the dry floor. A small fire burned nearby, oddly comfortable as it warmed his wet skin.

Miss Fealy appeared at Dr. Latimer's side, her face and lips pale. "Did Kat do this?"

"Focus, Miss Fealy." Dr. Latimer removed the cover from the device and placed the cylinder down on the ground beside Kat. "Time enough for that later."

He turned a knob in the back, and an arc of electricity shot around the cylinder, followed by a hum.

Kat had gone slack the moment she touched the ground. Slowly, she opened her eyes. "Stephen?"

He grabbed her hands, both chilled as ice.

The color drained from her face, leaving behind a cool, blue hue. "Y—you came back for me."

"Yes." He rubbed her knuckles, his stomach churning. As he watched, her lips grew pale. "I came back for you. I—Kat, I love you." He didn't know where the words came from, only that they were all he could think of as he watched her slip away.

Her face changed. "You love . . . me?" She went rigid.

"Dr. Latimer!"

"I'm going as fast as I can!"

She looked at Stephen, her breathing erratic, sweat beading her colorless face. "I don't know . . . how much longer . . . I can hold back. There is nothing left inside of me now—except for the monster. It wants out. It wants control!"

Stephen bent over her and looked into her eyes, her frozen hands still inside his. "Focus, Kat. Dr. Latimer is here. We're going to save you."

First one tear, then another rolled down her cheeks. "I . . . will try."

"Just look at me." She stared back. He had forgotten how beautiful her eyes were. "That's it. When this is done, we'll have a whole new life ahead of us."

"You mean together?"

"Yes."

She closed her eyes. "I would like that." Moments later, her body began to convulse.

Stephen's heart went into double beat. "Dr. Latimer! She's regressing! We need to do it now!"

"Make sure you're not touching her!" Dr. Latimer pulled the strange electric device nearer Kat. "I've never done this without opening the chest."

Stephen stared at him, horrified. "Open? You mean—?"

"I'm going to try and restart her heart without actually touching her physical heart. Miss Fealy, I need you to expose her chest."

"Doctor?"

"Remove the gown around her chest. I need to use the rods directly on her skin, in the middle of her chest and along her left ribcage. You've seen a surgical theater, correct?"

Miss Fealy nodded.

"Same thing. I will be performing something like an operation."

Miss Fealy looked at Kat and squared her shoulders. She went down on her knees and with the material between her fingers, tore the gown down the middle.

Stephen kept his gaze on Dr. Latimer as the doctor removed two long wires from the cylinder. At the end of each wire was a thin brass rod, like two small batons, which he held gingerly by their small handles. Electricity crackled across the larger cylinder behind them.

"She's ready, Doctor." Miss Fealy's voice was breathless as she pulled back. "I've kept her as modest as I can."

"All right, nobody touch Miss Bloodmayne, or you will be shocked as well. I am going to stop her heart first, then hopefully revive it."

Miss Fealy's head shot up. "You're going to stop her heart?"

"Yes. Then revive it."

Miss Fealy opened her mouth as if to argue.

"There is no time to debate, Miss Fealy. You must trust me."

Miss Fealy pressed her lips together in a fine line and nodded.

Dr. Latimer took a deep breath, then pressed the two batons to Kat's skin. Her whole body jumped into the air, then fell with a thud. Her head sagged to the side and lay still.

Dr. Latimer held the wires and batons back, keeping them well apart. "Miss Fealy, check her pulse."

The way Miss Fealy looked, Stephen was almost sure she would faint any moment. She placed her fingers along Kat's neck for a couple seconds. Her head dropped. "There is no pulse." She sniffed and adjusted the material across Kat's chest.

"Now, we wait." Dr. Latimer looked gray but resolute. "If my hypothesis is correct, her condition is a result of being pulled out of our element, our plane of existence, if you will. And given what I know of Dr. Bloodmayne's experiments, it was caused by death in the first place. So another kind of death should hopefully shift her back."

"Will it undo the damage that's been done to her soul?" Stephen asked.

Dr. Latimer sighed. "I don't know. Souls are God's province, not mine. If her soul is truly dead, then only God can bring her back to life. My only hope is to reset her physical body back into our world."

"And what if this doesn't work?"

"Then I revive her, and I will continue to study her condition with what limited time we have left." He gave Stephen a frank look. "That is, if I *can* revive her. I was only in the experimental stage of this process and never used it to stop a heart, only to start a heart."

Stephen stared down at Kat. Every tick from a clock nearby marked off Kat's life. His fingers slowly curled up across the floor. The rain had stopped, but the air still held that awful smell of burnt flesh and incense. Bells rang far away. They didn't have much time before either the firemen or police arrived.

Just when he thought he would go mad with waiting, Dr. Latimer moved. "All right." He brought the small, slender brass batons out. "Time to revive her. Make sure you're not touching her."

Stephen clenched his hands, his knees numb beneath him. *God, please let this work. Let Kat be all right.* He continued to chant those words as Dr. Latimer placed the batons across Kat's chest.

Her body bounced, then fell back to the ground. Everyone waited. She did not move.

Stephen dug his fingernails into his palms. *Please, God, please!*

Dr. Latimer waited, sweat beading along his forehead. "Again." The cylinder gave off a crackle as the batons touched Kat's skin. Her body jolted, then flopped to the ground.

There was a pause. Miss Fealy pressed her fingers to Kat's throat and shook her head.

"Again."

Stephen stood and walked away. His whole body shook with adrenaline and grief. His gaze fell on the bodies still smoldering in the middle of the vast room. He knew he should feel appalled by the violent death these men had succumbed to, but he was too angry.

Instead, he turned toward one of the pillars and, with a raised fist, hit the marble with all his might. "It's not fair!" he shouted. He slammed his fist again. "She didn't deserve this! Out of everyone, Kat was innocent. She shouldn't have to pay for what her father did to her! They drove her to this! And now . . ."

He sank to the floor, his throat tight. He squeezed his eyes shut as he heard Dr. Latimer say "again." He had never cried before. Not at his parent's graves, not at Aunt Milly's. But this time something broke past the walls he surrounded himself with and a single tear trickled down his cheek.

He looked up at the shattered glass dome. *Please, God. Don't let me live through another death. Please save Kat. You're the only one who can.*

CHAPTER
37

UNLIKE HER OTHER DREAMS, WHERE SHE WAS STRUGGLING, drowning in dark waters, this time she was already at the bottom. Total darkness eclipsed Kat's vision. She no longer breathed, no longer felt anything. She couldn't hear or see anything either. Was this death? Was her body finally dead? Or did her body still rampage on without her, and this was where deceased souls like hers went? To a place of nothingness?

But then why could she still think?

She was neither cold nor hot. She was . . . nothing. Nothing but thoughts.

Awake.

She looked up into the nothingness.

Awake, O sleeper.

Awake? Was she only dreaming? She closed her eyes. At least, it felt like she was closing her eyes. *Right. Time to wake up.* She focused on that thought. *Wake up, Kat! You're only dreaming.*

The darkness persisted.

Come on, Kat, you've fought this darkness before. You can do it again. Wake up!

Nothing.

Awake, O sleeper. Rise up from the dead.

That voice again. Like a tenor and bass rolling together. And those words. She knew them from somewhere . . .

That slip of paper inside the main medical tent. What did it say? Something about awakening, rising from the dead, and God's light. But why was she thinking about that now? Or was someone else here with her saying those words? She turned her head to and fro, but only darkness filled her vision.

Awake, O sleeper, rise up from the dead, and I will give you light.

"Who's there? Who's speaking to me? How do I wake up? Or am I—am I dead?" There was no echo to her voice, no bouncing of sound. As if she were in a wide-open space here in the darkness.

Your soul is dead. The words were spoken in gentle, somber tones—the voice that commanded her to rise up—not in the harsh cruelty of the monster.

My soul . . . is dead. Kat swallowed. Then it had finally happened. That last episode had been her final one. Everything—hope, will, determination—drained away. No matter how hard she had fought, she had lost in the end. She lifted a hand and wiped her cheek, then looked up into the dark abyss. "Who are you?"

I am the One who can awaken you. I am the One who can give you light.

Light. That one word spurred a deep longing inside her. More than anything she wanted light. Just to see again. Breathe again. Have life again. "I want that light," she whispered. "I don't want to be like this anymore." But wasn't it too late? Didn't the voice just say she was dead?

Then I will give it to you. It is time to awaken, child. It is time to rise up from the dead. Your soul was never meant to exist in a place like this.

A place like this? Did the voice mean outside of life, like Dr. Latimer had said? *I was never meant to exist here.*

In answer, a small pinprick of light appeared above her body.

Here is my light for your darkness.

The light expanded like a ball of white fire until she was bathed in it. There was nothing but bright light all around her. The warmth from the rays filled her being until something shifted inside her. A piercing heat entered her heart, so intense it took her breath away. It felt like all the broken parts inside were welding back together, piece by piece.

The light culminated in a blaze of heat and blinding brightness, forcing her eyes shut.

Thump. Thump.

Her heart beat again.

Her eyes fluttered open, and she pressed her hand to her chest. Her heart throbbed steadily beneath her fingertips. All around her, the light blazed with white intensity. "I'm alive," she whispered. She sucked in a quiet breath and savored the feel. *I'm alive!* Every touch, every sensation confirmed she was no longer dead inside. For the first time in a long time, she could feel again. No more numbness, no more darkness.

But what about the monster?

Her eyes widened. While holding her breath, she sank deep inside herself and searched for that dark presence. Nothing. She no longer sensed the other Kat or the taint that had hung like a shroud across her soul. The monster no longer waited inside her. It was gone, as if it had been burned up within the blazing light.

She looked up, then shied away from the intense glow. Was this real? Or was this place like the dark whirlpool from her dreams, just some vision inside her mind?

No. She breathed in deeply, relishing in the feel of her heartbeat. It was real, as real as the connection she had felt with matter. She couldn't see it, only feel it.

Awake, O sleeper, rise up from the dead, and God will give you light.

Those words again from that scrap of paper. That voice from moments ago spoke those same words.

Her heart gave a warble inside her and she clutched her hand to her chest. If that was what had just happened to her, if those words were really true, then . . .

She swallowed hard. This light around her, and the life now beating inside her, it had come from him.

From God.

She dared not look up again, but kept her hand where it was, next to her heart. Fear and awe waged war inside her. He had heard her. Her entire being tingled. He had *heard* her. Her cries for help had not been in vain. "Thank You," she whispered, her throat choked up. At the last moment, when she had lost everything, He had come for her.

The light began to pull away, but instead of leaving her in darkness, it drew her with it. She felt like she was drifting back toward reality, as if she were waking from a long, restful slumber. Only this time she was waking up a new woman.

CHAPTER
38

"AGAIN—WAIT."

The pure light morphed into a stormy gray. Kat groaned. She could feel her heart all right. It felt like it had been kicked by a horse and trampled on.

"She's awake!" Something heavy and coarse settled over the top half of her body, shielding her bare skin from the cold air.

She blinked and groaned again, placing a hand over her aching chest. The area around her was dark except for the pale light to her left streaming down from a hole in the ceiling.

Two people knelt beside her. She blinked. "Dr. Latimer?"

He nodded, his eyes bright. "Yes. How do you feel?"

She winced and closed her eyes. Tears welled up behind her eyelids. How could she summon up everything she felt at the moment? Tired, weak, yet strong and brimming with life.

"Kat?"

Her eyes shot open and she glanced to her right. A young woman with carrot-colored hair and a stained white lab coat knelt beside her. Her mouth opened and closed. "Marianne?" She brushed her forehead. "Perhaps I'm still dreaming."

"No." Marianne gave out a gurgled laugh. "It's me."

"But how . . . ?"

"It's a long story. I came with Dr. Latimer and Mr. Grey. We came to rescue you."

"Rescue me?"

"Let me help you put that coat on. You'll catch a chill in just that gown."

Dr. Latimer looked away as Marianne helped her sit up and pull the coat over her torn gown. Kat barely noticed. Like one of those new slide projectors, the last few days flashed across her mind, whipping through her memories at a frenzy pace of color and sound. Strapped to a metal table inside her father's private laboratories, presented before the World City Council, then . . .

The monster.

Kat straightened up and looked around her. "What happened?" Bit by bit, her eyes adjusted to the gloominess of the room. The air was filled with the acrid scent of smoke and burnt flesh. In the darkest corners, embers glowed with a deep red light. And in the middle, where pale light streamed down from the broken glass ceiling . . .

A sudden coldness hit her, chilling her from the inside out and washing away the euphoria from moments ago. As her gaze passed over each smoldering body, each charred figure, the chill inside her intensified. She had finally done it. The monster inside of her had unleashed its full power.

She hunched over as dizziness swept through her body, causing her stomach to revolt. "I never wanted to hurt anyone. But I—I couldn't control it." She pressed a cold hand to her face. "What have I done?" *Oh, God, what have I done? You healed me, but this . . .*

A figure knelt before her and lifted her chin with two fingers. A face she had come to love looked back. "Stephen," she whispered.

"Kat."

They stared at each other, the gentle sound of pattering rain nearby. Then Kat scrambled onto her knees, grabbed the front of his duster, and pressed her face into his shirt. Elation and grief mingled inside of her. She was finally free of the monster, but the cost had been great.

"I'm cured," she said with a sob. "He cured me."

Stephen rubbed her back. "I know. I watched Dr. Latim—"

"No. God did. He heard me, and He healed my soul. There's no more monster inside me. But . . ."

She lifted her face and looked to her left at the wreckage the monster had wrought. "I never wanted to harm anyone. Never! I wanted to help people. And Father . . ." She glanced toward the platform, her throat tight, her stomach quivering. "He hurt me exceedingly. And yet I still desired . . ." Her voice faltered and a sob clutched her throat. "I just wanted to be his daughter. And that will never happen now."

Kat pressed her face into Stephen's shoulder and cried. She cried for the little girl who would never be loved by her father. She cried for the tortured woman who lashed out. And she cried for the living soul inside her, a soul reborn of tragedy, but a new creation nevertheless.

There was a crashing sound behind her and shouts and gasps. Out of the corner of her eye, she saw Dr. Latimer stand and walk away. Marianne followed shortly afterward. Voices rose and fell with questions. She heard Dr. Latimer say something about an accident during the exhibition and that there was only one survivor.

Kat sat there with Stephen, her head pressed to his chest. She had stopped crying and now only listened.

"Stephen!" a man said above her. "What in the world are you doing here?"

"Patrick!" Stephen's voice rumbled through his chest. "I'm so glad to see you. Are you the officer in charge here?"

"I am. Blazes, Stephen, what happened here? This place looks like a war zone. And the city council . . ."

Stephen sighed. "It's a long story."

"So you know what happened?"

"I do."

"And the woman, is she the survivor?"

Kat never looked up.

"Yes."

"Well, you know the procedure, Stephen. We'll have to take both of you in for questioning, along with the other man and woman here."

"Very well, but I will accompany her during her questioning," Stephen said. "This woman is my client."

"Why am I not surprised? You always did find a way to be in the middle of things." Patrick sighed. "What a mess."

Kat tugged the coat that covered her closer and shivered.

Stephen pulled back and rose. "Let's get you to a warmer place."

Kat nodded, her senses dull from all the stimulation earlier. Stephen helped her to her feet. She kept the coat tightly wrapped around her frame, her bare feet chilled against the marble floor.

"Stephen, I need her brought to the precinct for questioning. This cannot wait. You understand."

"Yes."

"I'll send a couple officers with you," Patrick said. "As for the other lady and the doctor, I will send them shortly." He turned and started giving orders to the other police officers.

Stephen led Kat past the throng of policemen, many of whom acknowledged Stephen, past the firemen working on the few blazes, and past a reporter from the *Herald*. Outside, he hailed a cab and helped her inside.

Kat sank into the leather seat and propped her back against the corner. Part of her wanted to fall asleep and never wake up. Another part of her wanted to hide from all the people gathering outside the cab window.

How could she move past what she had done? And what would happen to her now? She had single-handedly murdered the entire city council.

It wasn't my fault. I couldn't control it.

But how could she prove it? Then again, who would even believe she had done it in the first place?

"I can tell what you're thinking. Your eyebrows are creased and your eyes are unfocused."

Kat glanced at Stephen.

"You're thinking about what happens next, aren't you?"

Did Stephen really know her that well? "Yes." Her gut clenched at all the possibilities. Would she be convicted of murder? Sentenced to prison? Or worse?

"One step at a time, Kat. One step at a time. As Dr. Latimer told the officer, it was an accident. And it was," he said, pressing a finger to her lips when she opened them to protest. "Right now, let us be thankful that you are alive and healed."

Kat paused. Stephen was right. All the tension left her body and her shoulders dropped. The taint across her soul was gone. She was a new woman. No matter what happened, inside she was free.

Nothing could touch that.

"And I'll be with you through the whole process."

His words struck a chord deep inside her being. Kat sucked in her lips. She wasn't going to cry. Instead, she looked out the window and felt him give her hand a tight squeeze.

Whatever happened next, she would not be facing it alone.

CHAPTER
39

WORLD CITY COUNCIL AND DR. BLOODMAYNE DEAD
AFTER EXPLOSION DURING A PRIVATE TOWER EXHIBITION.
ONE SURVIVOR, A WOMAN.

CORRUPTION DISCOVERED AMONG CITY COUNCIL AND HIGHEST
AUTHORITIES OF WORLD CITY. INVESTIGATION ENSUES.

BOUNTY HUNTER STEPHEN GREY CRACKS OLD "
REAPERS" CASE. WORLD CITY STREETS SAFE AGAIN.

DR. JOSHUA LATIMER NAMED NEW HEAD SCIENTIST
AT THE TOWER.

AFTER THREE DEADLY YEARS, WAR WITH AUSTRIUM
OFFICIALLY OVER AS PEACE TALKS CONCLUDE

Kat fingered each article trimmed from past editions of the *Herald*,
then placed them in a small pile on the desk. Whenever the guilt of
her past became too much, she would pull out the clippings from
the last year and reread them. They were reminders that life moved
on, and that she was no longer the woman with the monster inside.
But that didn't mean she didn't mourn all that had happened. The
scars of that year, and the years previous, would be forever etched
on her heart.

Next to the clippings was a leather-bound journal. Shortly after the tragedy at the Capitol building, Stephen bought her the journal and encouraged her to write. At first, the words came slowly. Writing about her experiences and thoughts were almost like reopening wounds best left untouched. But as the weeks went by, the words started gushing. As her story spread across the pages, she realized something—she had never been alone. Ms. Stuart had been there for her during her childhood, then Stephen after Ms. Stuart's death, even when he turned her in to the Tower. And others like Dr. Latimer and Marianne.

And God, though she hadn't realized it until the end.

Kat brushed her fingers across the journal. A piece of paper poked out along the top. The official verdict of her case. After multiple hearings, the event at the Capitol building had been deemed a tragic accident and the case closed. Soon afterward, the *Herald* covered all that came to light—her father's dark work, the City Council's approval of his corrupt methods, the truth behind the war, the greed of the elite of World City, and the death of countless poor at the hands of the Tower.

As for her, life went on after that. It was as if she had been reborn that day and given a new chance at life.

Kat gathered the clippings and tucked them inside the journal, then placed the journal next to the Grey family Bible. The clock in the hall chimed three o'clock. She stood, then paused, her hand on the edge of the desk. A photo stood inches from her fingertips. A smile crossed her lips. In the photograph, she stood behind Stephen, dressed in her mother's wedding gown, her hand resting on his shoulder. Their expressions were somber, but their wedding day had been anything but. Captain Grim and his crew had made sure of that.

Cricket let out a mechanical chirp and bobbed its head, its emerald eyes twinkling from behind gilded bars. Above the cage hung a painting of Helen Bloodmayne, one of the few portraits Kat had brought with her when she moved from the Bloodmayne mansion.

"I know, I know," Kat said to the automaton bird. "I don't want to be late."

It chirped again as if in agreement.

Her smile widened and the last of her morose spirit slipped away. Stephen was coming home today, and she did not want to be late in greeting him.

She grabbed her wrap and left their flat. Flowers poked through the cracks along the streets as spring made its way across World City. Airships glided through the bright blue sky and far off in the distance a train blew its whistle.

Twenty minutes later Kat reached the sky tower just as the *Lancelot* started docking along the walkway high above. The cylindrical structure swayed and creaked under the rush of wind brought down by the airship's propellers.

She kept a hand on the railing and made her way up the narrow stairway inside. With each step, her heart beat faster. Stephen had been gone for two weeks, but the time had felt so much longer.

At the top, she stepped out onto the dock. A wind cooled her heated face and blew back the few hairs that had escaped her chignon. She held onto her wrap, now whipping around her body, with one firm hand.

The airship dipped as the docking balloon expanded, exchanging places with the slowing propellers. Moments later, the ship rose again and leveled itself with the platform. Sailors scurried across the deck, securing the *Lancelot* to the sky tower and adjusting the gigantic balloon above the ship.

Stephen approached the railing and placed a hand on the wooden frame. His hair and duster settled as the last gusts of wind died with the rotors. His mustache was neatly trimmed, and he still had that patch of hair beneath his lower lip. His eyes came to rest on her, and a broad smile spread across his face.

At his look, a burst of sunshine erupted inside of her. She twisted the wrap between her fingers as a fluttering feeling filled her chest. She would never tire of seeing Stephen's smile after each mission.

The moment the plank bridged the gap between the ship and the walkway, Stephen jumped over the railing without waiting for the crew to unlock the opening and dashed across the board.

Kat's heart stopped as he ran across the plank, stories above the city. "Stephen! What are you—?"

Stephen grabbed her by her waist and swung her around. The city flew beneath her feet. Then he pulled her in close, wrapped his arms around her, and buried his face in her hair. "I missed you, Kat."

Kat closed her eyes and breathed in his scent. "I missed you, too."

A moment later, his lips were on hers. He pulled her hair loose from the chignon and let the wind take hold of the strands. Her wrap flew from her shoulders. She held onto the front of his duster and kissed him back, ignoring the shouts and cheers from the airship nearby.

A year ago she had been on the run, searching for a cure for the taint she carried inside her. Then she had been healed, awakened to something new.

To life and to love.

ABOUT THE AUTHOR

Morgan L. Busse is a writer by day and a mother by night. She is the author of the Follower of the Word series and the award-winning steampunk series, The Soul Chronicles. Her debut novel, *Daughter of Light*, was a Christy and Carol Award finalist. During her spare time she enjoys playing games, taking long walks, and dreaming about her next novel.

Find out more about Morgan and sign up for her newsletter at: *www.morganlbusse.com.*

Facebook: *facebook.com/MorganLBusseAuthor*
Twitter: *twitter.com/MorganLBusse*

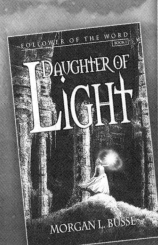